4/25

things that grow

Meredith Goldstein

Houghton Mifflin Harcourt

Boston   New York

For Jessica Douglas-Perez, who makes the best things bloom

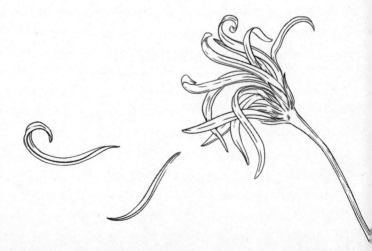

Chapter 1

We're the only two Jews—accompanied by one agnostic Christian—in Walsh's Funeral Home, a very Irish Catholic business near Hoppy's Liquor Store in Framingham.

My uncle Seth, my best friend, Chris, and I sit on one side of a stony gray conference table staring at the same horrendous thing: the massive crucifix hanging on the wall across from us.

"It's frightening," I whisper, because it is.

The cross, with Jesus pinned to it, has to be four feet tall and just as wide. Jesus's miserable face looks like it's made of porcelain. There are tiny cracks on his forehead, spreading like spiderwebs just under his thorny crown. Blood is coming from his eyes.

"Jeeeee-sus," Uncle Seth says, his own face sour as he narrows his eyes to examine Jesus's anguished expression.

"Indeed, it is," I say.

"He could not look more . . . *unpleasant*," Seth adds, waving his hand toward the sculpture.

"He's having a very bad day," I say, and Seth smirks at my understatement.

Seth's graying black hair sticks up in all directions. My uncle is the coolest person in my family, now that Grandma Sheryl is dead. He usually looks New York sleek, like a distinguished man in an advertisement for a watch, but right now he's red-eyed and messy, and so am I. I know from a recent trip to the funeral home bathroom that my cat eyeliner has spread across my face and is inching its way to my ears. I can smell my own armpits. There are hospital cafeteria blueberry muffin crumbs stuck between my teeth.

We're doing the best we can. We just lost our matriarch, the best person in the world.

Chris shifts in his seat next to me. Our commentary about Jesus has made him uncomfortable. He taps his foot on the floor before he responds.

"They can't make a crucifix where Jesus is, like, smiling," he says, keeping his voice just above a whisper. "He's literally dying on the cross."

Chris, whose family helped found the new Black church off Route 9, isn't sure what he believes anymore, but he knows the rules of Christianity and still tries to follow them when he can. He lives in the kind of house where you say grace before eating yogurt. He does not take the Lord's name in vain.

His mother, Grace Burke, is a tall woman with flawless dark brown skin and the world's highest cheekbones, which she passed down to her sons. She loves to remind me, like every few weeks, that Jesus was a Jew, and that when the "time comes" (by this, I like to assume, she means the alien apocalypse), I, too, will be saved. I tell her this is good to know.

Seth nods his acquiescence on the Jesus point but continues. "Okay, fine, he's being crucified, it's horrible, I get it, but who wants to look at this in a funeral home, of all places? It's so *bleak*."

"It's exactly where Christian people want to look at something like this," Chris—whose name is literally Christian—explains. "For somebody like my mom, a crucifix is a comfort. She believes it's a reminder that Jesus died to save us."

"I get that," I volunteer, "but I don't like that this *particular* Jesus has a body made of so many different materials. His face is clearly breakable, but his stomach is, like, plastic. His fingers are made of fabric. He's . . . Franken-Jesus."

Seth erupts, letting out an exhausted cackle. "Good line, Lor. You should write that down and use it for something."

And with that—even on what is probably one of the worst days of my life—I am floating. I am a ray of light. I am a genius.

Uncle Seth has written two novels and teaches creative writing to college students at some of the best schools in New York. He doesn't just throw out compliments, so when he likes my work, it makes me feel invincible. Like I can see my future. It looks a lot like his life, hopefully.

"Franken-Jesus," I repeat as I text it to myself so I don't forget.

"Let's try to keep it down," Chris says, noticing that people are walking by the door. "There are grieving families looking at coffins in the next room."

It's true. When we entered Walsh's Funeral Home, the three of us huddled together as if we were embarking on a haunted house tour, we passed a room full of coffins, with sad-looking families perusing them in rows. Most of the coffins had brownish wood with a soft satin interior — but there was one shiny white one with silver trim that reminded me of the cheesy white limos some kids rent for prom. I imagined that it might have fluorescent lights inside. Maybe when you close the lid of the white party coffin, it plays EDM.

I grin, hearing the coffin beats in my head, but I keep that thought to myself. I don't want to say anything else that will make Chris uncomfortable. There are crucifixes here, which means this is his world, not mine.

I take a closer look at him to see how he's holding up, and I can't help but notice his perfect ears. I would like to trace them with my finger.

I shake my head, as if the action will knock every forbidden thought I have about my best friend out of my system, and I focus on Uncle Seth instead. I can't figure out how he is related to my mom, let alone that he is her twin brother. They look the same, I guess. They have curly dark hair that's turning white at the same speed. They're both compact and fit.

But they couldn't be more opposite in every way that counts. Seth is hilarious and talented and dedicated to his one passion. He has the world's most perfect relationship with his partner, the very dashing — and very British — Ethan. Seth travels the world and sends me a keychain from every place he visits.

Meanwhile, my mom is, as Grandma Sheryl used to say, still searching for her rudder. She goes from job to job, claiming that each one is her destiny. She is a life coach who pretty much reads only self-help books, and she preaches about them to everyone around her. She's on her sixth boyfriend in five years, and goes *all in* with every single one of them.

She's so messy as a parent that she's *not even here* right now. Her own mother died more than twenty-four hours ago, and somehow she's still trying to figure out how she'll get from Maryland to Massachusetts. It's only eight hours away, and there are a zillion flights between Baltimore and Boston. Also, she *has a car.* This isn't that difficult.

Seth reads my mind and tries to soothe my anger. "Five bucks says Becca arrives tonight. In a matter of hours," he says, then tucks a stray piece of hair behind my ear. He gives me a sad smile.

"Ten says we don't even see her today," I tell him. "It's okay," I add. "You're doing a very good job."

Seth exhales.

"I know you probably have a lot of questions right now about what happens next," Seth says.

Chris's foot starts tapping as fast as a rabbit's. We both know this has been coming.

I've been living with Grandma Sheryl instead of with my mother since the start of high school. After Mom changed jobs and cities for the zillionth time, everyone agreed (albeit reluctantly, on my mom's part) that living with Grandma would give me stability. Mom would visit on weekends when she could. Honestly, letting me go is the best decision she's ever made.

But now, without Grandma Sheryl, where will I live? I have one more year left of high school, the most important one of all. I don't want to leave this place that has become home.

Seth watches me panic. I'm doing the thing where I pull on my eyebrows.

"Don't think about it now," he says. "It's not a question for today." He tries to change the subject. "How did you get so tall? As of this visit, you could absolutely take me in a fight."

I laugh because it's true. I am five foot nine now, which makes me as tall as Chris and about an inch taller than my uncle. Four inches taller than my mom, his twin, and I look nothing like either of them.

I'm blond and so pale that sometimes you can see the veins in my forehead. Also, I am not an athlete. Grandma Sheryl always said I was "full-figured—like the statue of a goddess!" but all that means is I can't go anywhere without a high-quality bra, and that if something is on a high shelf, I can usually reach it.

Based on what's available on the internet, I know I look more like my father, who works in sales, lives in Florida, and recently ran a 5K to benefit a colitis foundation. Good for him.

The door to the room swings open all the way, and the man who enters must be Mr. Walsh.

The owner of Walsh's Funeral Home looks exactly the way I

thought he would, based on our phone call: pasty white skin, dull white hair, an ill-fitting suit, a chin that blends into his neck. He wears a shamrock pin on his lapel.

"You must be the Seltzers," he says, wearing a sympathetic smile that must be plastered on his face all day in this kind of job. "Can I get anyone anything? Water? We have some individually wrapped bags of pretzels."

"No, thank you," Uncle Seth says. "I'm Seth Seltzer. This is my niece, Lori, and her friend, Chris."

Mr. Walsh shakes our hands, his eyes stopping at my purplish hair, which is in a messy bun. I did not intend to dye my hair purple, but what was "russet red" on the box turned out to be eggplant on me. The color won't wash out, and now my roots are coming in light blond again. Just a few hours before she died, Grandma Sheryl said that my head was beginning to remind her of a blackberry ice cream cone. That made me kind of like it.

"It's so nice to meet you, Lori," Mr. Walsh says, giving me the warmest smile and then turning to Seth. "I had such a lovely talk with your niece on the phone. It sounds like her grandmother — your mother — was a wonderful woman."

"She was," Seth says, his voice cracking.

"It also sounds like she was a voracious reader with quite a green thumb!" Mr. Walsh adds.

Seth looks too heartbroken to confirm this. He's barely nodding, so I come to his rescue.

"She was a retired English teacher who liked to garden," I say. "After she retired, it was all books and plants."

"Well, those are two wonderful things," Mr. Walsh responds.

He takes the seat across from us at the table, his body obscuring Jesus's so it now looks like he's the one on the crucifix. He places a laminated spiral notebook on the table, and it reminds me of a Cheesecake Factory menu. On the cover it says AFTER-LIFE in all capital letters over a picture of a harp.

The harp is surrounded by shamrocks.

"You guys really like shamrocks," I say, and Seth bites his lip, trying not to laugh.

"Sorry," I add to Mr. Walsh, knowing that he probably thinks I'm making fun of him. I truly was just noticing that they do really like shamrocks here. The sign out front has a shamrock in place of the apostrophe in *Walsh's*.

Sometimes I sound sarcastic when I don't mean to be.

"This catalogue outlines our array of services," Mr. Walsh says after a nod, and he opens the binder to the second page, where there's a cheesy cartoon drawing of an old man rowing a boat by himself.

Chris and I make eye contact as soon as we see it, and I can tell that he wants to redraw the picture on the spot. He's the best artist I know, and he illustrates everything I write. Our thing is fantasy and sci-fi, and we're the cofounders and editors of the *N-Files,* a short-story journal that comes out four times a year. We write our own stuff and accept submissions from other students.

Chris says he draws my ideas, but often it's the other way around. I'll come up with some story about sentient robots, or a population of superintelligent gnomes who spend their days undoing stupid decisions made by humans, but his illustrations wind up being so good that I end up rewriting the whole thing to match his vision. It's our process.

My best friend could make major improvements to the drawing of this man in the catalogue rowing himself into the afterlife. I can see Chris mapping out the work in his head, his eyebrows moving up and down with every new idea. His long fingers twitch, as if he's trying to stop himself from reaching for the pen I know is in his backpack. His self-restraint is adorable.

I am so horribly in love with Chris that I want to crawl into a coffin.

As if he's reading my mind, Mr. Walsh flips to the next page in the binder, which shows dozens of photographs of coffins, most of which are similar to the ones we saw in the front room of the funeral home. Each image has a price next to it—most of the coffins are $1,500 or more—and I silently thank Grandma Sheryl for bypassing this option. It seems like a waste, and it would stress me out to have to choose one of these boxes.

With another flip we're at a page that has pictures of white doves. Living, breathing, flying doves. Apparently you can have "doves of peace" released at your loved one's funeral.

One of the images shows a white middle-aged blond woman with a sensible haircut who is standing in a cemetery in the middle of a bunch of tombstones. She's holding her hands open, and two doves are flying right out of them. She looks delighted by the experience; she's actually beaming. I imagine her exclaiming, "My spouse is dead! But look at these fucking birds!"

My eyes go wide at the price next to the picture.

"Um—is it eight hundred dollars per dove, or does that money cover, like, multiple doves?" I ask, and Seth swallows a laugh. He thinks I'm just messing around, but a small part of me is desperate to release some doves in Grandma Sheryl's honor.

"Usually there are two for that price," Mr. Walsh says without looking up.

He knows we're not here to spend $800 on doves. He knows we're not even going to have a funeral.

"You said you plan to scatter Sheryl's remains?" he asks, trying to move this along.

We all nod.

"Well, like I said on the phone, Miss Seltzer, we can help you with that." Mr. Walsh smiles at me reassuringly. "Let me tell you how cremation works."

Chapter 2

This all started a week ago when Grandma Sheryl had some chest pains, which turned out to be a mild heart attack. Not the biggest deal, a nurse assured me, even though it sounded very scary. People have mild heart attacks and are just fine, she said. Now we could monitor her. It was better to know there was a problem.

Seth took a train from New York City to our Massachusetts suburb as soon as it happened, and the minute he got there, things felt manageable. Grandma needed to be in the hospital for a few days, so he took over at home. We went to Whole Foods and bought all these fancy groceries Grandma and I would never have had in the house. At night, after spending time with Grandma in the hospital all day, Seth and I watched TV and talked about our writing.

I felt terrible that Grandma was in the hospital, but having Seth in the house, all to myself, made the whole thing feel like one big sleepover party. In pajamas, over a plate of mochi ice cream, he told me he was ready to write his third book. I asked for details, but he said it was too early to talk about it.

"I'd like to write something literary . . . but more commercial, you know?" he told me just a few nights ago after he'd had a glass of wine.

I didn't know what he meant, but I wanted him to keep talking to me as if I were one of his writer friends, so I nodded.

My mom did offer to come up, but I told her that we had it under control. I was annoyed because she seemed relieved to be off the hook.

"Please let me know if anything changes," she said. "Seth promised he'd keep me posted. Make sure he does."

"*Okay,* Mom," I'd said.

Grandma *was* getting better by the day, becoming less sluggish and more of her usual feisty self. And then she was moved out of the ICU into a regular hospital room, which made things feel less urgent.

Seth even booked his train ticket back to New York. He planned to leave a few days after Grandma came home. Everything would be back to normal just in time for me to start senior year.

But then, twelve hours before she was supposed to be released, Grandma had gone into cardiac arrest and died. It happened just after two a.m. on Friday. Which I guess is technically still today. What a blur.

We weren't there when she died, but the hospital people assured us that she was probably sleeping when it happened. Seth and I rushed to the hospital and spent an hour staring at her dead body, which looked remarkably like her *alive* body. Like she might just wake up. Her short white hair framed her head with wild curls. She still had a little bit of blush lipstick on; she'd applied some earlier in the day to "feel like a person again." Her eyes were closed, and her long lashes had a touch of mascara. A book rested on her nightstand: Dorothy Parker's *Laments for the Living*.

"Well, that's on the nose," I whispered.

"It's perfect." Seth took my hand and squeezed it. "I'm gonna call Becca," he said then, and left the room to call my mom.

My instinct, in the moment, was to call Grandma Sheryl. Because when something bad or confusing happened, she was the person who explained it or took care of it. I imagined her talking me through it.

"What am I supposed to do now?" I asked her dead body.

I knew that, always the English teacher, she would say, "Sometimes the worst experiences make the best stories. Notice the details. Write them down. Also, go eat something. Make it protein."

I tried to notice as many of the details as I could. Grandma's still-perfect red-painted nails. The strange, fluorescent lighting in the hospital room that made her lips look that much rosier against her pale skin.

I wondered if she died with her eyes closed, or if someone closed them the way they do with dead people on TV.

Then Seth returned from his call, looking like he'd cried a lot more, and this time he was joined by a social worker who ushered us into a "family room" that had couches. The social worker, who held a clipboard, asked if we knew what we wanted to do with the body, and I said, "Reanimate it," which earned me a smile from Seth.

"Do you know if she had a will—or funeral instructions?" the social worker asked.

"Yes," Seth said. "There's a will in the safe with the important papers."

"Why don't you take a look at her instructions and give us a call tomorrow morning so we can start arrangements," she said. "We can keep her here, so there's no rush right now."

We walked like zombies out of the hospital, and then Seth called my mom a second time. He told her the immediate plan, and then I spoke to her for two seconds.

"Sweetheart," Mom said, crying, "I'm going to get there as soon as I can. Bill and I are talking about driving up. I think it might be good to have a car there. Better than flying and having to rent a car at the airport."

Of course she'd bring Bill, her latest boyfriend.

"It doesn't matter," I said, trying to give her the hint that instead of thinking about every single transportation option, she should probably just show up.

"Or maybe we could rent a car here in Maryland," she said. "My car's been rattling."

I heard a muffled male voice in the background. Bill weighing in.

"Lori, just sit tight. I'll be there soon. I love you, honey."

"I know," I told her.

When we got home, Seth called Ethan, and I crawled into Grandma's bed and texted Chris to let him know I was home. The last time I'd messaged him was to tell him we were on our way to the hospital because Grandma had gone into cardiac arrest. Then I'd put my phone away, so I'd missed a bunch of his messages.

"You okay?"

"What's happening now?"

"Check in when you can."

"Lori, are you sleeping?"

I didn't know what to write back so many awful hours later.

"She's dead," I finally responded.

My phone suggested I use the skull emoji when I typed the word *dead,* which caused me to let out a hysterical cackle. I added it to the message and hit send.

"I'm so sorry, Lori," Chris wrote back almost immediately, and I wondered if he'd stayed awake this whole time, waiting to hear from me. "You're going to be okay. I promise."

"Sure," I wrote back. "Going to sleep now."

I leaned into Grandma's pillow, which smelled like lavender-scented dryer sheets. Then, for hours, I tried to keep my eyes closed.

It was early morning when Uncle Seth and I reunited in the kitchen. He wore a New School sweatshirt and skinny jeans, and he'd pulled out a box of Honey Nut Cheerios, my main form of sustenance.

"Want some?" he asked.

"Yeah," I said, and dug my hands into the box as he held it for me. The Cheerios were so dry on my tongue that I opened the refrigerator and drank some orange juice straight from the carton.

"Sorry," I responded. "I don't have the energy to be hygienic today."

"First rule of shiva," Seth said, "you can drink from the carton."

"I thought the first rule of shiva was not to talk about shiva," I said, and then burped.

Seth laughed and then got quiet. "I'm going to go in and look at the paperwork," he said, and based on the way he eyed the door to Grandma's room, I could tell that he was freaked out about going in there. Or maybe he was scared to look at the will.

"Do you have any idea what it says?" I asked.

Seth ran his fingers through his hair.

"Only that it's a will and that she had named me as medical proxy."

"I know that part," I said. "Grandma told me once to call you if anything happened to her, like if I walked into the house and found her unconscious."

"That's morbid," Seth said, his eyebrows raised.

"Well, a year ago my guidance counselor told Grandma that kids who live with older grandparents, like, as guardians, should have some sort of instruction, just in case they drop dead," I explained. "This one kid, Blake Hartley, he lives with his grandpa, who's like ninety-two. Blake is fully trained in CPR."

"How many kids at your school live with their grandparents?" Seth asked.

"A bunch. Mostly it's kids who live with their parents *and* grandparents, but I can think of, like, ten kids in my class who live with just their grandma or grandpa."

"Interesting," Seth said, and we both took deep breaths.

"Well, let's do it," I said. Seth followed me into Grandma's room and opened her closet, where she kept her small safe of important papers.

I slid the safe out onto the carpet. It reminded me of a tiny metal suitcase, like what you'd put a bomb in if you were a villain in an action movie. Then we both sat crossed-legged on the pale blue carpeted floor as I used the combination, Dorothy Parker's birthday (8-22-93), to open it. Some arrangement of 8-22-93 was Grandma's password for everything.

"Oh my god," I said, looking at the numbers.

"What?" Seth asked, panicked.

"She died on Dorothy Parker's birthday. Eight twenty-two."

"Oh my god!" Seth's eyes pooled with tears. "Of course she did!"

Our knees touched as we clasped hands. Then he let go and wiped his eyes.

I started to laugh then, not because Grandma died on her favorite author's birthday, but because Seth was unknowingly sitting in front of about twenty-five photos of his own face. Grandma Sheryl's bedroom walls were covered in framed pictures of all of us—me, my mom, Seth—but the ones that surrounded Seth now were a series of his own school photos from kindergarten through high school.

Even as a toddler, Seth looked cool and confident, always flashing a relaxed grin at the camera. My mom's row of photos, on the other hand, are so embarrassing. It's like she tried a new style every year, and in every picture her bangs are higher, as if she put her finger in an electrical socket.

"Do you think she planned it somehow? That she wanted to die on Dorothy Parker's birthday?" Seth asked, the question bringing me back to reality. "That would be so on-brand for her."

"I don't think she planned to die right now," I said, shaking my head at all of Seth's faces. "I mean, we had plans to be with Mom in D.C. for Labor Day weekend. She was right in the middle of a book. She'd never want to die in the middle of reading a book. Also, she wouldn't want to leave us."

"Right," Seth agreed. "I guess I just want this to make sense in a way that it can't, you know?"

I nodded because I understood. It would be comforting to think that Grandma Sheryl was capable of orchestrating her own exit from the world. She was so good at planning everything else. But she didn't want this.

Seth pushed aside files labeled LORI'S BIRTH CERTIFICATE, INSURANCE DOCUMENTS, MEDICARE CHANGES, PENSION, and ESPRESSO MAKER WARRANTEE and found the one labeled WILL. I watched Seth, fearful that if he opened it too quickly, a bat might fly out.

He opened the folder, and I moved behind him so I could read too.

The first page was a lot of printed names, dates, and addresses. Then there was a typed message: "Assets and accounts to be split between Ms. Seltzer's son, Seth, and her daughter, Rebecca. Bequests: Rebecca shall receive all of Ms. Seltzer's jewelry, and Seth shall receive her collection of books."

Seth nodded through tears, and I felt a little bit of jealousy that he would get her library.

"You can take some of them," he said, reading my mind again.

"The Stephen King," we both said at the same time, and then laughed.

Seth isn't a fan of Stephen King, but I love him. My favorite is *Christine*.

The next page of the will looked even more important. It was called "Letter of Instruction" and had a lot of Grandma's handwriting on it.

Seth and I leaned in closer.

"I do not want a funeral!" Grandma Sheryl had written in her compact cursive script. "I would like to be cremated and placed near things that grow."

I stopped breathing for a second and read it again. Seth ran his fingers over his mother's words.

"'Things that grow.' I guess that's no surprise," he said with a smile, his eyes moving to the dozens of plants around her bedroom.

Then we noticed the asterisk at the end of the last sentence.

"* see reverse side."

On the back, where there was more space to write, the instructions continued.

"My dears," it said, and I whimpered.

"I would like to be placed in a lovely garden. I've listed four options below. Please do not get yourself in trouble as you scatter; I've been told the process requires permits, but if you are discreet, no one will interrupt. I'm grateful and love you all . . . And pick an appropriate reading, please."

I wiped my eyes with my dress collar, streaking the white fabric with my dark eyeliner. Seeing Grandma's handwriting had shaken me, reminding me of her body in that hospital bed and the fact that all this was real. I imagined how the instructions would sound in her voice, and then I realized I'd never hear her voice again.

Had I saved any of her voicemails?

"I don't know most of these places," Seth said, running a

finger down the list of gardens Grandma Sheryl had chosen for her remains.

Seth looked up to find me sobbing, and then he joined me.

Crying is like yawning, I guess; if one person does it, it catches on.

"I can't believe my mother is dead and that I'm supposed to cremate her and deposit her in a fucking garden," Seth said, speaking to the ceiling. "Where the hell is Becca?"

"Probably sitting on her bed reading some self-help book about what to do when a loved one dies—instead of actually doing anything you're supposed to do when a loved one dies."

"Fuck!" Seth shouted to no one.

"Is Ethan on his way?" I asked.

"I told him to wait until I knew our plan."

In that moment, despite the lines around his eyes and his graying hair, Seth looked like a child. Feeling like I should be more of a help, I took a deep breath and considered next steps. I needed to be his partner in this.

"She wants to be cremated, so let's cremate. I'm going to look up cremation places," I told him, pushing myself up from the floor.

"Lor, wait. The cremation thing seems like the adult task. I'll find a place that does it. There are other things you can do to help. And Becca will get here eventually and can take on some of the logistics."

"The cremation part is the thing I *want* to do. Look at me," I told him, motioning to my black leggings, my purple hair, and the vintage dress I bought because it reminded me of what a possessed doll would wear in a horror movie. "I write stories about zombies and ghosts. My eyeliner is threatening and severe. I am *all in* for finding out about cremation. What I *don't* want to have to do is call the Feldbergs and Cousin Helen. That's on you."

"Fair," Uncle Seth said, and then he fell backward onto the carpet, muttering, "Ugh, the fucking Feldbergs."

In my room, holding my phone above me, my arms outstretched with my back on the bed, I googled the temple where Grandma and I spent the High Holy Days every year, and I called the main number.

"Boker tov," a woman answered.

"You too!" I said, hoping that was the right response. "My name is Lori Seltzer. My grandmother and I come to your temple for Yom Kippur every year. Anyway, my grandma—she just passed away. I'm wondering . . . where do your members go for cremation?"

The woman on the line was silent for long seconds.

"Lori, can I speak to one of your parents?"

"She's not here right now," I said, annoyed by her assumption that my parents were around and that there were two of them.

"I'm just trying to help my family by getting some information about cremation services."

"I understand, sweetie. It's just that we don't do cremations."

"I know you don't do the actual cremations, like, in your temple," I said, "but can you recommend a place where we can go to get it done?"

"No, sweetie. What I mean is that Beth El doesn't recommend cremation services, because Jews don't cremate," she whispered into the phone. "It's not something we're supposed to do."

"Oh," I said. This was news to me. "Why?"

"It's against the rules," she said.

"Whose rules?"

"Well . . . the Talmud's, I guess."

"Oh. That's good to know."

"I'm sorry. I didn't mean to sound so flip," she continued, "but most Jewish people believe that we are forbidden to defile the body, and that includes cremation. That's why many Jews don't get tattoos and piercings—because many Jewish cemeteries don't allow them."

"Right," I said, running my fingers over the three small silver studs in my right ear.

"There's also the matter of the Holocaust," the woman continued.

"The *Holocaust?*" I whispered. That is how Grandma always said "the Holocaust"—in a very loud whisper.

"Yes. You see, many Jewish people object to the idea of

cremation because of the bodies burned en masse during the Holocaust."

"Oh," I said, feeling stupid. This woman had every reason to be offended by my phone call. I wondered if Grandma Sheryl had known any of this.

"I'm so sorry," I said. "I didn't know."

"It's okay, honey. If you'd like to come in, I'm sure Rabbi Grossman would be happy to sit down with you and your parents and talk about your options. But you should come today. The burial should happen Sunday. It's Friday now, so we'll need to set this up before we begin Shabbat."

"No, thank you," I said. "My grandma was really clear that she wants to be cremated; I just have to find a place to do it. I'm sorry if that's horrible and offensive and makes us bad Jews."

Silence.

I cleared my throat. "Um, I hate to ask, but do you know who *does* cremate? Like who else I could call?"

"Christians," the woman responded, her tone flat. "Cremation is something Christian people do."

"Fair enough," I said, and then thanked her before hanging up.

I considered walking down the street to talk to Chris's mom —she would be able to tell me everything about how Christian people cremate—but I knew that if I did, she'd feel responsible for helping me through the process, and she's always doing too much for everyone.

That's when I thought of Walsh's Funeral Home, which I'd

passed seven thousand times on the way to the thrift store that always has good Halloween costumes and vintages sunglasses. I remembered the big shamrock on the Walsh's sign, and the message underneath: AFFORDABLE BURIAL AND CREMATION SERVICES FOR YOUR FAMILY.

I called Walsh's, and after a man answered with a friendly hello, I blurted my questions. "Do you guys do cremation? Can Jewish people use your services? Do you have availability to cremate my grandma?"

"Well, yes. To all of that," he answered. "I'm James Walsh. Happy to help you. Would you like to stop by this afternoon?"

And that's how we got here.

⟐

Mr. Walsh flips the catalogue from the doves to the next page, which is all about the service we came for. The page is titled "Dust to Dust."

"These days, the majority of our business is cremation, as opposed to a more traditional burial," Mr. Walsh says. "People are very interested in limiting their carbon footprint. They want to be respectful of the space they take up in the world, even after death."

Mr. Walsh's eyes are huge and bright as he tells us this, and I smile because he loves his job. Good for him.

"We do the service off-site, in a crematorium in Chelmsford," he continues, "and we can have it completed within the next two days. We'll coordinate with the hospital morgue, so you won't have to worry about transporting the body."

He clears his throat.

"What we should talk about today is storage. There are many options for the disbursement of cremains, so let's take a look, and I can show you—"

My head pops up, as does Uncle Seth's.

"The *cremains?*" we say at the same time.

"Yes," Mr. Walsh continues. "You see, some families bury their loved one's cremains and have a traditional funeral service at a gravesite. Others choose to bring the cremains elsewhere . . .

"There's also the option of keeping the cremains in an urn."

He flips to a page that has a photo gallery of urns. Most of them are a solid color or have quiltlike designs on them, but one has a Red Sox logo. It's a baseball urn. I know Chris has spotted it, because he's swallowing a smile.

"I bet there are a lot of people around here who want that Red Sox urn," I say, trying to keep my voice even.

"Indeed," Mr. Walsh says. "We hope it's an alternative for the many people who want to bring their loved one's cremains to Fenway Park. That's not allowed, you know."

"People do that?" Seth asks, disgusted. "They bring ashes to a baseball stadium?"

"Oh yes," Mr. Walsh says with a chuckle. "My nephew used to lead tours at the ballpark, and at least once a week he'd catch someone depositing cremains on the turf or in the crevices of the bleacher seats. He stops people when he can, but some are too fast for him."

"That's so weird," Chris says.

"That's so gross," I say.

"Red Sox fans are eternal. I do warn ticket holders that most stadiums are covered with the cremains of the people who loved their team," Mr. Walsh says.

"Jesus," Seth says, and then we all look up at Franken-Jesus right there in front of us.

"For your purposes," Mr. Walsh continues, trying to get back to business, "we also have smaller urns, if you plan to divide the cremains among a group of people."

Every time Mr. Walsh says "cremains," I clench my jaw to keep it together. I can't look at Seth; I know he's about to laugh, too.

I must not be controlling my facial expressions very well, because Mr. Walsh looks uncomfortable and says, "Forgive me. Have I said something funny?"

"It's just that you keep saying 'cremains.'"

"Yes?" Mr. Walsh asks, confused.

"Is that what we're supposed to call the ashes?" Chris asks, and I'm relieved he's never heard the word either.

"Is 'ashes,' like, not politically correct to say anymore?" Seth chimes in.

Mr. Walsh pulls his chair closer. He's wearing a dark green

blazer, a wise wardrobe choice. Even though it's a humid ninety-eight degrees outside—the worst of Boston's late-August heat—the air conditioning inside the funeral home makes it uncomfortably cold. I'm freezing in the black tank dress I'd changed into before we left, and when I look at Chris's arms, they are covered in tiny goose bumps.

He's wearing a light blue T-shirt. Chris's closet is all jeans and solid-color T-shirts that are the same brand because he likes the softness. They all fit him the same way and flatter my favorite part of him.

I want to touch his clavicle.

"It's an industry term, I suppose," Mr. Walsh says, distracting me from my silent objectification of my best friend. "I believe we began using the word *cremains* to prepare the family for what they'll actually receive."

Uncle Seth is nervous. "What will we . . . actually receive?" he asks, cracking his knuckles.

"People hear 'ashes' and they expect just that. But . . . you're not getting ashes. Human remains don't look like what you see at the end of a cigarette or the ashes from a fire. Movies about cremation have led people to believe that when human bodies are oxidized, they take the form of gray dust."

"Like the end of *Infinity War*," Chris says, and Seth and I look at him, stunned that the only Jesus-knowing person in our party has invoked an Avengers movie in this funeral home.

"Sorry," Chris says, looking at the ground. "That was stupid."

"No, it isn't stupid! *Infinity War* is a great example!" Mr. Walsh says, tapping the table in front of Chris to give him credit. He looks so thrilled to be sharing a cultural reference with a teenager that I wonder if he has any non–funeral home friends.

"In *Infinity War,* people disintegrate into dusty ashes. But bodies," Mr. Walsh continues, "when they're oxidized—they don't look like that. We want people to understand that human remains —*cremains*—don't look like ashes at all."

"What do cremains look like?" Seth asks. His right hand grips the edge of the table.

"Human bones are made of calcium phosphate," Mr. Walsh says. "They're solid and strong and white. Almost like stone. Because of the bones, you should expect to see something much more like . . . gravel."

He is quiet as we all try to imagine Grandma Sheryl as gravel. My stomach does a backflip and my mouth goes dry.

"Would it help if I showed you a picture of what you'll see at the end of the process?" Mr. Walsh asks.

"No. No, thanks," Seth says before I can say yes.

I'm desperate to see a picture of cremains—to prepare for them—but I keep my mouth shut because Seth is not ready. His eyes are red, and he's starting to cry all over again. Mr. Walsh pulls a box of Kleenex from nowhere and places it in front of us.

Chris takes my hand in his under the table. He can sense that

I'm about to lose it, too. When he reads me like this, I am so in love with him that it makes me want to hide under my chair.

Before I can prevent my brain from doing what it shouldn't, I imagine having sex with Chris. I picture it happening in my bed, in his bed, on the football field at school, and in front of the Natick Mall—all in three seconds.

Then I imagine us old and dying in bed together.

Then I imagine us being cremated together and sharing that horrible, stupid Red Sox urn for the rest of eternity.

I turn to Chris, and his big brown eyes are already fixed on mine, as if I'm the center of his universe, but I know it's the other way around.

He is my best friend and my inspiration for everything good thing I write. He is my conscience, the person I want to know, forever. I can't risk screwing that up, this perfect thing we have. That is why I will push these feelings aside until they go away —so I can keep him.

We are supposed to start our senior year together in two weeks and put out our final four issues of the *N-Files*. We have so many stories we want to write. We've already come up with our Halloween costumes (we bought matching curly wigs so we can both go as Neil Gaiman). We have plans to skip homecoming and get our tarot cards read by real psychics in Salem.

But how can that happen now?

I take my hand out of Chris's so I can rub the makeup that's seeping into my eyes. Uncle Seth is also composing himself; he gives his hair a tussle and rubs his hand down his face.

"I feel like I should start from the beginning," Mr. Walsh says. "Everyone take a deep breath, I'll get us some pretzels, and then I'll tell you about how all this really works."

Chapter 3

Twenty-four hours later, Chris is sitting on my bedroom floor, drawing, like it's any other day. His back is against my bed, his notebook rests on his knees. His hair is its short summer length. From this angle I can see a few tiny hairs growing on his square jawline. They are delightful.

I'm lounging on the mattress above him, and when I prop myself up on my elbows, peering over his shoulder, I can see what he's creating. It's his Chris Burke signature style — the kind of polite ink drawing that would work as a classic children's book illustration — but the subject matter is deeply upsetting. Chris's favorite artist is Edward Gorey, who was the king of creepy ink illustrations. He made men with skeleton faces, bad things happening to cute children, people who look like they're stuck in an evil fairy tale. Chris has a framed print of a Gorey self-portrait on his wall, and sometimes when his mom passes it, she mutters, "That man," as if Edward Gorey himself is out to get her.

"Interesting," I mutter at Chris as I survey his work.

His drawing-in-progress is of a rocket ship that looks like a coffin. It has fire coming out of its bottom, and it's flying through space, past a round object that could be the moon. There's a little window at the top of the coffin in which Chris has drawn a tiny face with dead eyes illustrated with little x's.

He's using the colored pencils Grandma Sheryl got him for Christmas.

"Is that a space coffin for Grandma Sheryl?" I ask, noticing that there are black streaks on my white bedspread. God, my eyeliner is everywhere.

If Grandma were here, she would tell me that I'm asking for conjunctivitis, but I don't want to wash off the makeup she last saw me in. I just keep putting a new layer over the last one. It is not hygienic, but it feels right.

"Sheryl would never want a coffin this ostentatious," Chris says. "She's too classy. This is for those rich guys who want their body shot up into space just to prove they can pay for it. They should put this in the Walsh's Funeral Home catalogue just to see who asks for it."

Chris gives the body of the coffin rocket some definition and draws a price next to it, like the one we saw next to the picture of the doves. "Send your soul out of this world—for only one million dollars!" he writes.

"Mark that up," I say. "It should be at least *two* million to have space cremains."

"What's your story for the rocket coffin?" Chris asks, turning his head so he can give me a tentative smile.

I let my head rest on the bed, so now our faces are so close we could be kissing. It would only require one of us to lean in a few inches. I don't want to exhale, my breath is probably terrible, so I move my head before I answer him.

"You know I'm bad with space," I say, turning onto my back. "My alien stories are the worst."

"That's not true," Chris says. "What about 'Hayley's Comet'? That was awesome."

"That wasn't actually about space. It was about a girl who hates everybody. It's a story about feminine anger, not space."

"Whatever, it was great."

"Your illos made it great. Your pictures were the whole story."

Chris ignores the compliment. I stare at the ceiling—wanting to focus anywhere but on him—but he's up there, too.

For my birthday, he made me a massive drawing of the Natick Mall, which is within walking distance—albeit over a dangerous major thoroughfare—from our neighborhood. The mall is so big, and it continues to expand, with standalone strip malls and fancy condos all around it. It feels like it's going to suck us up like a black hole, as if our tiny, retro residential road will be absorbed by a new Shake Shack or a seven-floor furniture store, and our homes and families will disintegrate into nothingness.

Chris illustrated our anxiety about this by creating a massive sketch of the mall on a long sheet of poster paper. He drew a swirling hole of dark matter in the parking lot area.

"It's not a black hole," he explained, "it's a portal."

He told me that he believes the portal is really there, and if we found it, it would lead to another mall parking lot. He claims that all malls are connected. He called the drawing *Leaving Nord-strom*. I taped it to my ceiling that night. Now it's the last thing I see before I go to sleep.

"If I'm going to write a death-inspired sci-fi story right now, it won't take place in space," I tell him, because I know he's waiting for an answer. "I'd rather write about a guy like Mr. Walsh who runs a funeral home, but it turns out—and we won't know this until the end of the story—that he's dead. He's been dead the whole time."

"So he's like a zombie funeral home director?" Chris asks.

"Not a zombie, but a ghoul. He still has his full personality and brain. Like, it turns out he used so much of the weird chemicals in the funeral home—formaldehyde or whatever—that when he finally died, his body remained preserved, like canned goods. So he just keeps running the place because . . . what else is he supposed to do with his life?"

I turn over on my stomach again to watch Chris flip to the next blank page of his notebook. He starts sketching, and within a minute he's drawn a tiny Mr. Walsh, with more ghoulish features. He's wearing a button that says ASK ME ABOUT ETERNITY!

"That's good," I tell Chris. "Save that one. I actually want to write it."

"I'd read that," two voices say in unison, and I am reminded that other people are here.

Our closest friends, Jessica and Jason, sit side by side in the corner of my room. They wear matching track pants, and

T-shirts printed with our school logo (a very angry-looking bird), although I'm sure that's not planned. Jessica and Jason are inseparable, like Chris and me, but unlike us, they are a couple. They are allowed to kiss. I have asked Jessica a thousand times what will happen if they break up, and she just says, "We won't," as if she knows the future. As if there's no risk whatsoever.

Chris and I find it fascinating that Jessica and Jason kind of look like each other, the way people and their dogs do. You'd think that would be impossible, seeing that Jessica is short and Korean and Jason is tall and white and blond, but it's all in how they carry themselves. When Jessica grew out her long black hair last year, Jason's usually cropped cut suddenly went past his ears. When she got bangs, he let his hair fall just above his eyes. And because all they do is run—on the track team, for fun, on various community leagues, and as a way to get to school—they're almost always in athletic gear, and often, it matches.

They're unlikely friends for Chris and me, seeing as we're big on avoiding sporting events and prefer sitting around each other's bedrooms, but I think Jess and Jason know that no matter how far they run, we'll be there for them when they're done, ready to eat and watch movies. Jessica and Jason live in the fancy condos by the mall, so it's a pretty quick jog to our neighborhood—for them, at least.

They came over, not long after Chris's parents stopped by with baked goods, bottles of soda, and a bouquet of flowers to offer their condolences, which basically meant sitting on my floor and just being present. Jessica usually talks a lot more than Jason, but today he's taken the lead. All four of his grandparents are dead, so he knows what this is like. He's said more words to me today than he ever has. I like this version of my friend.

"Sheryl was the best," Jason said when they arrived, pulling me in for a big hug. He smelled like body odor and cinnamon, a surprisingly nice combination.

Jessica, standing behind him, whispered, "I'm so sorry, Lori," but she looked too uncomfortable to say anything else.

After we came upstairs, it started to feel like things were normal, but they aren't. We're all pretending that it's any afternoon, but it's not.

"My mom will be here soon," I announce all of a sudden, more to remind myself. She used to visit a lot when I first moved in with Grandma Sheryl, but for the past few months I've flown to see her instead. We were aiming for two visits a month, but that became monthly soon enough. Now that I think about it, it's late August, and I haven't seen her since July 4.

"Right," Jason says. "I guess we should probably go and let you deal with family."

"Unless you want us to stay," Jessica adds.

"Go," I tell them. "It's only going to get more depressing and boring here."

They stand up; Jessica looks relieved to be dismissed.

"Call if you need anything," Jason says. "And remember, it's going to be different every day. The grief—some days it's really easy, and other days it's like you can't get out of bed. I know you're not a runner, but you can always do a brisk walk. It might feel good."

"I love you," I tell him, "but I'm not going to do a brisk anything."

Jason laughs and hugs me again, and then he gives Chris this Rube Goldbergian six-step handshake that I'm always surprised Chris knows. We hear them jog downstairs, say goodbye to Seth, and then they're out the door.

Chris and I are alone.

"We could just run away," he says, and gives me a small smile.

Before I can ask him what that would entail, the doorbell rings.

Mom.

My body tenses, as if it's preparing for a fight, but Chris puts his hand on my arm to settle me.

"Try to be nice. Remember that *her* mom just died," he says, and I exhale. He's right.

Chris and I make our way down the stairs, him right behind me, and as soon as Becca Seltzer is close enough to reach me, her arms are around me tight.

Seeing my mother is sort of like the best and worst thing at the same time. I resent that her arms feel like home. That the smell of her—the distinct odor of her vegan, nontoxic lemon-cedar deodorant—reminds me of the way her car smelled when she used to pick me up from school in all the many towns we lived in together (five).

I resent that even though she doesn't act like a mom in the right ways, she's so *overwhelmingly my mother* that I can't help but lean into her embrace.

"My baby," she says, touching my hair and looking at its color with some confusion. "Aubergine?"

I also hate that she says *aubergine*.

"It's supposed to be dark red," I tell her.

"Well, it's a risk. I like it!" she says, which makes me want to dye it something else.

I look behind my mother and see that Bill is standing just inside the front door, his face in his phone. From the few times I've met him I know that this is his natural resting position in life —slumped over and scrolling.

"Honey," Mom says, squeezing my shoulders. "I'm so sorry I wasn't there when we lost her. It's both beautiful and traumatic to see a person's soul leave their body, and I wish I could have shared it with you."

This is a very Mom thing to say.

"We weren't there when she died either," says Seth, who appears from the kitchen. "I'm not sure anyone was there when her soul left her body."

"Well," Mom says, still taking me in, "she has passed on through all of us just them same."

This is what my mother believes—that when someone dies, pieces of their soul enter the bodies of those who loved them most. She got this from a self-help book called *The Dissolving of Spirit: How to Escape Mortality*. She bought it for Grandma Sheryl years ago for no good reason, and it's still sitting unopened on Grandma's bedroom bookshelf. I'd like to light that book on fire right now.

My mother is wearing an oversize brown dress with some sort of swirling turquoise pattern on the sleeves. It's boxy and confusing and reminds me of the clothing you'd find in an art museum gift shop. There is one reddish chunk of hair at the front of her graying brown bob. There is also a geode—like a full amethyst rock formation—hanging from her neck.

She catches me eyeing it.

"Isn't it lovely? Bill got it for me for our anniversary. It keeps out negative energy," she says. I don't know what anniversary she's talking about. She met Bill only about eight months ago.

Then Mom moves to Seth and they embrace, and I guess he can't fight it either. No matter how irritating you find Becca Seltzer, you can't reject her hugs. It takes Seth a few long seconds to pull away, straighten up, and clear his throat.

"There's lasagna and shit on the table," Seth says, and that wakes up Bill, who whooshes past us to the dining room.

"Nice to see you too, Bill," Seth mutters, and Mom gives him a light slap on the arm.

"He's been driving for ten hours in traffic," she says. "Be kind."

Then we're all around the oval dining room table, and at first glance, we look like a pretty typical family that might eat dinners at a table like this, even though that hasn't happened since before I moved in. There's Mom, Bill, Seth, Chris, and me. No one is sitting in Grandma's chair at the head of the table, the one that always put her closest to the kitchen. We all take turns glancing at it.

In the uncomfortable silence I notice that Bill is growing sideburns, which is a choice, I guess. Bill is balding, about my height, and looks like a lot of other people. If you put ten white, baldish men in front of me, it might take me a few long seconds to recognize him. Perhaps the sideburns will give him an identity of some kind. Like when you put a random bumper sticker on your very basic-looking car so you know you'll be able to find it in a Target parking lot.

I don't know much about Bill, other than that he likes sports a lot, and I can't say that makes him unique. It's his conversation entry point with me, even though I do not like sports at all and have told him as much.

Still, he'll say things like "Your Sox look good this year," to which I respond, "I literally have no idea," because I literally don't, and then I feel bad because he's just trying to make small talk.

Bill owns a small chain of dry cleaners in Maryland. My

mom, who has lived right outside of Washington, D.C., for about a year now, met him at some self-help business class where you were supposed to "learn how to be your own best manager." Mom said that she and Bill spent the seminar as partners and asked each other questions all day to help determine their most important social qualities (hers turned out to be "verbal communication" and his was "paying attention," so that worked out for them), and then they had a four-hour lunch that turned into dinner.

Bill does seem to have a number of good qualities, especially if you keep the bar low. For instance, he's very good at showing up. He's picked me up from the airport twice, on time. A solid showing, compared with Mom's last boyfriend, Declan. I'm quite sure the delay in my mom's arrival in Natick is not Bill's fault.

But the thing that that excites my mother most about Bill is what he comes with: free dry cleaning. My mother has mentioned this a lot.

"I've always avoided buying anything that was dry-clean only, and now I don't have to!" she said just before I met him for the first time.

"I didn't realize you were depriving yourself," I said. "I'm really happy you finally have this in a relationship."

"Honey," she said, "don't be mean."

"I'm not trying to be mean."

"Uh huh," she said, and gave me one of her looks.

I am sarcastic about Bill only because there have been a lot of Bills. There was Jeff and Luis and David and Sam. There was Lance, who turned out to be married.

When I was younger, we moved around for some of these guys—or didn't when we should have—until Grandma put a stop to it and said it was time for me to move in with her. My mom's love life—and her may career changes—became more palatable after I left. Meeting a new boyfriend wasn't so high stakes.

I suppose this all started with my dad, who was also temporary. He and my mom had an on-and-off thing until she got pregnant. He told her he'd help financially, but she declined, thinking it would be better to keep clear boundaries if he didn't want to be involved. She told him she'd find love elsewhere.

Chris thinks it's weird that I don't reach out to my dad, but I don't know what I'd say. I do check his LinkedIn profile sometimes, and I looked to see his special skills, which are things like "sponsorships" and "personnel management," but I always hope he'll add something like tightrope walking.

I am still hoping that Bill will reveal a special skill that actually makes my mother a better parent. So far, no one's done that.

One of the most notable things I learned about Bill when I first visited his apartment is that he collects expensive corkscrews, which he displays on tiny hooks all over the wall in his kitchen. They look like serial killer weapons. I intend to write a truly terrifying story about them, but I can't figure out what the plot would be.

The most upsetting thing about Bill's corkscrew collection is that he *barely drinks wine*. He prefers beer. My mom told me that once, casually, and I freaked out. It made the whole thing so much more troubling, but also awesome.

Why would you collect hundreds of corkscrews and put them on your wall if you don't ever plan to use them? What are you trying to unscrew, Bill?

"Hey, Bill, good sideburns," I say, because I haven't formally greeted him yet.

"Thanks," he says, and he looks up from his phone, beaming. "So sorry about Sheryl."

"Me too," I say.

"Double-header today," he adds.

"Sure is," I say. I know he's trying.

Mom scoots her chair closer to the table. "So, how's everyone feeling?" she asks, like she's licensed to help us.

"Like our mother just died," Seth says, and Mom takes a deep breath.

"Christopher," she says, finally acknowledging Chris. He's in the chair next to me, tapping his foot near mine. "It's so lovely to see you. Thank you for being here for Lori right now."

"You're welcome, Ms. Seltzer," Chris says, because he's too nice.

"Christian," I snap. "My best friend's name is Christian."

Mom has the decency to look embarrassed, at least.

"I'm sorry," she says. "It's been a long few days."

"No problem," Chris says.

"Honey," Mom says, looking at me while holding onto her neck geode, "we have to talk about practicalities here. We're going to have to get you enrolled and set up at a school in Maryland."

"Mom," I say, wanting to cover my ears and scream like a kid. I try to breathe.

"I know I just arrived and we're all processing the shock of this, but school starts very soon, and we're going to have to deal with the house."

"I bet you'll get a lot for it," Bill says, surveying the room for a second, and then I know he sees my look of death because he wilts into his chair.

"I don't want to move," I say.

"I'm not ready to sell the house," Seth says at the same time.

"Of course you don't," Mom says, "but that's the only option on the table. She's gone, Lor. My work is in Maryland, and I can't see any reason for us to hold on to an empty house, Seth. I know there's a lot of history here — for all of us. We're all going to have to make some adjustments."

"Just let me think," I say, and Chris puts his hand on my hand, which is clenched in a fist. He takes each of my fingers and extends them, making me feel even less relaxed because now I'm not only furious, I'm also feeling a riot of aggressive butterflies in my stomach. He has touched me so many times in the past few days that I can barely focus.

"You can't just expect me to pick up and leave," I say.

"Not today—but very soon," Mom says. "Before school."

"You don't even have a real second bedroom," I remind her.

When I stay with her, I sleep in a tiny office space that doesn't have a window. She said that the sublet would be temporary, but she's been there for more than a year.

"Bill has a three-bedroom condo," Mom says. "The public high school in his town is very good."

My head snaps up. Now it's clear. Mom is moving in with Bill after less than a year of dating him. Of course she is.

"I'm not living with Bill," I say, and then I see Bill pretending not to hear, staring at his phone. "No offense, Bill."

"None taken," he whispers, and scratches the shiny part of his head.

"You're springing this on me now? That you're moving in with another boyfriend?"

"He is more than just another boyfriend, Lori," Mom says.

"Sure! He comes with free dry cleaning!" I say, and I regret it as soon as the words are out of my mouth. There is no reason to be cruel to Bill.

"Sorry again, Bill," I say. "This is not about you."

"Honestly, no problem," he says, and smiles.

"I didn't want to have to fight about this," Mom says. "There's no alternative, Lori."

"I'll be eighteen this December."

Chris's foot taps at hummingbird speed.

Mom leans forward. "Are you saying you want to live here on your own?"

I shrug.

"Out of the question," she says with a laugh. "You are one hundred percent seventeen, and even if you weren't, we wouldn't allow you to live in a three-bedroom suburban home by yourself."

Fair.

"Well, we're at an impasse then, because I can't go. Chris and I have a year of issues of the *N-Files* planned. I have strong relationships with teachers who'll be giving me recommendations for college—which I'll be applying to in just a few months. I'm a writing lab aide for Miss Checka, which is going to look great on my applications. You can't pull me out now."

"Miss Checka is still there?" Seth says, his mouth full of lemon cake. "Becca, you remember Miss Checka?"

Sometimes it's hard to believe that Mom and Seth lived in this house and went to my high school, even though it was in an older, smaller building back then.

"She was so elegant," Seth says, smirking. "Is she still elegant? She looked like a movie star."

"She really is," I say. "She always wears these ornate scarves."

"Yes, the scarves," Seth says. "I wanted to be her."

Chris and I smile. We have long fantasized about the secret personal life of Miss Checka. My mom looks irritated, but before we can get back to the matter at hand, the doorbell rings, and I'm saved, at least for now.

I assume it will be the food basket delivery from the Feldbergs, who told Seth they were having some sent all the way from Chicago, but when I swing open the door, I see a group of people who are staring at me as if we've met before.

There are five of them — four women and one man. The man wears a shirt with a beaver on it that says DAM!

"Who are they?" whispers Seth, who has followed me into the hallway.

Before I can guess, they confirm.

"We're the Garden Girls," says the woman at the front of the pack. She has white, spiky hair and is dressed in jeans and a beige tank top. Despite her hair color, I think she might be a lot younger than Grandma. She walks in, the others trailing behind her, and goes to Seth.

"You must be the prodigal son!"

"I am," he says.

Another woman — she has black and gray dreads and is holding a pan of lasagna — chimes in. "I read your book, Seth. It was lovely. Very depressing, but I suppose all the best books are."

"Which book?" Seth asks.

"The one about Sheryl," the woman says.

"It wasn't technically about her —" Seth starts, but the woman has passed us and is on her way to the kitchen.

"You must be Lori," says the man in the DAM! T-shirt. He

looks way too young to be in this group, like maybe he's not even in his thirties. "We've all heard so much about you," he tells me.

"You too," I say, because I have.

When Grandma Sheryl retired from being a public school English teacher, there seemed to be so many more hours in the day, she told me. She tried joining a few book clubs, but she said she was a know-it-all in them. Always lecturing. She said she'd rather read her favorites on her own. So she took up her other hobby and signed up to volunteer for the parks department. Through that work, she met the Garden Girls, and that's where she got to be social, maybe for the first time since my grandpa died.

The Garden Girls had meetings and did community projects such as tending to the trees around town hall or teaching a class about herb growing to people at the senior center.

I've always known about the Girls, as well as the names of the members — I know the one man in the group is Kevin, and I always assumed he was some old widower and that he texted Grandma Sheryl a lot because he was in love.

I was wrong, apparently.

In the three years I've lived here, I've had no reason to meet them. Most of the stuff they do together is during the day while I'm at school or on weekends when I'm with Chris and Jess and Jason.

Sometimes they take these long day trips to see, like, *one tree*.

"Jill found a gorgeous spruce on Instagram in Portsmouth,

New Hampshire, so we're going to take a drive," Grandma would say, and then she'd be off for the day.

It's not like I was ever going to join them for that.

The last three Girls file in, clogging the hallway, some of their summer sandals clicking on the wood floor.

"You're all here," I say, overwhelmed, and I hope they don't take that to mean I want them out of my house.

"What's left of us," the woman with the spiky white hair says from the living room. "There were ten of us just two years ago, and then six. Five now, I suppose. She was the best of us, your Sheryl."

"She was, wasn't she?" another woman says. "Not the greenest thumb of us, but certainly the sharpest mind."

Kevin tears up and wipes his eyes, which makes me wipe mine.

"You should all have lemon cake," I say.

"I'm Jill, by the way," says the woman with the spiky gray hair. "That's Kevin."

"I figured," I whisper to him, and he smiles because I've heard of him.

"I'm Deb," the woman with the dreads and the lasagna calls from the kitchen.

The last two Garden Girls—a tall, elegant older woman in a navy sundress, and a short woman around the same age wearing ill-fitting jeans and a T-shirt with a cat on it—introduce themselves as Rochelle and Lenny respectively. I cannot imagine a world where Rochelle and Lenny are friends, but they seem to be a pair, and honestly, kudos to the Garden Girls for bringing this crew together.

"Don't worry about feeding us," Jill calls to me; she's moved to the living room. "We're here to work."

"Work what?" I ask.

Rochelle and Lenny are on the move then, too, toward the kitchen, with a confused Seth at their heels. I follow behind Jill, who makes a beeline for the massive tree Grandma Sheryl kept by the living room window. Kevin heads upstairs. Seth and I whirl around in circles, seeing how the house has been taken over.

I put my focus back on Jill, who puts two fingers in the tree soil.

"Kev?" she yells. "Can you bring me two cups?"

"Just give me one second," he yells from somewhere on the second floor. "We have a small emergency here."

Seth and I follow Jill upstairs, where Kevin is next to a plant Grandma kept on a table under a skylight in the hallway. The plant has pink lines all over its green leaves, but you wouldn't know that, because it looks very dead.

"Too much sun, not enough water," he says, looking at me and then at Seth as if we did a murder.

"I haven't even thought of the plants," I admit.

"Don't worry," Kevin says. "I can save it."

We follow Jill back downstairs and into the dining room, where my mother, Bill, and Chris look bewildered while the other Garden Girls buzz about them like fairy godmothers.

"You must be Becca," Jill says, and her tone is a little too flat to be kind.

My mom sticks out her hand, and Jill gives it a lukewarm shake.

"Are you going to be able to keep up with all this?" Jill asks me.

"The Fittonia might sag quickly, but that doesn't mean you should give it more water," Kevin tells me now that he's returned to the first floor. "Try putting an ice cube at its base."

"Which one is the Fittonia?" Seth and I ask at the same time, which makes all the Garden Girls pause and stare at us.

"The one upstairs," he says, as if this is obvious. "The pink one."

Our question makes them nervous. The Garden Girls are worried that we're going to kill the plants, and they're right, we might. But honestly, does it matter?

"She'd want the plants to thrive," Jill says, reading my mind. Rochelle and Lenny, who have gathered in the dining room with us, nod behind her.

"Would it be better if we took some of them?" Deb asks. "To care for them so you don't have the responsibility?"

"No!" I snap. I don't want to start giving away Grandma Sheryl's things. I don't want to feel less permanent here.

"Oh, I'm sorry," Deb says. "I don't know where my head is. We're being so rude."

"I wouldn't say that," Jill says.

"Of course you wouldn't," Kevin says, smirking at her.

"We can write down some instructions," Jill tells me, ignoring Kevin.

My mom stands up from the table and makes an announcement. A pointed one, in Jill's direction.

"You know," she says, "this is so kind of you to help. But at the moment, I think we need to make a *family* plan. For *arrangements*."

The hint is clear—but it is not taken.

"You're right," Kevin says, and he and Jill grab chairs from the kitchen and set them up near the dining room table.

Seth smirks at this, as do Chris and I. Mom not so much.

Then, with everyone around the long table—Grandma's chosen family in place—it looks like some sort of *Game of Thrones* military planning session.

Chris pokes at my arm to slide his chair closer to mine, making room for our new friends. I am close enough to inhale him. I close my eyes when the smell of him hits me.

Mom looks at the two of us, eyeing me with a question in her head, and I'm angry. If she saw me more often, she'd know there's nothing going on here.

Seth shifts his chair so that it's inch closer to mine than my mom's. I don't know why, but it means everything. It feels like we're a team.

"Okay. So . . . does everyone know?" Mom says, swallowing. "Have we made all the necessary phone calls?"

"No one called us," Jill says.

We're sheepish.

"I'm sorry. I should have gone through her phone. That's on me," I say. "I know how much she loves you guys."

"Don't spend a second feeling bad about that," Jill says. "Your grandma was texting from the hospital, and when she stopped, we started calling to get her patient condition. Kevin called last, and then—he told us."

Kevin's eyes get red at the memory.

"I called the Feldbergs," Seth says.

"Oh god—the Feldbergs," Mom says with an eye roll, and at least we can all agree about that.

"Who are the Feldbergs?" Chris whispers.

"My second cousins," I say.

"They're *my* second cousins, twice removed," Seth says.

"I thought they were Great Aunt Susan's kids," Mom says.

"Grandma knows who they are," I say.

Then it's weird, because she's not there to explain it to us. Perhaps we'll never know who the Feldbergs are.

"We arranged the cremation," I tell Mom, to move the conversation along.

"When will we be able to pick up the ashes?" she asks.

"Cremains," Seth and I say at the same time, and then burst out laughing.

Mom gives us a confused look.

"They're called cremains," Seth tells her. "*No one* says ashes anymore, Becca. We can get the cremains tomorrow."

"Okay then," she says, annoyed by our inside joke collusion. "Does the funeral home provide an urn for the *cremains?*"

"Grandma doesn't want to be in an urn," I say, already defensive. "She wrote in her will that she wants to be placed near things that grow."

"Oh," Mom says. Her voice is small. "She said that? In those words?"

"I can show you," I say.

"No, I believe you. It's just . . . well, it's beautiful." Mom stares at the table.

"You okay, Mom?" I ask. As much as I don't always like her, I love her, and her mom just died.

"'Things that grow,'" Mom says. "You know, there are some beautiful gardens near Bill's house in Maryland. Where did you take me on our second date, Bill?"

"Brookside Gardens," Bill says without looking up from his phone.

"We're not bringing Grandma to Maryland," I snap.

"Please don't yell at me," Mom says.

"Sorry," I say. "It's just that she made a list. We know exactly where she wants to be. It's not just any place with plants. She had favorite gardens."

"Okay, then," Mom says, on the defense.

I know she feels left out of the loop. But that's what you get when you show up late.

"We're going to take her to each place on her list," Seth explains before I can respond. "We have four boxes of her to scatter. We might as well bring her to all her favorite places."

"Four boxes?" Mom asks, surprised. "Why are there four boxes of ashes?"

"*Cremains*," Seth and I say again.

Mom glares at us and waits for an explanation. There isn't a great one.

At Walsh's, after we'd been given the basic information about cremation — and a price of $1,400, which seems like a lot of money to blow on something — we were asked how we wanted to split the cremains.

"How many boxes?" Mr. Walsh had said.

"You put it in boxes?" Seth had asked.

"If you're not storing the cremains in an urn — if you plan to scatter your loved one — we pack the contents into a thick plastic bag and place the bag inside a cardboard box. We can prepare the cremains in one box or split them into multiple boxes. Some families choose a few boxes so they can share the cremains or take them to more than one location."

"Does it cost more to get more than one box?" I asked.

"No. It's all covered under one price," Mr. Walsh said.

"Then we'll take the maximum number of boxes, obviously," Uncle Seth said with confidence.

"We will?" I asked my uncle.

"It's the best deal, right?" Seth said. "Why wouldn't we get all the boxes we can."

"I don't want fifty tiny boxes of Grandma Sheryl," I said. "That's kind of gross, don't you think?"

"It's not going to be fifty," Seth responded, and then turned to Mr. Walsh. "It's not, right?"

"It would only be four," Mr. Walsh said. "Our maximum is four."

"Then we want four," Seth said.

It sounded reasonable at the time—four small boxes of cremains to bring to beautiful locations—but Mom clearly thinks we've overdone it.

"It seems a little unnecessary to bring her to four different places," Mom says. "Could we bring all the boxes to one place? The best place on her list? That way it feels like there's a real monument to her life. One tree—or park. Is one of the gardens more —I don't know—interesting than the others?"

"She went to the trouble of making the list," I say, "and all the gardens are close by. And . . . I don't want Grandma to have to sit with the same scenery for eternity."

I'm speaking like I believe in something—as if I buy into the idea that the spirit of my dead grandmother will be present to experience the plants around her incinerated body, and for a second, I wonder if I do.

I do believe in some things. I absolutely believe there is alien life elsewhere in the universe—because to assume otherwise is narcissism. I also believe there is power and energy in the world that we can't see. Like the way I sometimes know that Chris is in a room before I can see him. Like the way I can tell when he's looking at me. I believe that love gives you a sixth and maybe seventh sense.

But I do not believe in heaven or hell, or that there are rules when it comes to death. I don't believe that if you get your ears pierced, you've screwed up a lifetime of being Jewish.

At least I don't think I do.

But after extensive googling, there was one Jewish thing that seemed real to me. A rule I wanted to follow.

"I think it's important that we bring Grandma's remains to these gardens sooner than later," I say. "Grandma asked to be cremated, which is not a very Jewish thing to do, but I think we should follow the rules about timing. Jews are really specific about not waiting to bury people. Technically, we should be putting her in the ground *right now.* Or tomorrow, because I guess today is Shabbat. We should scatter the boxes as quickly as possible."

"I've never understood why we Jews do funerals so quickly," Seth says. "Is there an actual reason—or is it just because Jews don't do a wake, so we don't have to dress the body up and put on stage makeup?"

"I'd be really good at doing funeral makeup," I say. "I could make dead bodies look so great."

Chris coughs through his discomfort, but I also know I've probably given him an idea for an illustration.

"I don't see a need to rush any of this, Lori," Mom says. "The wonderful thing about cremation is that we can wait to scatter her ashes until it feels right. We have so many things to do over the next few weeks. I know you don't want to talk about this right now . . . but the reality is that we are going to have to pack up this place and move you. I know that everyone wants to take their time, but it's August and there's school. We really can't wait. Although . . . this house will be a project."

Mom looks around at the books and tiny sculptures and closets, which we all know are packed with clothes as well as a generation's worth of belongings.

"We can't even think about selling it before we get rid of all of this stuff," she says. "I should start dumping and organizing things while I'm here. We all should."

"You know I get the books, right?" Seth says. "The books are mine."

"I'm not trying to take your books," Mom says. "I want you to have her things. I have to be back for coaching sessions by Tuesday, but Seth, if you can stay for the next few days, we can come up again at the end of the week. Bill, when we get home, we'll have to clean out that guest room closet for Lori. Bill, are you listening? Bill!"

I'm sure my face is blank as I listen to this. I can't process it.

"Bill, what's the name of the school she'll go to?"

"Atholton High School," he says, looking up from his phone. "I'll google the public school start date right now."

"Thank you."

They are going to pull me out of my high school and away from my friends. They are going to make me go to—

"Wait, what is it called?" I ask.

"Atholton High School," Bill says.

"Asshole-Town?" Seth says.

"Atholton. With a *t-h,*" Bill says.

"Great," I say. "Wonderful."

"Lori, I'm really excited to have you with us in the house," Bill says, which is nice, but it doesn't make this any better. I imagine Grandma Sheryl telling me that things look different after you take just one full breath, so I do.

"Can we get back to the cremains for a sec?" I say, not wanting to face the reality of how my life will be uprooted over the next week. "You know, there's a very specific reason Jewish people do funerals quickly," I say, and Mom gives me a questioning look. I've had no Jewish education, and suddenly I sound like WikiJew.

"Jews bury people quickly, Mom, because between death and burial, the soul is unsettled. Expelled from its home," I say, and my voice sounds a little bit like the rabbi I watched in an online tutorial I found on some website. "The body must be returned to the earth in order for the soul to be at peace."

Everybody, even Chris, goes quiet and stares at me.

"Did you just get possessed?" Seth asks.

"No, really!" I continue. "I've done a lot of Jewish research in the last day, and I buy into a lot of it. I don't want to wait on this. Jewish people believe that the soul can't get into heaven until the body is buried. It's just stranded out there, floating."

"I thought Jews didn't even believe in heaven and hell," Seth says.

"Well, the website talked about heaven."

"What was this website?" Seth says, smiling.

"BuryyourJewishgrandmadotcom," I joke. "I don't remember. It was a legit website, though, I swear. It had Hebrew on it."

"Catholic people cremate," Bill says, placing his phone facedown on the table. "We cremated my grandparents, but we still buried them. They're in a family plot in Virginia. The priest told me it was okay, as long as the body was buried." Then he lights up. "Here's a fun fact—my grandparents are in the same cemetery as Patsy Cline!"

I don't know who that is, but Bill seems thrilled about it. We give him weak smiles, but no one responds.

"What are the gardens on Mom's list?" Mom asks, sounding exhausted, like we're putting her out.

I shoot up from my chair and run to Grandma's bedroom to grab the will. Then I bring it to Seth, and the Garden Girls jump out of their chairs to stand behind him. This is what they were waiting for.

Jill clutches her heart and lets out a gasp. "Oh, my sweet, dear Sheryl," she says.

"What?" I say.

"This list is lovely," Jill says. "We went to these places together. Kev, look—she's got The Mount here."

Kevin takes Jill's hand. "Of course she does. And look—her favorite Tapestry Garden, although Lord knows how you're going to get her there."

Before I can ask about these places, Mom speaks up.

"If you don't mind, Jill—Garden Girls, all of you, I have a bit of a migraine, and I think I need to talk to my family in private for a bit."

I give her my angriest look. These people were Grandma's closest friends, and to kick them out—I can't believe she's being so rude.

"No, of course," Jill says. "We understand. Come on, girls."

"I guess that means I should go too," Chris says, and then I'm really furious.

"Chris, you don't have to—"

"No, Lor, it's cool. I'll just run upstairs and grab my stuff."

And with that, the Garden Girls follow Jill to the door and I see them out.

"I'm sorry," I tell Jill.

"Don't be," she says. "We don't want to overstay, and we'll come back to check on the plants, if you don't mind."

"Of course," I tell her. "Please do."

"In the meantime," Jill says, "Rochelle, do you have the book?"

"Oh yes," the glamorous Rochelle says, and reaches into her navy woven bag to retrieve a shiny paperback edition of *An Illustrated World of Plants and Flowers*.

"It's your grandmother's," Rochelle explains. "I was borrowing it."

"It looks familiar," I say, taking it.

"Yes," Deb says. "It was her favorite field guide. If you have questions about what you have in the house, what you see at gardens, you'll learn a lot from this."

"Thanks," I say, and I feel as if I'm holding something more important than the Torah.

"Keep us posted, my sweet," Jill says, squeezing my shoulder.

Kevin approaches me. "Do you have your phone?"

I take it from my pocket and hand it to him. He thumbs work fast as he enters information.

"This is us," he says when he's done. "Text us with any questions, and let us know . . . let us know where she is, okay?"

He's crying now, and I say, "okay," as he wooshes past me out the door.

"Girls!" I hear him yell, his voice harsh. "Take me home. It's too much."

They crowd around him, arms around shoulders as they disappear down the driveway.

Determined, I return to the dining room.

"Here's the thing, Mom," I say before she can start. "I know we have to deal with a lot of stuff. But I want to bring Grandma to her favorite places. All of them. Now."

"Lori, I'm not saying—" she starts, but I cut her off.

"You're the spiritual one, Mom. You of all people should get it. I need to put her to rest."

Seth sits up straighter, his brown eyes bright, and I can tell he's with me.

"She's right," he says. "Mom wanted this. She listed four gardens, and we have four boxes. We have at least a week before Lori starts school—somewhere. If you have career coaching sessions with your clients, go home. I can take Lori to the gardens. We can bring Mom around and deposit her with things that grow, just like she asked. I can even get going on packing up the house."

Mom holds her geode chain again.

"This won't take us long," Seth continues. "Go clear out her new room. Sign her up for Asshole Academy."

"Atholton," Bill whispers.

"Meanwhile," Seth says, "Lori and I will get this done. She doesn't want Mom to linger in Jewish purgatory, and neither do I."

He reaches for my hand across the table, which is dramatic, but I like it.

"I never get time with my niece. Mom would want this

—she'd want us to do this together. Lori and I will scatter the boxes. Go home, Becca. We've got this."

"Don't you have to get back to New York, Seth?" Mom asks. "When do you start teaching? What about Ethan?"

These are fair questions. Seth teaches writing at a bunch of colleges around the city, which is his main job, other than working on his third novel for a long time.

Uncle Seth waves off Mom's question.

"The classes are online," he tells her. "It's a syllabus I've taught a bunch of times. And Ethan can fend for himself. Honestly, we don't need to be so . . . on top of each other all the time."

It's a dig at my mother's relationships. I appreciate it.

"Really, Becca, if Lori doesn't want to pick up and run to some random town in Maryland days after her grandmother died, she shouldn't have to. You're not the one who gets to decide how we get closure. *I* want to distribute the four boxes now, too."

"These gardens are all local? You could visit them this week?" Mom asks.

Seth places the list of gardens in front of Mom so she can see it. She gets quiet, and her eyes are glassy. I know it's weird for her to see her mother's handwriting. It was so hard for us too.

Mom reads the local sites aloud.

"Arnold Arboretum. Tapestry Garden. The Mount. Brayton House (Rhode Island).

"Oh, sweetie, I'd love for you to see the arboretum," Mom continues.

"I've seen it a bunch of times," I say before I realize that she's talking to Bill, not me.

"What a beautiful place for the craisins," Mom adds.

The room gets quiet, and then Seth and I explode with laughter. Bill is trying to keep it in, but he can't.

"What?" Mom says.

"You said *craisins*, honey," Bill says, stifling a laugh.

"They said that's what the ashes are called!" Mom yells, which only makes me laugh harder. Her face is turning red. Like a Craisin.

"It's *cremains*, honey," Bill says.

"Craisins are dried cranberries," I say. "Like what they have at the salad bar. Or in a cookie."

Mom realizes her mistake and lets herself laugh—a little. "Fine, make fun of your mother."

I wipe my eyes, this time full of the laughing kind of tears.

It's so exhausting, all this laughing and crying—and then the periodic panic about what will happen next.

Grandma Sheryl would tell me I should be drinking more water.

"Seth," Mom says, "are you up for this? Do you really want to stay in Natick for another week and take Lori to all these gardens? *And* pack up the house?"

She's skeptical. Seth has never been able to keep himself in Natick for very long. The last time he spent four days in a row here, it was because he got the flu during a visit, and by now he's on day eight or nine.

Bill looks up from his phone. "It'd be great if you could," he tells Seth. "Hon, if Seth stays here with Lori, we'd be able to focus on prepping the house. We need all hands on deck."

Mom nods. This is starting to sound like logic.

"We could start calling some Realtors. We could come back up next weekend and help with the packing," she says. "Then we could drive Lori back with us."

I can accept that plan for now. It gives me just a little more time to figure out if there are any other options.

"Well," Mom says, "can I at least join you for one of the boxes? She was my mother, after all."

Then I feel terrible.

"Mom, we didn't mean you shouldn't come," I say. "Of course you should be there for a box. We can do the arboretum first. Tomorrow. You can show it to Bill."

"Thank you," she says, knowing it's hard for me to be nice to her sometimes. She walks to her small suitcase, which she left in the front hallway. "We should check into the hotel, Bill. I'm wiped out, and I'd like to meditate."

Mom and Bill gather their things, and she and I pause at the door.

"Where are you staying?" I ask.

"A hotel by the mall," she says.

"Which side?" I ask.

"Neiman Marcus," she says, because that's the compass. Neiman Marcus, Nordstrom, Sears, and Macy's.

"I know you don't want to talk about moving, but it's in your best interest to be part of this discussion," she says. "I'd like as much of your input as possible."

I take one step backwards. I can't right now.

"One thing at a time," I say. "All this just happened, Mom"

"I know it will be hard to leave this house—and your *friend*," she says, and I shoot her an offended look. She understands nothing about my relationship with Chris.

"It's fine," I say, which is what I always say when things are not fine at all.

She nods; she knows the discussion is over.

Bill walks past her, grabbing her bag, and then I see him on the other side of the screen door, getting into the car and starting the engine. Seth follows Mom outside, standing with her on the front step, and they close the door behind them. They think they're having a private, grown-up conversation that no one can hear, but they don't understand that the sound from the front of the house travels right through the window in the living room. I don't even have to walk over to it to eavesdrop.

"Becca, you've got to give her a second to breathe. This is hard enough for you and me, but Lori was *living* with Mom. She's the one who brought her to the hospital with chest pains. She's a wreck," Seth says.

"How can you tell? She always defaults to being stoic and sarcastic. God forbid she shows her vulnerability. She's just like Mom. It's eerie sometimes."

"Well, she's cried plenty in front of me. Also, Bec, you have to look in the right places. You have to look for the chin acne," he says. "I used to get it whenever I was anxious as a teen. You did, too. It's a Seltzer trait."

I feel the small city of zits growing under my chin, embarrassed that Seth has noticed. I really have to wash my face.

"Becca, all I'm asking is that you behave like the sensitive empath you claim to be. If Mom had pulled you out of school right before senior year, you would have chained yourself to a tree in protest. God forbid she had pulled you away from Matt Ellis."

"How dare you invoke Matt Ellis," she says, but she's laughing.

"Isn't it sad that he remains the most attractive man you've ever dated?" Seth asks.

"He wasn't a man; he was *seventeen*."

They pause.

"Bec, I'm just telling you to give her the week before you start planning the rest of her life."

"Fine," Mom says. "You know everything, and I'm a terrible parent."

"That's not what I'm saying."

"I know," she tells him. "I'm just wondering when I get to feel part of the inner circle here. I'm always on the outs."

I roll my eyes. She is the one who chooses to move everywhere. She is the one who stays away from any circle that doesn't involve a boyfriend.

They're both quiet for a long moment, and I can't tell what's happening.

"Ba-ba, our mom is dead," Seth says, using the nickname he invented for Mom when they were little, before he could say the *c*'s in my mom's name.

"I don't even think it's hit me yet," Mom says with an exhausted cry, and I am reminded of what we've lost, and I start to cry too, before I can stop myself.

"We're orphans," Mom says dramatically.

Seth laughs.

"We're almost fifty, Bec, I don't think you can be an orphan when you're this old. We just have two dead parents. That's different."

"It doesn't feel different," Mom says.

"Go get some sleep," Seth says. "I'll see you tomorrow."

❧

The car pulls away, and then I hear Seth call Ethan from the front stoop. The conversation is quick, and I can hear only the one side.

"I'm going to stay for a bit."

"Yes. We'll do all the gardens in a week or so."

"That would be great."

"Yes."

"Yes, that would be helpful."

"Anywhere close to The Mount works. Sure."

"Okay. Okay."

The call ends, and Seth comes back inside.

"Thanks for backing me up with the cremains," I say.

"The craisins, you mean," he says, laughing. "You're right, though. We should bury her now. Or scatter her? I guess it's a scatter. Otherwise we'll spend the rest of our lives trying to coordinate when to do it."

"You really don't mind staying in Natick for an extra week?"

"For this? For you? Of course not," he says.

The air feels breathable now that my mom is gone, and I feel bad for thinking that. It's just hard with her agenda filling up the room.

"Ethan will meet us at The Mount," he says. "He'll get us a hotel."

"Can Chris come with us?" I ask.

"It's no big deal if I can't—"

As if out of nowhere, Chris is coming down the stairs, his backpack on. I guess he was waiting up there until it was safe to leave.

"I don't want to intrude on family stuff."

"Of course you can come," Seth tells him. "As long as your mom says it's okay. One of these gardens is in Rhode Island. Two of them are kind of a drive, come to think of it."

"I'm sure she'll say it's okay," Chris says, walking toward the door, and as much as I don't want him to go anywhere, I know it's time to be alone. To sleep. To think about how this week is going to change my life.

"You'll come tomorrow? For the first box? So I don't have to deal with my mom without you?" I ask.

"Of course," Chris says, and pulls me into a hug. Feeling bold for a second, I put my hands on his chest.

"Thanks for everything, *Christopher,*" I say, mimicking my mom.

"No problem, Lucy," he says, which is what my math teacher, Mrs. Williams, called me for an entire year.

After he's gone and Seth retreats to the spare room, I walk to Grandma's bookshelves and find her favorites.

She asked in her will for an appropriate reading, and I know who she'll want to hear.

I hope Dorothy Parker has something meaningful to say about gardens. Or death.

Chapter 4

After an almost reasonable night of sleep and my first shower in days, I am a new person. I watched days of makeup swirl down the drain. I shaved my legs and my armpits. My eyes are no longer red, and I can focus. I feel like myself.

Of course, seeing things clearly only makes reality seem uglier.

Seth passes me in the hallway and shoots me a smile, which helps. Today is going to be weird. I like the way we can be comfortable in the house without talking. We slide by each other, me on breakfast, grabbing cereal and coffee and orange juice, and him making his midmorning coffee and sending emails from his phone, like we have a rhythm. It's not what I had with Grandma, but it feels right.

An hour later, it's time to move. I'm standing in the driveway with a pack of people who qualify as my immediate family, but we all look like we've dressed for different events.

Seth is wearing dark jeans and a T-shirt that says MONTREAL on it. He wears sunglasses that look expensive, and his sneakers have a cool paisley pattern. He could be going to a reading at a bookstore. He could be going to a restaurant downtown.

Mom, meanwhile, is in one of her flowing hippie sack dresses and a large mesh sun hat that, like her dress, is made from some sort of burlap. Her geode necklace is back, but she's added a rose quartz beaded choker to the mix. The woman loves stones.

Bill is in a long-sleeve formal suit, even though it's ninety-four degrees outside. I don't know where he thinks he's going. Did he think we were having a real funeral?

Chris is in black pants and a matching T-shirt, like he's dressed to be a stagehand in a theater production. Another baffling choice.

I am wearing a white A-line dress with birds on it that I bought at a thrift store in Cambridge. I look like I should be on an indie rock album cover, which is predictable, but the way I like it.

I suppose we never talked about the dress code for the day, but together, we look ridiculous.

"What is this ensemble?" I ask Chris.

"I know it's not a funeral, but my mom said I should be respectful," he says, embarrassed. "I went with all black."

"Very respectful," I say.

"You're making fun of me."

"No. I mean, it'll be good for the miming portion of the burial," I tell him.

"Are you sure I should be here?" Chris asks me.

"I'm so grateful you're here. I can't believe your mom let you miss church."

"And the clothing drive," Chris says.

My chest gets tight when I realize what day it is.

"The clothing drive!" I yell, and rub my forehead.

Over the past year, Grandma and I tried to do more volunteering with Chris's family, joining the activities put together by their church. It was kind of weird — partly because we were two rando white Jewish ladies tagging along with the Burkes' church friends, but mostly because I'd never done stuff like that. My mom and I never had enough time in one place to get to know big groups of people and give back.

Grandma and I were supposed to be sorting clothes today. We were supposed to be organizing donations for people who need nice things to wear to job interviews.

We would have been there right now, in Chris's church's basement, if things were normal.

"The clothing drive," I say again, and I blink tears away.

"My mom's got it, Lor," Chris says, placing his hand on my shoulder. "There are fifty volunteers over there. I didn't mean to make you feel bad. All I meant was that I didn't want to get in the way of a private family moment today. I'm honored to be here."

"Grandma would want you to be part of this," I say.

"You're part of our family, Christopher," Mom tells him, because she's overhead.

"Christian!" Seth and I say.

"Oh yes, I'm so sorry," she says, and gets into the passenger seat of her car with Bill.

"Meet at the Bussey Street Gate," Mom yells out the window.

Seth gives her a thumbs-up as she pulls away, and then he notices the house across the street.

"What is up with that kid?" he asks.

"Who?" I ask.

"That kid," he says, pointing to the middle schooler on the trampoline on our across-the-street neighbor's long front lawn. "He's been jumping on that trampoline every day since I've been here, like, all day. He's on that thing when I wake up and when I go to bed. Literally, the only time he hasn't been on it was when we came back from the hospital at three a.m., and frankly, he might have been on it then too, but I didn't think to look."

Seth is talking about Devin Coogan, the youngest of three brothers who live across the street. When I moved in, I asked Grandma Sheryl the same thing about Devin Coogan. Even a few years ago, he would hop on that fancy trampoline as soon as he got home from school, bouncing for hours, and sometimes for an hour or two before he left in the morning.

"He's committed to his jumping; that's all I know," Grandma had said.

Chris had filled me in at the time, and I looked to him now to explain it all to Seth.

"Devin Coogan loves soccer," Chris says. "He wants to be a famous player, and he practices all day, every day. See how there's a net around the trampoline? He's usually out there with a ball, and he'll be kicking it against the net and catching it over and over and over. Sharpening his reflexes. It's a little compulsive, I guess, but he knows what he wants."

"I could put him in a book," Seth says. "Honestly, that's the kind of great suburban character I tell my students about."

"Lori and I wrote a story about him once," Chris tells him as he slides into the back seat and Seth and I take the two seats up front. Seth hasn't driven in years, so he's to my right.

"Tell me about it," Seth says, and looks to me with a smile.

"We called it 'Bouncing Boy,'" I tell him. "It was about a boy who's always jumping on a trampoline, getting better and better at doing flips and kicks, until one day, after a series of somersaults, he bounces so high he never comes back down. His parents search for him but find nothing. After years, they give up—until one day he falls back down onto the trampoline. But he's the same age. Like, for him, it was just one high jump. Seconds of time. The story sort of worked, but we were never sure if it was a metaphor or just a cool idea."

"I'd love to read it," Seth says, and I beam.

As we back out of the driveway, I see Devin in my rearview mirror. I have taken it for granted that I'll get to see his weird jumping every day.

"I wish I liked anything as much as that kid loves that trampoline," Seth says with a little bit of reverence. I stop the car to let him look.

"Hey, Devin," Chris yells through his open window. I love that he is the kind of person who yells hellos. He is so social and easygoing, as long as he's not in a big crowd. That's when he gets shy. "You're looking swift, like Ronaldo," Chris tells him.

"I'm done with him," Devin says, his voice cracking as he leaps. "I like Messi."

"He's got the moves for your height," Chris says, "Keep kicking, man."

"How do you know who these soccer players are?" I ask Chris. "I've literally never seen you watch soccer."

"I don't know," Chris says, shrugging. "I guess I just hear stuff."

Chris always knows sports things even though he doesn't watch or do sports things. I have no idea how that works.

"Where are the craisins?" I ask then, remembering why we're in the car.

"There's a box in the trunk of your mom's car," Seth says. "I took the other three boxes up to the spare room closet."

I don't like the thought of boxes of cremains in a closet, but I'm not sure where else I'd put them. I can tell Mom and Seth have been divvying up this adult resposibility all moring.

Twenty-two minutes later we are technically in Boston, but you wouldn't know it. It doesn't look like a city here. The Arnold Arboretum is a massive open space that runs through a couple neighborhoods in the city, sort of like Central Park in New

York, I guess, but probably not as cool because it's Boston and not New York. I have driven through the arboretum with Grandma—the cut-through road is something we've taken into the city—but I haven't spent a ton of time on the grounds. Grandma asked me if I wanted to visit the gardens many times, and even though I always told her I'd be willing *someday,* I never made it happen for more than a quick drive. She always went with the Girls.

"Do you know what an arboretum is, Lori? Chris?" Bill asks us as he gets out of my mom's car.

I am staring at him. He's taken off his formal suit jacket and thrown it into the back seat. He has massive armpit stains on his white shirt, and they're only getting worse. I worry for a second that he might die by suffocation from his own outfit; I'm overheated, and this dress is one of the lightest things I own.

Chris is standing next to me, and I feel the warmth of him at my side. He's brought his sketchpad and pencils so he can draw whatever site we choose for Grandma.

Chris shakes his head, and I think he probably does know what an arboretum is, but he wants to be nice and let Bill explain. But I am less nice. I answer Bill by lifting my arms and motioning to what's in front of us. We're at one of the gates of the Arnold Arboretum. Acres of trees and plants lie beyond. I mean, we're looking at it.

"This," I say, waving my hand at the gate. "This is an arboretum."

It's like he's asked us if we've ever seen an amusement park while we're standing across from an amusement park. But I know he means well, so I work to keep my tone as even as possible.

"Yes," Bill says with a chuckle. I notice that he's cut his face shaving. There are a few large dots of dried blood near his new sideburns. Poor guy.

"But do you know *why* we have arboretums?"

Bill really wants to give me some answers here.

"No, Bill," I say. "Why do we have arboretums?"

"It's not just any old trees," he says. "Most arboretums are for study—so scientists can watch them. I looked up the Arnold Arboretum this morning, and it's run by *Harvard*."

Bill says *Harvard* like it's the most impressive word he's ever uttered.

"There are thousands of plants and trees here, and many of them are native to other countries," he says. "It's like a museum of trees—you don't have to travel, because it's all right here. More than two hundred acres of flora from all over the world!"

Bill has made the arboretum sound majestic, but I can't ignore that there's a car being parallel parked behind ours, and that the kid in the back seat is licking the window.

"That's really cool," I tell him, and I suppose it is. I like the idea of a tree museum. This is one of those moments when I appreciate Bill's kindness and simplicity. He did not tell me about the arboretum to lecture me or prove that he's wise. He just wanted to share a cool thing. Most of mom's boyfriends have pretended that they know everything, or they've ignored me, but Bill wants to communicate. I can't imagine he'll be around forever, but I have to admit he's the best she's found so far.

Mom pops open the trunk of the car, and when she walks around back and lifts the lid, I hold my breath. I think we all do. When she slams it shut, we all look and see that she's holding a shopping bag from Chico's, a store in the mall where they sell big, shapeless dresses that make up most of my mom's wardrobe. I'm sure Chico's sells other stuff too, but whenever I pass the one in the Natick Mall and see a mannequin wearing a massive burlap sack with a belt around it, I think of my mother. She loves a formless garment.

"Where are the craisins?" Seth asks her, and then we lock eyes and grin.

"In here," Mom says, lifting the Chico's bag and giving it a shake.

We're all stunned. Even Bill looks appalled.

"You put Grandma in a Chico's bag?" I ask, and let out a sharp laugh. Chris drops his water bottle, which is probably his brother's because it has tiny Miles Moraleses on it, and scrambles to pick it up. My mom doesn't seem to understand why this is off-putting.

"The craisins are still in their own box," she says in a loud whisper. "We can't walk around an arboretum with a bag that says Walsh's Funeral Home on it, can we? I had this stray Chico's bag in the trunk. I figured it would make the process a little more inconspicuous."

"But Chico's—" I say. "Who wants to be caught dead in a Chico's bag?"

"Lori!" my mom says, and this is where our senses of humor diverge. She does not like to joke about things like death—but I can see that Bill is laughing. Chris has turned his entire body away from us, pretending to look at a tree, so I know he's losing it, too.

"The bag has sturdy handles, which is something we need right now," she says. "Apart from that," she snaps, "there is nothing wrong with Chico's. Half of my closet is Chico's."

"Well, we know that's true, Becca," Seth says.

"Sick burn," I say, and we high-five.

My mom storms ahead of us, down the path, into the thick of this tree museum.

"I guess we should be nice," Seth groans, and we follow.

❦

As we walk up the paved path through what's labeled the Bussey Gate, I'm overwhelmed by the beauty of this place. The wildness of it all. Every tree is different from the next, and the farther in we get, the more the arboretum feels never-ending. I smell pine and grass. It's a clear day. I'm going to get a sunburn, but it feels good. It's a dry heat.

We've come from the suburbs to the city, but the air smells cleaner here.

"How will you guys pick a location?" Chris asks me.

"I don't know," I say. "I guess we just go with something that looks pretty, but permanent. I don't want her to, like, get blown away by a lawn mower or anything."

"Yikes, I hadn't thought of that," Chris says.

"Why have we never come here together?" I ask Chris. "This is a good fantasy setting—if you removed all the people. It'd be good for stories. Witches could live here."

"I don't know," he says, and when I look at him, his eyes are on the tallest trees. "I can see why Sheryl picked it, though."

We wander off the paved path, weaving in and out of this mismatching forest, and we all start slowing down to stop and look at the signs in front of each tree to learn their names. There are so many trees with fancy names.

"That's so perfect," Chris says, pointing to a narrow creek that runs next to the path. "Lor, look," he says, pointing to a small wooden bridge that takes you over the water to more open space and growing things. He walks over, and I follow. I sense the rest of the family behind us.

We wander until we stop under the shade of a circle of trees. It's peaceful here.

"Oh, this is beautiful, honey," my mom says. "What a great spot."

She is walking up to us, smiling, looking determined, and it's clear she believes that after ten minutes of wandering around a three-hundred-acre arboretum, we're going to put Grandma Sheryl under the first mildly attractive tree.

"We're not stopping here," I say. "This isn't the right place. These trees are too basic."

"But it's so lovely," she says, motioning to, yes, what is probably the most scenic landscape I've ever seen. "These are beautiful trees."

"There are a zillion gorgeous spots in this arboretum, and we're not stopping at the first one just because you're ready to drive home with Bill."

"Lori," she says sharply. "I'm not trying to rush this. I'm only saying you've found a very lovely, private-looking spot. I don't see why we wouldn't take advantage of it."

"Lori's not wrong, Becca," Seth tells her. "This place is huge. Can you give us a chance to walk a little bit? I'd like to see if other parts of the arboretum call to us. This isn't the time for efficiency."

Chris takes two steps away from the family and pretends to be focused on a tag identifying another tree. I know how much he hates conflict, how listening to all this ugliness probably makes him want to disappear into whatever shrubbery he can find.

"I'm not trying to be efficient," Mom says. "It just happens that this is an incredibly gorgeous spot. We're not far from that babbling brook!"

She points in the direction of the bridge we took.

"That was just water. A stream," Seth says. "I don't think it qualifies as babbling."

"Oh, I can hear some babbling," Mom says to her brother, and Bill looks at her as if she's grown fangs or something. My mom is usually so self-helpish, so touchy-feely, but Seth brings out the sibling in her.

"Let's just keep walking," I say. "Seth and I will know the right spot when we see it."

I pass them and set out farther into the wooded area, snaking through patches of grass under sagging branches. I can hear my mom, Seth, Bill, and Chris following behind, which makes me feel like the Pied Piper of death.

I stop abruptly because I can sense her shadow. "Jesus, Mom, I almost feel your feet on the back of my heels. It's like you're chasing me," I say.

She looks like I've struck her. "You are not the only person who is grieving, Lori," she snaps. "It's not just you and Seth here."

But it is, I think.

The thing Seth and I keep thinking but not saying is that he was much closer to Grandma than my mom was. *I* was much closer to Grandma Sheryl even before I moved in with her. Seth and Grandma could talk for hours on the phone about books and whatever else they were interested in. Seth asked about her life, whereas my mom always "checked in." Their conversations and visits were a series of obligatory questions about money, health, the usual. It does feel as if Seth and I have more invested in where Grandma will be put to rest.

"Fine. Just forget it," I say. I'm frustrated that she doesn't seem to understand this, and I'm about to march away from her when I hear someone mutter, "Excuse me."

Mom and I freeze — and then look down. There is a very old man on the ground, only inches from our feet, and he appears to have been sitting there for a while. There is a bottle of water on a tray in front of him.

I think he might be a hundred and fifty years old, and he's wearing tan cargo shorts with many pockets and a dark green T-shirt that says ENERGY.

His nose is sunburned, and it makes me think of what a wizard would look like if he fell asleep on the beach. His white hair goes down to his waist, and the branches of the tree he's leaning against are peppered with white petals, so he's basically in camouflage, which is probably why we didn't notice him. He's wearing glasses that look like goggles. There are twigs stuck to the sleeve of his shirt and a pack of sunflower seeds tucked into his sock.

"Well, hello there," my mother says, and her voice, now light and airy, suggests that she thinks she has found a magical gnome. She bends over to continue. "I'm so sorry we didn't see you there."

The man, who I am very much hoping is a certifiable spell-caster, does not return my mother's smile, and that makes me like him.

"I understand we're in a public space," he says, his voice reminding me of the texture of granola, "and that there are no specific rules about conversation in the arboretum, but we're in the middle of a forest bathing activity, and we're hoping you can respect the quiet, at least in this immediate area."

"Forest bathing," I say, testing the words.

Seth, who has Chris and Bill behind him, asks before I can.

"What's forest bathing?"

"Oh, hey there! Watch your step, everybody," Bill says, and then we look at our feet and realize that this Gandalf-esque man by the tree is not alone.

To my left there's a young man leaning against another tree, a backpack in his lap. The bark looks rough, but he seems comfortable, not quite asleep, but resting.

A few feet from him, two women are on their backs, side by side in the grass. They're holding hands. One is humming.

Now that we're looking around, we can see that there are probably twenty people here, draped all over the landscape as if they live here.

"What is this?" Seth whispers to me. "Is it a cult?"

He moves his head in the direction of the backpack guy, who, actually, seems like he might be sleeping, to make sure I've noticed. "Is he dead?" Seth whispers.

"He's taking a forest shower," I whisper back. It's the only explanation we've been given.

Hearing me, the Gandalf man says, "Forest *bathing*. It's the Japanese practice of *shinrin-yoku*."

He stands up and motions for us to walk with him so we're a few feet away from where the others are lounging.

"I'm Kel. I'm a part-time forest therapy guide, and I'm guiding today's forest bathing exercise. You're welcome to join the group, but if not, I ask that you try to be respectful of the others who are working in partnership with the forest."

"I'm so sorry," I say. Kel clearly cares about whatever this spiritual practice is, and my family has basically stepped on all of it.

I want to make it right.

"My grandma just died, and we're here honoring her today —in partnership with the land too, I guess—and it's really hot out and we probably are tired and cranky, but we will absolutely stop yelling at each other and get out of your way," I say, probably in one breath.

Kel's face softens, and then he looks at the Chico's bag in my mother's hands. He's probably judging it, too. Kel is pretty stylish for his age.

"I would be happy to have you join us in forest bathing in honor of your grandmother."

"That's okay. I don't think we—"

"Yes!" my mom says, because forest bathing is exactly the kind of thing she'd be into. "I'd love to learn more."

I'm about to protest, but Seth leans into my ear. "Always say yes to seemingly weird activities. It's good material."

And with that, I am no longer annoyed. Let Mom lead us into some mindless mindfulness activity. Seth has now made it a writing project.

Maybe Chris and I can write something about a man who talks to trees.

"Take a seat wherever you can find space," Kel says.

We all plop down in the same general area, trying to spread out. Chris is on his back, many feet away, not nearly as close as I'd like.

"Everyone lie back," Kel says, so I do.

"We're going to do some exercises to keep us present in this space," Kel tells the entire group.

He asks us to notice what it feels like to breathe. Sometimes he "invites us" to open our eyes and focus on one point. Other times he tells us to keep our eyes closed so we can listen to the sounds of the arboretum. I hear some planes overhead, but mostly it's just the breeze rustling the leaves and the rhythm of my own breathing. I do feel more relaxed. There probably is something to this.

But then Kel invites us to communicate with one of the trees, to see if we can get support from a tree, and I squirm a little.

I want to make fun of this exercise. I want to sit up and look at Chris to see if he feels the same.

But when I take a second and force myself to try, I find

myself imagining communication with the trees overhead. I picture myself admitting to these trees—all the green, willowing giants surrounding me right now—that I never did come to see them with Grandma. She asked me to do so many things with her, and I guess I did a lot of them. I went with her to the symphony, even though classical music isn't my thing. I went grocery shopping with her every week and carried all the bags from the car. I watched so much television with her, *so many* British mystery shows, because I knew she needed someone to talk to about who might be the murderer.

I let her tell me everything about her reading, about the books that shaped her life. She was an English teacher—the world's best, from what I know. She taught one town over, at the high school, for most of her life. I grew up knowing the big family story about how she challenged the school district about reading requirements for students, why there were so many mandatory reading list books by white men rather than women—specifically women of color. It was a whole thing, and there's a *Boston Globe* newspaper article about it framed on her wall.

Grandma Sheryl could read anything for pleasure, she used to say, but she did have favorite authors who she imagined might be friends if she had met them in real life. Her favorite was Dorothy Parker, who she said became an imaginary best friend after Grandpa died. She was living in Natick with two young twins, long before the internet, she told me once. She taught all day, leaving the kids with her own mother until they were old enough for school, and then, as the world got more expensive and her house became more difficult to afford, she began tutoring after hours. She prepared students for standardized tests and AP exams and used the extra money to keep the family afloat. She didn't have time for friends, but late at night, she could read.

That's when she'd hang out with Dorothy and Edith Wharton and Zora Neale Hurston and Tillie Olsen. I've tried to read them, the ones she said were her BFFs, and I've desperately tried to like their work, but it's all too real.

"There is an astounding absence of dragons and time travel in this book," I'd told her during my only attempt at reading *The Age of Innocence.* "I'm not this kind of reader. Unless these characters are stuck in a time loop or something."

"There's no shame in your favorites," she told me. She was never a snob about reading preferences. "Go back to your fairies."

For her, reading was company. It felt like hanging out.

I wish I'd known more about *this,* though—this arboretum, why she liked these things that grow. She got something important from all the plants in the house, but I never asked about it.

I feel someone lie down next to me and wonder if it's Chris moving closer, but when I open my eyes, I see Kel, and he is smiling at me. He's also like three inches from my face and smells like dried fruit.

"Did you know," he says quietly, "that trees release chemicals when they feel they are in danger?"

I don't say anything. I stay silent and let him be weird. This *is* excellent material.

"It's been scientifically proven," he continues. "They release volatile organic compounds."

"Oh," I say, because I don't know how else to respond.

And then I get it. He wants to tell me something about me—about my family. He wants to liken me to a tree because I yelled at my mom. Because when we stumbled upon Kel, we were releasing some volatility ourselves.

"Sometimes we have to release our negative energy when we're scared and upset," he continues, hammering home the metaphor, and I do my best to nod, my head lolling toward him on the ground. "It can feel good to let out the toxins and breathe in something pure.

"Forest bathing isn't just meditation or rest or communing with nature. It's proven to be good for your health. They've done tests on people before and after this kind of exercise, and over time, after those people were finished forest bathing, their immune function was stronger. I believe that when we commune with the trees, they give us this gift. Inhaling their phytoncides—what the trees release to protect themselves—can be good for our own bodies."

"That's really cool," I say, and I'm being serious. It really is.

I sit up, and he follows my lead. I can see my mom a few yards away, and she's seated in her favorite yoga pose. She's forest bathing as if she's done it thousands of times before. I can tell by the set of her mouth that she might be speaking some sort of wellness prayer or something. Bill is on his back by her side. His sweat stains have only gotten bigger. His shirt is more wet than dry.

"Do houseplants release the same chemicals?" I ask Kel. "Do they give off photons, or whatever, when they're happy or threatened?"

"Phytoncides," he repeats, smiling. "I don't think so. But they look nice."

"I just wondered. My grandma had a lot of houseplants, and I'm realizing that I never saw her get angry. Maybe it was the plants keeping her calm."

Kel smiles. "Maybe so.

"May I make a request?" Kel asks then, and I nod. "These trees are all quite sensitive, especially those that aren't native to this part of the world. You would think that human remains would be good for nature and for soil. But the body has a lot of chemicals in it. After cremation, the pH levels can be high and toxic."

I stare at his big woodland wizard eyes.

"How did you know?"

"I'm in this arboretum many hours a day. I'm only a part-time freelance instructor—I don't work for the arboretum. But I'm here, and I enjoy working in this space whenever I can," he says. "When someone tells me they've just lost a relative and they come in a group and they're holding a bag, I can make a pretty good guess about their intentions."

"The Chico's bag," I whisper.

"Personally, I believe in the right to bring loved ones to a place like this. I don't believe in permits. We're all of this earth. But people should protect the land, and we have to respect the needs of these trees and of Harvard, which is doing its best to preserve this property. Do you understand?"

"You're saying we can't put the ashes here."

"I'm asking that you don't put them *right* here, in this spot, near the trees. But you might find that there are some beautiful patches of flowers up the hill. There are also some nice shady areas with a great view. I would never recommend that you do any kind of scattering in the arboretum—I have no authority here—but if you were *going* to, that might be the place."

I do like the idea of a good view.

Kel smiles, takes a map from his back pocket, and opens it for me, pointing to where we are and where he wants us to go, illegally, with our human remains. He's a good sport.

"There might be some rose of Sharon somewhere up there," he says. "Very lovely."

"I don't know," I say. "Roses are kind of basic, right?"

"Rose of Sharon is not *basic* at all," Kel says. "It doesn't look like the kind of rose you'd buy in a dozen. Technically, it's more like a hibiscus."

"Hold, please," I tell Kel, and I reach for my bag, which has the book given to me by Jill from the Garden Girls. I find a picture of a hibiscus right there under *H,* and the flowers are super cute and colorful. Thank goodness for this book.

"Rose of Sharon can come in beautiful blues and purples," Kel tells me.

"That sounds perfect," I say. "Thank you."

He smiles, and there are so many lines around his mouth that they remind me of the inside of one of these trees. Then he rings a tiny bell—like a dinner bell—that must have been sitting on the ground next to him this whole time.

He rings the bell two more times, and the forest bathers understand. Slowly, they pull themselves upright and sit crossed-legged, facing Kel. I see my family and Chris look around, nervously taking cues from the others. Chris sees that I've been talking to Kel and flashes a look of surprise. A few feet away, Seth's eyes are red, and I realize that at some point during the exercise he must have been crying. I wonder what happened when he closed his eyes—what he told his tree.

"Friends, I'm going to invite you to do some walking on your own," Kel tells the group. "Those who want to peel off can do so now."

He gives me a knowing look, hands me his small paper map, and when the group follows their leader, my family is left behind. Mom, Bill, Chris, and Seth, who has composed himself, walk over to me, and Mom asks, "What was that all about? What did he say to you?"

"We're going to bring Grandma somewhere else. Maybe to a rose of Sharon. Which is apparently a hibiscus."

"Sweet," Seth says. "Lead the way."

We walk for about ten minutes, mostly in silence. The path takes us up a hill, past patches of so many blooming things and trees, until I see a patch of shady grass covered in pretty green plants. It's not far from a sign that says EXPLORERS GARDEN, which is something I bet Grandma liked. This patch of grass and already-bloomed buds is a small oasis on a hill that has a good view. Like a little hiding place close to the center of the arboreal action.

"This is it," I say, and I feel it. She'll be able to see everything from here.

"Oh, honey, this — this spot is beautiful," Mom says, and Bill walks to her and holds her hand.

"I don't know if this is a rose of Sharon, but I love it. She'd love it," I add.

"I know she would," Seth says, and I see that he's holding the Chico's bag now.

We all agree. We're not fighting, and I believe the trees have helped us make peace with one another, at least for the afternoon.

We all sit down near the one patch of grass and supernatural-looking shimmering leaves — which could be weeds, for all I know — coming from the ground, surrounding them as best we can. A couple with a double stroller passes us, but after they disappear, we're on our own. The closest arboretum visitors are

far in the distance. Most people probably opted for air conditioning today.

"We should do this while we have some privacy," Seth says.

Without asking for permission, Chris takes an art knife out
of his backpack—the kind he'd use to make a stencil—and outlines a circle in the dirt in the center of the space. Then he uses
his hands to dig.

I sit down next to him and watch. The adults surround us.

Chris looks up and then stops. "I didn't mean to overstep. I
just wanted to help make a place for you to do . . . what you need
to do."

"It's a perfect spot," Mom says.

"Thank you, Chris," Seth says. "I think we're all a bit unsure
about what to do here. This is a help."

I will never stop appreciating Chris's perfect friendship.

Once he's made a deep pocket in the ground, Seth reaches
into the Chico's bag and removes a white cardboard box the size
of a peanut butter jar. It reminds me of the kind of box you'd put
a cupcake in. There's a gold sticker on top that says WALSH'S, with
that shamrock in place of the apostrophe.

I hear a rustling next to me, and when I turn, I see that
Chris cannot help himself; he's fumbling with his backpack
again, putting the knife away and taking out his sketchpad, and
now he's drawing. It's compulsive behavior with him, and one
of the reasons I love him so much, because this is how he proc-
esses the world, putting it into a spiral sketchbook and changing

it into something he can understand. I guess that's also why I write.

Seth's hands are shaky and fumbling, so it takes him longer than it should to open the box. No one breathes as he pops the top and pulls out what's inside.

The plastic bag is clear, but it's very thick, so the contents inside look a little fuzzy. We all get a muted look at the gravel-like cremains. They're a darker color than I thought they'd be, but I see the white pieces.

Tiny white pieces. Tiny pieces of bones.

Mom starts crying.

"Oh, Mom," she says, and Bill pulls out a pile of tissues from his shirt pocket. I appreciate that he is a person who thinks to bring tissues.

Then Seth takes Mom's hand, and they both cry together. Bill hands Seth more tissues, and we all wait until they compose themselves.

I'm not crying. I don't know why.

What I feel is weirdly more like . . . euphoria. For a moment I think about how lucky I am that I knew this person, that I got to live with her. I think about our mutual love of kettle corn and how she always trusted me. That for a while, when I thought college might be a waste of time for someone like me, she didn't push back. She told me it wasn't for everybody, and it was a really expensive thing to sign up for if you're not all in. Then she looked up which of my favorite writers had college degrees, which turned out to be all of them. But the point was, she made it so we could figure it out together.

She was really funny and kind, and I was lucky to know her.

I think that when I die, I want to be cremated too and placed wherever she is.

Seth doesn't seem to be able to move. He's just clutching the bag of craisins like it's a stuffed animal. He can't take the next step. Grandma Sheryl would want me to help him.

I reach out and place my hands on Seth's, and he looks at me like a scared kid.

"What are you doing?" he says as I try to take the bag from him.

"Helping," I whisper.

"Lori," Mom says, "you don't have to do this. We'll do it."

"I know I don't have to," I say. "But I don't mind. You guys just be her kids today."

And then I realize that this might be why I'm not crying, at least not right this second. One of the things about grandparents is that even if they're on the young side, you know they're not designed to be part of your life forever. You don't get to have them for a chunk of your life, because you weren't around for a chunk of theirs. It's a relationship with a clear end; even if everyone lives to be a hundred, you still get only a window.

It's different with parents. No matter how I feel about my mom, I can't imagine her ever being elderly or gone from the world. It would never feel right. She and Seth probably feel the same about Grandma.

As soon as Mom realizes I'm trying to be nice and sensitive, she relaxes her shoulders and nods. Seth releases his tight grip on the bag.

I find the hole Chris made in the ground and open the bag, prepared to pour it in. For a second, I wonder if I should have brought gloves to do this so I don't get gross craisin residue on my hands, but I also think I *want* to touch the craisins, to know what they feel like. I don't care if they're toxic.

But before I stick my hand in, Mom has something to say.

"Did you read *Wild*?" she interrupts.

"Hmm?" Seth mutters.

"Cheryl Strayed's book *Wild*. It was very popular, Seth."

"Grandma read it," I tell Seth. I remember seeing the book next to her bed. It had a big hiking boot on it. I think she also saw the movie.

"I know what it is," Seth says in Mom's direction, annoyed.

"I bought it up because the author did this TED Talk about radical sincerity," Mom says.

"Right. Her TED Talk," Seth says, and takes the biggest breath to calm himself. "She's not famous for her TED Talk, Becca. You know, she started as a novelist. I've read her *novel*."

I love when Seth pretends that nonfiction doesn't exist.

"*Wild*! That's Reese Witherspoon!" Bill adds. "I saw the movie."

"Yes, honey," Mom says. "But the book is all about the death of her mother and how she hikes the Pacific Palisades."

"The Pacific Crest Trail," Seth mutters.

"Right," Mom replies, ignoring his tone. "The Pacific Crest Trail. Anyway, she has her mother's ashes with her, and she eats them."

Chris's head snaps up, and his jaw drops, as does Seth's.

"Why would she do that?" Seth asks.

"I believe it was to have her mother inside her, just like she had once been inside of her mother. It was very poetic, from what I remember. Something like that, I think."

I look into the bag. The craisins look chalky and hard and not at all digestible.

"Are you suggesting we eat our mother?" Seth says, pushing his hair from his forehead. It's extra springy with the humidity; my mom's is too.

Chris's hand starts moving feverishly on the page, and I assume he's now drawing someone eating remains and becoming a possessed golem or something.

"I'll do it if you do it," I challenge Mom.

"I'm not suggesting we do that, Lori, I'm just remembering the book," Mom says.

"I'm not sure it would be healthy," Bill offers with a shrug.

"Let's just move on," I say. Sweat is running down my legs.

"I do recommend the TED Talk," Mom says.

Chris bites his lip.

"Okay, enough. Let's move this along," Seth says. "Before someone official walks by and demands to see our permit."

Then we're all silent and staring at one another. Actually, everyone's staring at me. I'm the one holding the bag.

"Okay," I say. "I'm doing it. Now."

"Good. Great," Seth says, and he sounds scared. "Do it."

I begin to pour.

The first thing I realize is that this hole is not big enough to fit what's in this bag. The divot in the ground is overflowing in seconds, so I have to stop, cover it with some nearby dirt, and look for other places to put it.

"Do you want another hole?" Chris asks. "I can make that one bigger."

"No," I say. "I'm just going to spread it around."

The bag is a little lighter now, and I begin pouring the rest of the ashes around the roots of these green plants, using my hands to cover the ashes with the soil. I go out of my way not to touch the cremains, although I'm sure I come in contact with them. I try not to think about it. I feel better about putting her here, where she'll be surrounded by beautiful trees and plants, but where her body won't get in the way of letting things grow.

I want to give Grandma Sheryl variety, so I stand up and move a few feet away, where you can see more of what's below the hill. My hands are a mess, but I don't care. I close my eyes and rub the pieces into my palm, as if she might seep into me. It feels right to have her on my skin.

It's not until I notice the others staring at me that I return to the group and sit down, waiting for whatever's next.

"Is it time to say something?" Seth asks after an emotional cough.

Grandma had asked for a reading, and I'd found one, but before I can grab my notebook to start, Mom begins to speak.

"Mother," Mom says, without preamble, "we love you. We miss you. We are here today to honor your life, your love of all beautiful things, whether it be words or flowers—or . . . this gorgeous grass."

"It's not just grass," I whisper.

"I'd call it greenery," Bill says.

"Right," I say. "Sure."

"Whatever!" Mom snaps. "Anyway. Mom, today we hope to bring you a very good view. We will miss you always."

Then she looks at us for a response.

"Anything you want to add, Seth?"

"Yeah, the actual reading, Becca," Seth says. "Mom wanted us to read something from a book."

Mom looks hurt, Seth responds by looking contrite, and the whole exchange is fast and awkward.

"It's okay," I say. "I've got the reading."

I open my bag and take out my latest notebook. It's a red spiral one, and I've been using purple ink on the white pages. I open to the latest page, where I've made notes.

I let myself breathe and then start.

"Sheryl Miller Seltzer was born in Boston in 1944. She was a teacher and, in later years, a gardener. She also liked British shows about murders, especially if the murderer character was a woman.

"Most of all, Grandma Sheryl loved books. She loved women writers, especially the funny ones. She died on Dorothy Parker's birthday."

Mom gasps. She hadn't realized this. I give her a moment to recover. She takes Seth's hand.

"Today," I continue, "for Grandma Sheryl, I'd like to read some Dorothy Parker."

I look up, and they're all crying now, except for Chris, who has paused his drawing out of respect, I assume. He's looking down solemnly at his sketchpad. I assume it's his church face.

"Go ahead, Lor," Seth says, and sniffles.

I flip to the next page and clear my throat. I want to give a good reading, loud and clear, for Grandma. I move to speak directly to the place where the craisins now live. I bend my head, as if Grandma's remains might hear me.

"'You can lead a horticulture,'" I shout, "'but you can't make her think!'"

There is silence for a beat.

"What was that?" Mom says.

"Dorothy Parker," I say.

"*Jesus,* Lori," Seth says, but he's already laughing. Then he's laughing louder, and the rest of us join him. I know Grandma would find this hilarious, too. That was sort of the point.

"Wasn't there any other, I don't know, more *poignant* Dorothy Parker passage?" Seth asks, beaming at me.

"It's the one that seemed most relevant," I respond. "Most of her writing is about sex, men being stupid, and society women being terrible."

"I liked it!" Bill says.

"I don't know if I get it," Chris says.

"You know, *hor-ti-culture,*" I say.

"Oh," Chris says. "Oh!"

Then he blushes.

"Dorothy Parker would have been so good at social media," Seth says.

"Lori," Mom says. "I'd like you to wash your hands."

And with that, she has ended the moment.

She's already standing up, preparing to leave.

"I guess that's it for Box One," Seth says, and Chris gathers his things.

Before we go, I take a bunch of pictures with my phone—of the EXPLORERS GARDEN sign, of the patch where Grandma now lives, and a shot of the view from above. I send them to the text group that is the Garden Girls. I see that they're responding with prayer emojis and hearts.

Jill says, "Good girl. That spot will be gorgeous in May."

I want to tell this to everyone, but I see that they're already walking away, back to our cars to start the process of saying goodbye.

When we make it back to where we started, all of us almost as sweaty as Bill, me with the dirtiest hands, Mom calls me over to give me the facts.

"I just have a few coaching sessions this week, and then I'll be back to help you pack."

I say nothing.

"You'll make new friends, and of course you can keep in touch with the ones you've made here," she says. "Bill's spare room has a nice big closet."

I narrow my eyes at her. Closet space is not what I'm looking for in life.

"I think we'd benefit from a year together, Lori," she says.

Then she smiles at Bill, and I think that this is not about me. I'm an accessory, as usual with her. Like a geode necklace, but perhaps less meaningful.

She hugs me, and it feels like a countdown clock has started ticking.

Everyone waves as Mom and Bill pull out of their parking space, headed for the highway. I'm focused on Chris, though, and thinking of a plan.

Chapter 5

That afternoon I go over to Chris's house and ring the doorbell. Chris's younger brother, Adam, answers. He's not looking at me, though. He just swings open the door, his eyes on what's in his hands.

"You know, I could be been an intruder," I tell him. "Or a kidnapper. You should look up at a person before you let them in."

"Murderers don't ring the doorbell," he says.

At ten, Adam looks like a mini-Chris, but his personality is all his own. Whereas Chris is polite and helpful and is always apologizing for putting anyone out — as if he ever does — Adam does whatever he wants and figures he'll talk his way out of it later. He is already an expert at batting his eyelashes in a way that demands forgiveness.

The only person who scares him is his mother. If Mrs. Burke gets angry with Adam and says three specific words — "Try that again" — his lip starts to tremble and he breaks into a performance of groveling that ends with his being sent to his room to think about what he did. He cries so much at that point, trembling with fear, that you'd think he'd been sent somewhere awful, as opposed to his room, which has actual toys all over it. Once he emerges, usually after about twenty minutes, he sits on Mrs. Burke's lap and she calls him her Snugglepuss and all is forgiven. I have seen the cycle play out many times.

Chris and I wrote a story about it once. We imagined what Adam experiences in that room when he's sent there, and we decided that once he shuts the door, Mrs. Burke summons all of Adam's inner demons and they spend that entire twenty minutes taunting him and calling him names. Edward Gorey–style characters with scarier faces. They scream at him about his behavior until he can't take it anymore. We called the story "Time Out."

I have lost all track of days, which is sort of a late-August thing anyway, but time has been particularly weird since Grandma died. Adam has now reminded me that today is, in fact, a Sunday.

Mrs. Burke does this thing where Adam is allowed to play games on his tablet only on Sundays, after church, and he can only play until the battery runs out. She charges the tablet on Saturday night, and when they get home, he wakes up and runs to it. It's an old tablet, so it has about three hours of life in it. Adam has no self-control, and he plays the thing for hours, taking it with him to the bathroom because he doesn't want to waste a second. When the tablet dies, he lets out a small whimper. But he knows the rules. He would never challenge them.

"You look like the life is being sucked out of you when you're on that thing," I tell Adam, whose eyes are all weird and possessed.

He ignores me and takes a seat on the round leather ottoman next to the couch.

"What game?" I ask.

"*Battle Astra,*" Adam mutters.

I nod like this means something to me.

I hear shuffling and see Mrs. Burke coming down the steps, and I get a hug before I can say hello. She smells like pretty perfume. She's in gray yoga pants and a blue sweatshirt. She's also wearing beautiful red lipstick and mascara, probably left over from a dressier morning at church and then the clothing drive. Her hair is in a perfect ponytail. She's wearing a simple solitaire necklace with a clear stone that catches the light from the window. My mother's necklace could eat this necklace.

Mrs. Burke could not be more different from my mother. I love her.

She takes a long look at me.

"My Lori," she says, and I melt inside. This is why I'm here. "How are you holding up?"

"It's sucks," I tell her before I can censor myself. This is not a *suck* house. "I'm sorry I said suck."

"You get a pass this week," she says. "You must be missing Sheryl so much right now."

"Not yet," I admit. "It doesn't even feel like she's gone. Her smell is still in the house, you know?"

"Oh, the smells. Smell is so important. Do you know that

when my mother died, I put her favorite robe in a large Ziploc bag?" Mrs. Burke tells me. "Once a year, on her birthday, I open it up and smell it. It might be silly, but even though the smell is mostly gone, it makes me feel close to her."

"That's a really good idea," I say, making a note to myself to put some of Grandma's clothes in something I can seal tight.

"How was the clothing drive?" I ask.

"We collected and sorted more than five hundred suits. Pant-suits. Skirt suits. I'd call that a success."

"I know Grandma wanted to help," I say.

"I know she did, sweetheart," Mrs. Burke says. "Christian is helping his dad put up some shelves in Adam's room," she adds, changing the subject.

Right on cue, there's the sound of a hammer, and then Chris's dad comes down the stairs.

"He's going to put a hole right through that wall," he says to Mrs. Burke before he notices me.

"Hello, Lori, dear."

"Hi, Mr. Burke," I say.

"How are you holding up?" he asks, echoing his wife without knowing it, and this time I have a better answer.

"Okay, considering," I say.

"Well," Mr. Burke says, "anything you need, we're here."

Then he goes into the kitchen.

"Let me call for Chris," Mrs. Burke tells me.

"Actually," I say, "I came to talk to you."

"Oh. Of course," she says, and leads me to the couch.

Nearby, Adam screams, "No!" and Mrs. Burke and I both jump up, startled. Then we realize he's yelling at the tablet.

"Adam!" Mrs. Burke yells at the same time that Mr. Burke yells the same thing from the kitchen.

"Sorry," he yells back. "I just died."

"Young man!" Mrs. Burke yells in his direction, but that's the end of the sentence—she doesn't say anything else. He shoots her an apologetic look, probably thinking about "time-out," and then settles into the ottoman again, his expression contrite.

Mr. Burke smiles, rolling his eyes as he passes us to go back upstairs to his project.

"What game is that?" Mrs. Burke asks Adam.

"I borrowed it from Sammy," he says, not telling her that the name of the game is *Battle Astra*.

"It better not be guns or war," Mrs. Burke says.

"It's not a gun game," Adam swears.

"If it is, Adam, you better switch it to Zelda—" she starts.

"Mom, there are no guns, I swear," he says.

"Then how did you die?"

"A blaster!" he says.

Mrs. Burke is quiet, and I know she's probably deciding whether a blaster is some kind of gun, which it most likely is, but she exhales, gives Adam a long look, and decides not to pursue this fight.

"What can I do for you, Lori?" she asks.

"Well . . ." I start. "First, thank you for letting Chris be around so much and to miss church and everything today. It helped to have him with me."

"Of course," she says. "No need to thank me. You two are peas in a pod. And Sheryl was always here for me."

"She was?" I ask.

"Always," Mrs. Burke says. "When Gary and I moved here years ago, we were both working in the city. I was taking the commuter rail into Boston every day, running back and forth to pick up Chris from daycare. We didn't know one single neighbor. No one went out of their way to make our acquaintance. One day Sheryl saw me with groceries in one arm and Chris in the other. I was close to dropping everything, and the next thing I knew, there she was, taking the bags, carrying them inside, making me laugh.

"No one tells couples how lonely it can be when you first have kids. Our friends were all in the city still. We were tired all the time. Sheryl started showing up at our door with books for us to borrow, and it was a lifeline."

Mrs. Burke smiles.

"That's why it was so serendipitous when you showed up for Chris. We'd hoped to introduce you at some point, but then there you were, finding each other on your own."

"Right," I say, and take a breath. This is my opening. "About that . . . with Grandma Sheryl gone, my school situation is sort of up in the air. I'm almost eighteen, but not yet, so it's not legal for me to live on my own in the house."

"Oh, honey, that's not a good idea, even if you were eighteen," Mrs. Burke says, folding her hands in her lap. "It wouldn't be safe, you all alone in that big house."

"Right. Of course," I say. "But I really don't want to move. My whole life is here. Chris and I have a lot of plans for our writing and applying to colleges. Two peas in a pod, like you said. I don't want to move to some random place in Maryland and miss *N-Files* and Senior Internship."

Senior Internship is a program at the end of senior year where you get to take a week off from school to shadow a job. Miss Checka told Chris and me that she has a friend who'll be able to hook us up with a publisher in Boston that puts out some of the real books we love.

Mrs. Burke shifts in her seat. Maybe she knows what's coming.

"I thought maybe I could stay here for the year," I say. "With you. In this house."

"Lori."

"I'm over here so much anyway, and I'm sure I could get my mom to give you money for food and expenses, and whatever I might need. Mostly I keep to myself when I'm at home anyway. I was thinking that Chris could move into Adam's room, or maybe, if Mr. Burke isn't using his office that much, I could set up there. I wouldn't even have to bring much stuff."

"My room is *my room*," Adam mutters to himself. "No one else in my room."

"Lori," Mrs. Burke says again, and I can tell she's choosing her words carefully.

"I also think this would be best for Chris," I say, trying another strategy quickly before she can give me an answer. "He'll need a good portfolio for colleges, and I can help him with that. Like, at this point our portfolio is shared, with my stories and his art. We'd use the time to make it better and to help each other with college applications."

I'm hoping the more I say "college," the more she'll be open to this. I don't expect a yes right now, but I'm aiming for an "I'll think about it." I'm just trying to avoid a no.

"And you'd get a bonus babysitter for Adam!" I say.

"I'm allowed to stay home alone now," Adam says.

"Not at night you're not," Mrs. Burke tells him.

I am distracted when I hear a light tapping noise, and I look over Mrs. Burke's shoulder and see that Chris has come downstairs and is in the hallway. He's hiding behind the wall that separates the living room from the kitchen, and he doesn't know I can see him.

He looks tense.

I didn't talk to him about this idea, and maybe I should have, just to get his thoughts on how to persuade his mom, but I'm the better negotiator. Also, it came to me out of nowhere when I got home from the arboretum. I didn't want to waste any time.

He looks shocked by my request.

"Lori . . ." Mrs. Burke says again, bringing my attention back to the couch.

"I know this is something you'd have to think about—and talk to my mother about. I don't expect you to have an answer right this second," I assure her.

I can see Chris cover his mouth with his hand. He's tense from anticipation. So am I.

"Lori," Mrs. Burke says, "I *do* have an answer right now. I'm sorry, but the answer is no."

"No?"

"No."

I imagine multiple version of the word floating through the room like smoke rings.

"It's not a good idea," she says, and her tone makes it clear that this is a final answer.

Mrs. Burke starts to talk, but I can't listen. I am distracted because my best friend—who's just heard his mother's rejection of my plan to move in—could not look more relieved. With no idea that I can see him or that I know he's listening, he exhales and wipes his forehead, as if he's a comic book character with a thought bubble that says "Phew!"

My breathing feels weak. Chris takes a few steps back, and now he's out of sight.

"Lori, are you all right?"

"What?"

Oh, right. Mrs. Burke.

"Can you explain that again?" I ask. I want to hear her reasoning. For a second, I compartmentalize Chris's relief.

"Really, it's just what I said. I've spoken to your mother. She's thrilled to have you in Maryland. Apart from that, you kids need attention and parenting, even though you think you're beyond it. Chris and Adam need my undivided attention. I need to be there for Chris, specifically, as he applies for colleges and makes big plans for the rest of his life.

"That doesn't mean I don't adore you, Lori. It doesn't mean I don't want you visiting and being an essential part of my son's life. It only means that I can't be your *guardian*. That's a big thing —to be responsible for someone else's child. It's a responsibility I can't take on, but that reality has nothing to do with how much I love you."

This is a totally lovely and rational explanation, but I am frozen, still, because it doesn't explain why Chris wouldn't want me here. I want to ask her about his reaction, tell her what I just saw, but I don't.

"Do you need some water, Lori? You look flushed. There have been heat advisories for days. Have you all been drinking water while you've been running around outside? Adam, go get Lori a glass of water."

"I'm okay," I whisper.

"Adam," Mrs. Burke says, "water for Lori."

"Yes, Mom," Adam says, sulking as he stands up, still playing his game, and slides his feet into the kitchen.

"Lori, I'm sorry if you expected a different answer," Mrs. Burke says, taking my hand in hers, "but you need to be with your family. It will mean sacrifices, but also new opportunities. Your mom told me all about where you'll live —"

"When did you talk to my mom?"

"She and Seth stopped by early this morning. They wanted to know if I had any real estate contacts, and I do. There's a lovely man at church who's going to help them prepare the house for sale."

"Right," I say.

I don't want to hear how we're going to sell the house.

Mrs. Burke waits for me to close the conversation. Maybe to say "you're right" or some other polite response, but I can't form the words. Maybe I didn't believe I'd really have to move — to leave my life — until this moment.

I take my hand from hers and stand up. I need to get out of here. Just then, Adam returns, holding a full glass of water in one hand.

"Oh, no thank you, Adam," I say, and he responds without looking up, saying, "No prob." He takes a sip from the glass himself and tucks it under his armpit so he can return to his game with both hands.

"Adam Burke, hold that water with two hands," Mrs. Burke says, rising.

"I have to go," I tell them.

"Lori, if you want to talk more . . ." Mrs. Burke starts.

"No. I shouldn't have asked," I say. "It's fine. I should get back to the house. We're planning our next garden trip, and I need to check in with Seth."

"Of course," she says, but there's pity in her voice. Or something. Then Adam drops the water glass.

"Adam!" Mrs. Burke says, turning to him, and I'm happy she's distracted so I can leave.

I mumble a goodbye as I run out, the door latching behind me. As I make my way down the driveway, I glance up at Chris's window to see if he's watching, but he's not there.

At home, Seth is standing in the kitchen next to the open refrigerator.

"No more lasagna," he says, and shuts it. "What do you want?" he asks.

"P. F. Changs," I say without hesitation.

"Do they deliver?" he asks.

"Everything delivers," I say.

We are the one residential street trapped in the center of acres of chain stores and every kind of commerce, but whenever Seth visits, I can tell he still thinks of Natick as the tiny town he grew up in. Like it will never catch up to what he has in New York.

"Natick is a hub of services," I say. "I can't imagine what it was like when you were a kid."

"Natick was a dry town when I was your age," he says.

"What do you mean?"

"No alcohol," he says. "Not in restaurants, at least."

"Weird. What did they do at the mall? Like at the Cheesecake Factory?"

"There was no Cheesecake Factory."

"Wow. Olden days," I say.

"Be nice to your aging uncle," he tells me.

I want to laugh, but my body would rather collapse, I think.

"You're upset," Seth says.

I groan. "It's not you," I say.

Seth takes a long look at me, and I squirm a little because he's really paying attention, the way Grandma Sheryl used to. I'm not sure I want anyone to see me right now.

"The last week has been a mess," he says after a beat. "You order food. I'm going to run out and get wine because Natick is no longer a dry town and I deserve a nice glass of something. Maybe a few glasses. Let's have a night."

❧

I've never had wine like this. I mean, I haven't had much wine in general. The few times I've had alcohol, it's been beer, mostly.

I have no big thoughts about alcohol being good or bad, but

this wine tastes like dessert, and I did not know that was possible. I like this wine, and I like that I get to have it with Seth, who has decided that our evening of "writer's self-care" will be eating crab rangoon, pairing it with this alcohol, and processing all that's happened.

He thinks my mood is about Grandma, and technically it's related to that, but it's really that I will never be able to erase Chris's reaction in the hallway from my brain. His response to my not moving in—to my moving away for good—was relief.

"I want to know what my mother was watching before she died," Seth says, distracting me. "Let's watch what she was watching."

We lay out the food and turn on the television. It turns out that the last thing Grandma was watching was what I feared it might be, and I groan.

"What?" Seth says. "What is it?"

"It's *Poldark*," I say, and fall back onto the couch. "The last thing she saw was *Poldark*."

"I don't know what that is."

I explain to Seth that it is a public television series about a man in Revolutionary War times who comes home to England to find out that his girlfriend is marrying somebody else. I've seen many episodes with Grandma. The show manages to be sexy and boring at the same time.

"What is Poldark, though?" he asks. "The house? Or the person?"

"Him. He's Poldark. Like the family name. Ross Poldark. Like Seth Seltzer. You'd just be Seltzer."

"Hmm," Seth says.

We start watching an episode, and Seth is riveted, of course. He and Grandma had the same taste.

"I don't know why you don't like this," he says.

"I don't like history unless there's time travel, and even then, it's usually too many women characters wearing petticoats, or whatever, and not having any rights."

Seth points to the actor onscreen. "That's not the point," he says. "Look at him, shirt off, nipples out, thrashing his grain."

I start laughing really hard, and the wine makes it a cackle. It is baffling to me that Mrs. Burke, Mom, and Seth are around the same age. Mrs. Burke is the ultimate calm, dependable parent, Mom is the opposite, but Seth is like . . . cool and hilarious and like a friend.

"Why isn't Mom like you?" I ask him, slurring a little.

Seth sits up from his stretched-out position on the couch. I'm in my favorite spot, the worn-out, cushiony love seat that Grandma kept threatening to replace.

"What do you mean?" he says.

"You're twins, but you're, like, *human* in a way Mom isn't. Instead of just being a person, she reads all those stupid books about how to be a person. It's so annoying."

"Everybody thinks their mom is annoying," Seth says. "It's human nature."

"You had Grandma Sheryl as your mother," I protest.

"And I thought she was annoying, at least when I was your age. Maybe not as annoying as your mom, but there were definitely years when I locked myself in my room," Seth says. "And anyway, your mother loved you from the moment you were born. I didn't pay attention to you from the age of, like, seven to thirteen. You were annoying and weird those years, and I had no interest. Your mom was into you the whole time."

I always forget that. How Seth sort of went away.

"You got interesting again, by the way. Good for you," he says.

"I was always interesting!" I say.

"You *thought* you were interesting," Seth says. "All kids think they're interesting, but really, they're not. Most children are very boring."

"I got suspended in middle school for a day for telling kids not to stand for the pledge! Because it was fascist! Mom had to take me to the superintendent; it was when we were living in New Jersey. That was totally interesting!"

"Eh," Seth says.

I know he's teasing.

"What happened at Chris's?" he asks then.

I must look surprised.

"You ran over there and came back all sulky and weird," he explains. "I want to know *everything*."

I take a deep breath, and then I tell him everything that happened at the Burke's. It's embarrassing to say it out loud, to recount how happy Chris looked to hear his mom reject my proposal.

"Lori," Seth says after some consideration. "It would have been a struggle for you to live there."

"Why? It would have been ideal. The Burkes are perfect parents. I could have used that."

"Look, I love the Burkes. They seem great. But you're clearly into Chris, like obsessed with him, and I just don't see living with a crush—in a very rule-abiding traditional house, by the way—as being pleasurable or healthy for you. It would be a repressed nightmare, to be honest."

"I'm not obsessed with Chris," I say.

"You look at him like I'm looking at this man thrashing his grain," Seth says, pointing to the television.

"We're story partners," I say. "He illustrates my stories."

"Is that what you call it?"

"We're best friends."

Seth doesn't believe me. I have no energy to lie anymore, to him or myself.

"I do like him like that," I say, "but it won't happen, so it doesn't matter."

"Does he not feel the same way?" Seth asks. "It seems like he cares about you a lot. Has he ever hinted about romantic feelings?"

"We've only talked about it once," I say. "Like, not long after we met, when I first started here. We were working on a story, and I was getting a weird vibe from him, and I was probably giving off weird energy too. I asked him if he'd ever thought about it—being together—and he said yes, and then we sort of talked it out and decided there was too much to lose."

I've never had to articulate this before. It's not easy.

"I love Chris as a friend, as more than a friend, but that friendship, and the way we create things together, that's what I need forever. I can have feelings for other people and be with them and break up with them, but I can't do that with Chris, because I choose for him to be permanent, you know? He's too important to turn into some short-lived romantic thing. He felt the same way when we talked about it. We're best friends. Whatever attraction is there is less important than the other ways we connect, you know?

"Honestly," I add, thinking about it, "it's the most responsible decision I've ever made."

"Have you dated other people?"

I laugh. I don't know what he means by dating.

"I was hooking up with this guy Frankie on the lacrosse team for a while in the fall, but then we got bored, I think," I say.

"Lacrosse player. Good for you," Seth says.

"Chris was with this girl in his math class for like three weeks last year, but it wasn't a big deal. I think we're both just into our work, you know? He's pretty introverted. We like our alone time, or just hanging out with Jess and Jason. Whatever romantic feelings I have for him—and I mean, yeah, sometimes they're excruciating, especially lately. But I can ignore them to make this last. We're good with how we are."

"That sounds good . . . I guess," Seth says. "Deeply frustrating but good."

"That's why I'm mad at him. I work so hard every second I'm with him not to act on the way I feel about him, so we never have to break up. Our friendship and stories are the most important thing in our lives. Why wouldn't he want me to stay with him —so we can do what we love, together, for senior year? This year is supposed to be *everything*."

"Maybe you should ask him."

Seth is right. But I wonder about putting Chris on the spot. I wonder whether he'd be honest with me if it might hurt my feelings.

"Think of it this way," Seth adds. "If you're in Maryland, you won't have to manage lust over him in person. You can continue your relationship by text and keep a shared Google Doc if you still want to write together. Plus, it's only one year. You could wind up in college together. Maybe this space will be good."

I want to argue, but we're interrupted because Poldark is yelling.

"What's he upset about?" Seth says.

"Poldark is upset about a lot of things every episode," I say.

I stand up to get some water and then jump when I see a

silhouette of a person pass by the window. The shade is down, so all I see is the body.

"Someone's here," I yell to Seth, scrambling back to the center of the living room.

Seth jumps up too.

"Just stay where you are," he says. "It's probably some kid playing outside or something."

He pulls the string to raise the shade, and we see the Garden Girls in the backyard. All five of them are there, at sunset. Kevin, who's closest to the window, has taken the hose attached to the back of the house and is walking it to Grandma's small garden.

They're watering the plants back there. We wouldn't have thought to do it.

"Look at that," Seth says.

Jill, who's inspecting a bed of tulips, sees us in the window and waves.

They're not ready to let go of the house — or Grandma — either. Seth and I give them a wave back and lower the blind to give them privacy.

Seth falls back onto the couch. He closes his eyes.

I need to get water. Even with the wine, my body is not ready to relax. I need to come up with a new plan.

Even the foggiest version of my brain — even the part of it that is angry with Chris and hurt by his private rejection — tells me it's best for both of us if I stay right here.

Chapter 6

August in Natick is good for no one.

Even if you like summer heat, you will be suffocated by the humid steaminess. There is no escape from it. Not here, where there is no water to make a breeze, and where the asphalt draws the sun to the ground like a laser. I vaguely remember our short stint in Cleveland being worse—that was middle school—but Natick is still pretty bad.

At night, though, I can take it. I almost like it.

Grandma never had many rules for me, but she was clear about two of them: I was not allowed alone outside after ten p.m., and the door was to be locked at all times, especially if I was home by myself. Our street looks very safe, but people are people, Grandma would say. One never knows.

But she's not here anymore, and after tonight, now that Seth is fast asleep in the spare bedroom, maybe dreaming of Ross Poldark, I need air, and I need to break a rule. To think about everything that's happened. To think about that face Chris made, his look of relief that I will never be able to delete from my memory for as long as I live. There is too much in my brain right now, because the second I compartmentalize Chris's reaction this afternoon, I think about the cremains, and the evidence of how small we all get when we are gone. Remains aren't much to leave behind. They are easily stepped on.

I imagine more families with strollers walking around our perfect patch of green, dogs peeing on it, people stomping around and having picnics near it, not knowing what's beneath them. Less than two weeks ago my grandmother was watching *Poldark*. Now she is fertilizer. Toxic fertilizer, according to Kel.

I can't lie in bed and think about it anymore. I can't stare at the ceiling—or, more specifically, Chris's fictional mall portal to another dimension, because he wouldn't want to join me there, apparently.

I slide out of my room as quietly as possible, stopping to put on flip-flops. I can't imagine that Seth would enforce Grandma's rules or even know them, but I don't want him to see me sneaking out of the house after eleven. Mainly because he might try to join me, and as much as he is the best company I can imagine right now, I want to be by myself.

I take my keys so that I can lock up behind me. I'll follow that rule, at least.

Outside, the street is empty. I hear crickets. The heat is like a blanket. I can smell that someone had a barbecue. Probably the Rodmans three doors down.

This is the first place I've lived where I've known the names of my neighbors.

It's so dark on our street when it's this late. I can see the glow coming from Route 9 and the mall in the distance. It looks ethereal, like something religious might be happening over there. I know I'm being dramatic, but it seems to be calling me. I want to be there. It's been kind of like a North Star for three years, how I know I'm close to home.

It's not that far to the mall, but the walk is a little awkward. I have to cross this crazy part of Route 9 to get there. At least during the day, cars are moving slowly. There's so much traffic to get into the shopping centers it's unlikely that someone will come plowing toward you. But at night it feels risky, like I should run. If a car comes out of nowhere, the driver won't get much of a chance to see me and slow down.

It takes me about fifteen minutes to get to the dangerous part, and then I sprint right over it. As soon as I'm on the other side, I feel like an idiot for not bringing an ID or a phone or a wallet. All I have is my keys in the pockets of my thin sweatpants.

I have to admit that even though I'd rather buy things at small stores that sell vintage stuff—clothing that has a backstory (so it might be haunted)—I like this mall and the way it's designed. There's been a mall like this near every town I've lived in, but the one in Natick kind of looks like a castle. The outside of Neiman Marcus reminds me of a big metal wave, as if they were trying to make it look like an important monument, as opposed to a place where you can buy a purse.

I walk by that Neiman Marcus now, feeling small, and move to where I'll be farther from the street and any cars that might pass.

I like the feel of the paved parking lot under my flip-flops. I like the smell here, some oily combination of chain restaurant food and gasoline. There are a few abandoned cars in the lot, probably left by people who are still at the movie theater or maybe had dinner at one of the mall restaurants and were too drunk to drive home.

I've never been here this late. I don't know why I'm loving it so much, but it seems like a supernatural event has happened and everyone has disappeared. There is an old movie called *Night of the Comet*—Chris and I have watched it twice—where everyone gets wiped away by an astrological event, but some teens are left behind and they spend one long scene in a mall just taking whatever they want.

I think of that now as I play imaginary hopscotch through the parking spaces, my flip-flops slapping against the back of my feet.

"I am here," I say out loud as I jump.

I walk to the center of one of the open spaces and lie down. This is my property right now. It is my parking lot kingdom. The concrete is surprisingly soft, and the asphalt smells even sweeter down here. I am sure the back of my light blue tank top and gray sweatpants are covered in parking lot grease, but I don't care. There is no one around to yell at me about it.

I open my arms and legs wide and pretend to make a mall

parking lot snow angel. I feel a nice light scratch through the cotton on the back of my legs.

I wonder if I'll get the chance to be inside the mall one last time. I'm sure the mall near Bill's place in Maryland has some of the same stuff, but I will miss this particular Cheesecake Factory and California Pizza Kitchen because I went to them with Grandma.

I close my eyes. I could actually take a nap right here—finally, I'm tired enough to sleep—but then I hear a brush of something and footsteps, and I shoot to my feet, imagining that everything Grandma told me about Natick after dark is true, that there's some man who's about to kidnap me, and everyone will say, "Well, that's what she got for being alone after midnight in a mall parking lot without her phone."

I imagine a headline: THE GIRL WHO DISAPPEARED AT NEIMAN MARCUS.

There's a body coming toward me from the road. *Shit.*

It's a slight outline but tallish, and I think I should run, but where do I go? I can't bolt toward the highway, back in the direction of the house, because the person is approaching from there. I don't want to run toward the other side of the mall. It'll only be more secluded over there.

I decide to stay put. I am not capable of taking part in a chase. I'm wearing a bra without underwire, which is basically a non-bra for someone like me, and even when I have excellent support, I am a very slow runner.

The only thing I can think to do is creep to one of the empty cars and disappear behind it, so I do. It's a large sedan, which provides some good cover.

I can't see anything now, the car is blocking my view, so I freeze in my squatting position and try not to breathe. But I can hear the footsteps closer and closer. And then I realize that I'm an idiot. Maybe the person coming toward me *owns* this sedan and is coming to retrieve his car.

Maybe he's someone who went to Dave & Busters or something, and now he just wants to drive home.

Honestly, I should not be out of the house at this hour.

Tap tap tap.

The man — I assume he's a man, although I can't be sure — is tapping on the car window. I hold my breath.

He taps again, three times.

"Oh god," I whisper.

"Hello," he says.

I exhale, relief flooding my entire body. The voice is not a stranger's.

"Excuse me, madame," Chris says. "Are you stealing this car?"

I stand up, and after squatting for that long, my legs feel like jelly.

"What if I am?" I say, putting my hands on my hips.

"This car feels too business-casual for you," he says. "I picture you stealing something retro, like a big van."

"A school bus we could paint."

"Maybe an old VW," Chris says.

It's easier to look him straight in the eyes at night. During the day I find myself wanting to look anywhere else, usually at his clavicle, because to look at him directly makes my chest feel as if it will collapse into itself. But here, he cannot see how much I want him and how baffled I am about what to do about it.

Right now, he can't see how much he hurt me this afternoon.

"Lor, what are you doing out here in the middle of the night?"

"What are *you* doing out here?"

"I couldn't sleep, so I started drawing. Then I looked out the window and saw a pale ghost wandering past my house. And I figured the ghost was probably my best friend and I was worried about her, so I followed her."

I am mad at him. I don't want him to make me feel good right now.

"How bad was today for you?" he asks.

"Terrible," I say. I know he's talking about the arboretum and the craisins and my mom, but I'm talking about his horrible relieved face in the house.

"I mean, it could have been worse," I continue, wanting to answer his real question. "I liked where we put her. I think it was the right place, out of the way but close to beautiful things."

He comes closer. "Jeez, Lori, are you out here in just pajamas? Did you bring your phone?"

I shrug.

"You've lost your mind. Why would you do that? It's not safe this late."

"I was upset," I say, and I hope he gets the hint that he is my problem right now.

He shakes his head. "I brought us something," he says.

Chris has his backpack with him, and he puts it on the ground to open it. He pulls out something white, and when my eyes focus in the dark, I can make out a pair of roller skates. He hands them to me and then pulls out another.

I look down at the swinging skates, holding them by their shoelaces.

"Whose are these?"

"My parents'. Didn't you know? They met at roller-skating rink."

I smile. Of course they did. Chris's parents are so dreamy.

"I knew they met in high school," I say. "I just didn't know how."

"I can't believe my mom hasn't told you this story fifty thousand times."

He takes a deep, dramatic breath to prepare his delivery.

"You see," he says, mimicking his mom's voice for a second, "they went to neighboring high schools, but they both went to some Friday-night skate thing. The place was called Skate Island. He asked her to be his partner for a couples' skate. But then they never stopped couples skating, and they held hands for the rest of the night. Their first skate was to the song 'Endless Summer Nights' by Richard Marx. That's why they danced to the song on their wedding."

I can tell, even as he tries to sound unmoved by the details, that he also loves this story and thinks it's adorable, too.

"Anyway, sometimes they skate on their anniversary. My mom wears my dad's old jacket. It's a whole thing."

He motions to the skates.

"Put 'em on," he says.

I look around the mostly abandoned lot.

"Is this safe? To be skating around a parking lot this late, after the mall has closed?"

"Safe for *you*," Chris says with an exhausted laugh, and now I realize I should be extra worried about what a mall security guard might do or say if they notice us. "But restaurants are still open. Anyway, it's safer for me with you, so just stay close."

I can do close, I think as I reach for the skates.

"Are they even my size?" I ask, trying to find a number on the sole. "Your mom's feet are probably like dainty and perfect and size seven."

I look; they are a 9, only half a size smaller than mine.

"But I don't have socks on," I say.

"You're also in your pajamas, but that doesn't seem to bother you."

Fair enough.

I follow him over to a nearby curb and we sit side by side,

shoving our feet into skates that have been broken in by other people. Mine fit better than I thought they would; they're snug, but they don't hurt.

I try to stand up in them, but I fall back down, my rear end landing hard on the parking lot curb. "Of course I'm terrible at this."

"Can you not skate?"

"I don't think I've ever done it," I confess. "I tried ice skating when we lived in Cleveland, but I was really bad. Shouldn't this be easier?"

I stand up again, this time more carefully, and Chris, whose skates are on and seem to fit perfectly, moves in front of me, taking my hands to hold me steady.

All of a sudden, because we're closer, I'm more self-conscious about my pajamas and my crappy bra. This Target loungewear is so thin, and I feel a little naked.

At least I'm wearing eyeliner.

Chris is dressed similarly. He's in a long Natick Arts T-shirt, something he'd wear to school, and thin sweatpants.

"What do I do?" I ask, and I'm not sure if I mean on these roller skates or with my entire life.

"Let's skate," he says.

"Okay," I say.

I have never lived in Natick without knowing Chris.

I moved in on a Sunday, only two weeks after Grandma Sheryl convinced Mom that sending me to live here wouldn't make her a bad parent — that it would sort of be like sending me to a boarding school.

No more moving around, Grandma told her. I needed consistency, especially for high school.

Mom had started studying to be a life coach, which I guess is someone who, ironically, helps other people make responsible decisions, but it was going to involve a lot of time out of the house, and after I had gone through so much change and so many moves, Grandma was assertive. I was thrilled to join her.

Grandma's house was where I could talk about books and television. Grandma Sheryl treated me like a writer. She even set me up at Seth's old desk.

I had managed my expectations about school in Natick. I mean, most suburban schools are kind of the same, but high school would be different no matter where I was, and this one seemed even bigger than the ones in Cleveland or New Jersey. Once I started, I realized that some kids looked really old. The hallways were crowded. There was a moderately angry woman working the desk in the front office, and she behaved as though every person who walked in with a question had been put on this earth for the sole purpose of inconveniencing her.

"I'm just looking for a map," I told her on my first day. Other kids had taken tours and had orientations. I'd never been inside. Plus, I was starting three weeks late. Everyone else had already had their first days of school.

She didn't answer.

"Fine. I'm just looking for the library."

The library is where I would relax during lunch whenever I felt stressed out at all of my middle schools. I also figured I could find a librarian who was nice enough to tell me where my classes were. A lesson you learn if you move a lot — you will always be better off getting information from someone in the library.

I had tucked myself away, behind a display of science fiction, and that was where I found Chris, sitting at a desk, his sketchpad in front of him, a pencil behind his ear. There was a Supreme sticker on his backpack (he peeled it off not long after we met). His long fingers held a piece of charcoal. I could see ink on his nails. His hair was short, but not shaven. I figured I was taller than him, and at that point I still was. Our heights would even out months later.

He looked thin but very fit, like the kind of guy who doesn't play sports or lift weights but runs around a lot anyway.

"Hi," I said. I wasn't ready to talk to someone yet, but I wanted to see what he was making.

"You live on Sudbury Terrace," he said, his voice lower than I expected. It gave me the good kind of chills.

"How did you know?" I asked, my voice too high.

"I live there, too."

"Oh," I said.

"I keep seeing you run in and out of the house. Miss Sheryl is your grandma?"

"You call her Miss Sheryl?"

"I have since I was little," he said. "She's friends with my parents. She actually used to come watch me sometimes when I was super little, when my parents were doing work or church stuff. My mom borrows her books a lot. Your grandma's house is like a library. I'm Chris."

"Lori," I answered, afraid that if I said too many words, I'd ruin this very normal social interaction with someone who seemed kind of great. It usually took me weeks or months to meet someone great.

"That's a lot of notes for the first day of school," he said, eyeing my full notebook and the ink marks all over my fingers. I loved that we were both messy with pens.

"It's where I write stories," I said. "I like to write sci-fi stuff and fan fiction."

"Fan fiction for what?" he asked.

"Depends. Sometimes random ghost or zombie stuff, but also, like, stories for random *Dark Materials* characters."

"Cool," he said. "What story are you working on now?"

I couldn't come up with a lie, so I said the truth.

"A story about a guy who becomes a human mood ring. Like, when he's mad, he glows red, or when he's calm, he glows blue. He can't hide any of his feelings. So basically it's sort of about how people treat him when he can't lie about how he feels. He can't pretend he's blue when he's red."

"What color is he when he's happy?" Chris asked.

"Pink, I think. I haven't gotten that far."

"What do you call it?" he asked.

"I don't know," I said. "Maybe just 'Mood Man.' Something like that."

I sat down next to Chris as he pulled a small box out of his backpack and opened it to reveal a bunch of colored pencils. This was before he had the fancier case he works with now.

He began to draw, feverishly. Fast.

It was the Mood Man, but it was Chris. Same brown skin. Same dark blue shirt. Same short black hair. Same backpack covered in patches designed by his favorite artists. Those eyebrows with one freckle over the right one.

Chris made a halo of pink all around his body. "He's happy," he said.

"That's really good," I said. "You did that in like five seconds."

"My best ideas usually come first," he said. "I draw it up fast because it only goes downhill from there."

"Cool," I said, and then asked, "Why are you here during lunch?"

I regretted asking the question as soon as the words were out of my mouth. The question sounded rude. It's just that I knew why *I* was hiding in the library, but I didn't know what brought him here, with a turkey sandwich resting on the backpack next to him.

He looked up and smiled. "Lunch is a lot," he said.

"A lot of food?"

Chris smiled again. "A lot of people."

"Are people terrible in Natick?" I asked, wondering who he might be hiding from. In that moment I wanted to punish anyone who might be mean to this wonderful person.

"No, no," he said. "I mean, in some cases, sure. I just like quiet sometimes. My best friends are on a different lunch shift. In the lunchroom, it's just a lot. I can get anxious. Quiet makes me happy. I can draw better here."

He glanced at the clock. Fifteen minutes left of this peaceful, blissful lunch we were sharing.

"We should do another one," he said, looking happy for me to be there, which felt like the world's biggest win.

"Cool," I said, and opened my notebook, trying to look unaffected. "Can you make a banshee?"

As we start to skate, I am thinking about our meeting, mostly because I imagine Chris radiating pink right now. I am so confused at this point that I'm radiating a rainbow.

I have never known Chris Burke to skate—he's never

mentioned doing it—but apparently it's just another thing he's amazing at, because he lets go of my hands and takes off, immediately moving backwards toward the other side of the parking lot. "Come on," he says, as if I'll be able to follow.

I lean forward, hoping it's enough to get me somewhere, but I move only about an inch.

"You have to lift your feet," he says, skating back toward me. When he gets close, I can see him grinning. "It's like walking. Lift your feet and push back."

I try again, lifting each skate and pushing myself a few feet forward. When I finally start to roll, I lose my balance again and lean back to keep myself from doing a face-plant on the pavement.

Chris circles behind me, and I feel him grab my waist.

His hands are right there, perhaps only three inches from my mostly unprotected breasts, and I stop breathing. He is so close. To breasts. Mine.

"Relax," he says. Of course he's noticed that I'm tense enough to snap. He just doesn't know why.

He lets go and rolls himself in front of me, facing me. Then he takes both my hands in his—and we're off.

He's skating backwards, pulling me, weaving from side to side, and I'm doing very little besides saying, "Oh my god, oh my god, slow down," but after I get used to how it feels, I try to keep up. He is setting the pace and our path, and he has my hands in a firm grip, which means all I have to think about is lifting my feet.

I become more confident, and my feet begin to move on their own. I dare to look up. We're right by Lord & Taylor now, and in this section of the parking lot there are more abandoned cars. Chris weaves around them as if they're part of an obstacle course designed for us.

"How are you so good at this?" I ask.

"I guess it's in my genes," he said. "I am a child born of Skate Island."

He drops one of my hands so we can skate side by side. I am confident now, and I can probably go fast on my own, but being connected to his body feels so good. I fear that if we make it around the mall once, the night will be over, and I want it to never end.

In the back of my mind, I know I am angry with him. I have been rejected by him. But in this moment he wants me here, and I feel totally understood by him.

We're holding hands like we're dancing, and it will never be more romantic and intimate than this.

Chris starts singing, but I can't place the song.

"What is that?"

He laughs. "It's *the* song. The one my parents skated to. It's a cheesy song. They play it sometimes, though, and then it gets stuck in my head."

"Oh," I say.

"'I remember how you loved me . . .'" Chris sings, ending with something about endless summer nights, but he's pretty tone-deaf, so I wouldn't recognize the tune even if I knew it. I guess he's not good at *everything,* but I love that too.

"I literally have never heard this song," I say.

"Come on," he says, grabbing my two hands again, and then we're moving fast. I hold my breath as we see more of the mall.

"Jeez, from this angle, it looks like a castle," I say, and by "it" I mean the Cheesecake Factory. The lights there are off, but under the glow of the lights around it, the restaurant looks medieval. Royal.

There are a few people in the parking lot on this side of the mall, probably coming out of late movies and restaurants, and when Chris spies them, he ducks and spins us back around so we can retrace our route. I'm quiet for this second loop, until we slow down back at Neiman Marcus.

"Why haven't we snuck out for mall fun like this more often?" Chris asks, a little out of breath, and I hate that everything he says is starting to feel like a goodbye.

"Because you can't roller-skate and draw at the same time."

His pace slows, and my stomach flips, not in a good way. Or maybe in a good way, which is why it's bad.

We are still a little out of breath when we roll back to where we started, and where Chris has left his backpack and my keys under some mall shrubbery.

He drops to the curb and begins taking his skates off, so I do, too.

We walk back to our street, mostly in silence. He tries to take my hand to lead me along the scary parts of the road, but I shoo him away.

When we get to my house, I think about confronting him. But he moves to leave.

"I should get back," he says. "If my mom notices I'm gone, there's no way she'll let me go with you guys for two more boxes."

He has permission to come with us to Rhode Island for Box Two and to The Mount for Box Four, even though it's an overnight trip. At this point I should make everything less confusing and tell him to stay home. To give myself some space. But I don't.

"Go," I tell him. "'I'll see you tomorrow.'"

"Brayton Estate," he says.

"Right," I confirm as he runs off.

I walk upstairs and see that Seth is now asleep in Grandma's room and that he's left the door open.

He's been here for only a little over a week now, but he's spread out all over the house, sometimes sleeping in Grandma's room, sometimes in the spare room, which was my mom's growing up.

There are a bunch of his T-shirts on a drying rack in the spare room. There are about fifteen bottles of vitamin supplements on the bathroom counter.

Next to him, on Grandma's bedside table, is his notebook for ideas. It's a lot like mine, but the cover isn't as colorful.

I know he must be having trouble with his third book because it's been years since his second came out. Grandma said he seemed to be lacking inspiration.

I imagine that writing whole novels is really hard and lonely. I do not write alone; I always have Chris to work with, and our stories are short.

I see a pen sticking out of Seth's notebook, and it looks like he had things to put on paper tonight. I'm tempted to grab it to see what he's working on — what has inspired him.

Maybe it's easier for him to write in Natick.

He feels my presence in the doorway and wakes up.

"Lor," he says. "You okay?"

"I'm fine," I say. "We're all fine here."

He closes his eyes again and smiles.

Chapter 7

"The Big Whale is still open," Seth says at my door, which is the kind of announcement that wakes a person up.

Seth is already dressed and ready, wearing another university T-shirt (Fordham) and nautical-looking navy shorts. He's waiting for an enthusiastic response. I sit up and wipe the gunk from my eyes.

"I've never been," I say of the tiny bar, "as I am seventeen."

"I can't believe it's still around," Seth says, sitting on the end of my bed. "It was the reunion bar back when I was in college. Everyone would turn twenty-one or get a fake ID, and when they came home for Thanksgiving, they'd go to the Whale to see everybody. It was an absolute scene."

"I can't imagine I'll ever have a reason to go there now," I say. "If I move and we don't own the house anymore, I won't be back here for reunions."

Seth leans back against the wall, propping himself up against my large pillow that's in the shape of an avocado. It was a gift from him last Hanukkah.

"I only wanted to see one person—Jake Gunther," Seth says. "He played soccer, his jaw was so square he looked like a damn

G.I. Joe doll, and his voice was deep. And Jake Gunther was not *remotely homophobic.* He was this ridiculously hot soccer player who could have been toxic to everyone because it was the 1990s and everyone was mad and in flannel, but he was welcoming. I could not have been more out, and he never avoided me. In fact, he flirted with me. Or maybe that was all in my mind, but my god, shit like that made my life easier back then. People cared what he thought."

Seth sighs. "There was this era, back when I was your age, when all the best-looking boys were named Jake. It's like if you were born a Jake, it was your destiny to be a magnet for success, sexual and otherwise."

"Our popular guys are Tylers," I tell him. "There are three. There's also a Stephan."

"The Tylers are all hot?"

I want to tell him that the Tylers aren't my type, but it's Seth and I trust him, so I wind up admitting that I have recurring fantasies about all the Tylers, even though they call each other "bro" and do not seem very welcoming.

I hate that I want the Tylers to notice me, and that I was thrilled when they were nicer to me during the three weeks I dated a lacrosse player. I tell him that the worst Tyler is Tyler Rych (yes, pronounced "rich"), who's in my social studies class, who sometimes just stares at my boobs without being shy about it. I hate that I have a fantasy where he begs me to go to prom with him and I tell him no.

"Hmm." Seth stands up all of a sudden. "God, I regress in this house. Look at me; I just went from almost fifty to sixteen. You do know your bedroom was my bedroom, right?"

I did know that, but it's easy to forget that Seth has a whole history here. He and my mom moved here when they were six. This is more his home than mine.

I look at the desk across the room, which was also his. Seth became a writer sitting on that hard wooden chair that's covered in white paint that's bubbling up and peeling.

"You'll probably have some feelings about selling this house," I say, baiting him a little. "The memories and all."

Seth raises an eyebrow. "I don't have much love for this house. I was desperate to get out of it when I actually lived in it."

That's not the answer I want to hear.

"But your memories of Grandma are here."

"I guess that's true," he says, and smiles.

I grab my phone from where it's plugged in next to my bed. There's a message from Chris confirming that after he finishes watching Adam for a few hours, he'll join us on the drive to Rhode Island to scatter the second box.

Seeing his name makes the memory of last night come back to me, and I'm baffled by how romantic it felt. My neck is probably getting blotchy, which is what happens when I feel embarrassment, but Seth doesn't notice. He's staring out my window, and I imagine he's thinking about Grandma or the house, or maybe Jake Gunther.

Seth is on the phone with Ethan, behind a closed door, when the doorbell rings. I assume it's Chris and that he's early, but when I open the door, it is Jessica. Alone. Which is weird, and she seems to know it. I look behind her to see if Jason is obscured by something, but he's missing.

I realize that I've never seen Jess without him, apart from when she and I use a public restroom at the same time, or when we happen to pass each other in the hall.

"Where's Jason?" I ask.

"I do exist without him," she says, smiling.

"Really?" I answer with a smirk.

"As much as you exist without Chris," she says, and that comment knocks my heart around in my chest.

Jessica's wearing thin purple athletic shorts and a blue tank top that says RUN in big letters, and I feels like it's shouting at me. Her black hair is in a high ponytail. She's wearing the fancy watch she got for Christmas. She and Jason both asked their parents for these expensive watches that track every change in their pulse, as well as a bunch of other athletic things. I cannot imagine wanting to know that much about what's happening inside my body.

"How many steps have you taken today?" I ask.

She looks at her wrist and hits a button.

"Sixteen thousand," she says.

"It's only one in the afternoon," I say, and she shrugs.

"So," I say, trying not to sound awkward, "what's up?"

She's carrying two big cloth bags, which she brings into my kitchen.

"Sorry, these are heavy," she explains.

I follow her and watch her take out long Pyrex trays. "From my mom," she explains.

"Lasagna?" I ask.

Last night, two random neighbors left lasagna on our porch. "These will be known as our lasagna days," Seth had said before putting them in the freezer.

Jessica crinkles her nose at my question.

"Are you kidding?" she says, and begins to remove a series of plastic containers filled with Korean food. There are enough scallion pancakes to feed us for weeks, and a vat of the clear noodle and chicken thing I've eaten at her house.

"I love your mother," I tell Jessica as I survey the spread. "I love everybody else's mother. I've never eaten so well as I have over these last few days. I wish Grandma were here just to eat this stuff too."

Jessica turns to me, and for a second, I am overwhelmed by her. She is pretty and smart and athletic and easy going, so many things I'm not. She is popular with everyone at school, but she doesn't seem to care, and she has always prioritized our little group. When I make judgments about kids who seem like dicks, she jumps to defend them.

"His dad is horrible to him," Jess once told me when I went off about this menacing bully kid who I caught peeing on a geeky kid's car. "That kind of behavior starts at home."

I never think much about my friendship with Jess, because winning her over never took much effort; she and Jason already knew Chris through middle school, so when I met him, they were part of the package. But looking at her now, I know I'll miss her too. She's a really good editor. She's usually the first person who reads our stories, and she always has cool things to say about them.

I should have spent more alone time with her. I shouldn't have thought of her and Jason as extensions of Chris.

She has finished making a tower of Pyrex in our refrigerator, and she closes the refrigerator door, leaning her back against it, her arms across her chest.

"I'm sorry I was awkward that shiva day," she says. "I've been thinking about it ever since we left. I can talk about a lot of things, but I never know what to say when someone dies. Jason was so good at being comforting, but I couldn't come up with the words."

"You were great," I say. "There is no right thing to say, really. It just sucks."

She nods.

"Chris told me you've already spread some of the ashes," she says.

"We'll spread the second box today," I tell her.

"Was it horrible?" Jessica asks, her voice quiet.

"Which part?"

"Seeing it—the ashes." She blows her breath up into her bangs. She's uncomfortable.

"It was strange," I confess. "I mean, none of this feels real yet. It doesn't feel like she actually died—like she'll come home after all this and it'll just be normal again. I can't really picture her as ashes."

Jessica nods. She gives me a sad smile and then opens her mouth and closes it again.

"What?" I say, because she has something to get off her chest. She does the bangs thing again.

"What?" I say. "Just tell me. Please."

"It's just . . . remember Winston?"

"How could I forget Winston?"

Winston was Jessica's family's German shorthaired pointer who died over the holidays our sophomore year. The unspoken thing at the time was that even though Jessica was miserable—inconsolable, really—in the weeks after Winston's death, I could tell her parents were totally okay with it and maybe even relieved to let him go. By the end, Winston was so old that he was peeing everywhere, and they had him walking around the house in a doggie diaper. Winston couldn't hear and couldn't see, and sometimes he'd bark at nothing. He'd regularly gallop straight into their family's curio cabinet, not noticing all the breakable glass inside. He looked miserable.

Jessica hadn't wanted to accept that it was his time. Her grief was epic. So her parents threw this big memorial dinner after he was gone, so she could feel like her pet had really been laid to rest.

The meal, which included a lot of the kind of noodles Jessica just put in my fridge, was probably nine courses. We all made speeches. I talked about how warm it felt when Winston put his head in my lap.

But Chris did the best thing; his contribution was what helped Jess really move on.

He drew a portrait of Winston that now hangs in Jessica's bedroom. It doesn't look exactly like Winston, of course; Chris had imagined the dog reincarnated as a human man. His afterlife version of Winston was a tall, strapping farmer with skin and hair the color of Winton's dark brown coat. This Winston stood on a farm, tending to vegetables. Chris named the illustration *Winston Reborn*.

"He *would* be a farmer in another life," Jessica had said, crying, when she first saw the illustration. "He loved carrots."

"I know, Jess," Chris had said.

"Thank you, Chris. It's beautiful."

They'd hugged then, and I was jealous because the hug lasted several long seconds and he rubbed his hand up and down her back twice. That's when I started to realize how my feelings for him had grown. I couldn't even watch two longtime platonic friends hug without being an idiot about it. I realized that no one other than Chris could be so thoughtful, that not even Jessica's parents could make the kind of picture that would help her let go of her beloved pet without having to feel that he was really gone.

"What about Winston?" I ask her now. After that night, we pretty much never spoke of him.

"Well, we cremated him," she says.

"Oh. I thought you buried him in a pet cemetery," I say.

"We did—he's on a plot in Middleborough—but we cremated him first."

"Oh."

I don't know what she's trying to tell me. She rubs the back of her neck under her ponytail. I don't want her to compare the loss of Winston with the death of my grandmother.

"The vet took Winston's body somewhere for cremation," she continues, "and when we went to pick him up, they gave us a bag."

"Of his remains."

"Yeah, a bag of Winston. I just wondered how it was for you, because when we got the bag, it wasn't what I expected. I don't think any of us expected it."

"Expected what? That a body doesn't look like ashes?" I say. "I knew it was going to look like gravel. Bone is white. We learned all about it at the funeral home."

"Right," Jessica says. "It is sort of white, I guess. But that's not what upset me."

"Oh."

"Well," Jessica says, her voice soft. "I asked my mom and dad if I could bring Winston down to the cemetery myself, like, to hold him one more time. Like, hold him in my arms."

She blinks a tear away.

"Anyway," she says, "it was *heavy*."

"Death is ridiculously heavy," I agree.

"No, I mean, the ashes were heavy. Like, literally. The bag of ashes—what we got from the vet—it was . . . *huge*. I was just so freaked out that the bag was so massive. It felt like I was carrying a dead weight, and I guess I was. I don't know why I thought it would be light and airy. The feel of it made it all seem so much more final. It was a *body*. Like a full dead body."

"Oh," I say, my brain blank.

"I asked my mom about it, and she said she was surprised, too. You hear *ashes* and you think of something light, like feathers that used to be a body, but that's not how it feels."

I nod because I don't know what else to say.

"I guess my point is that Winston was, like, a forty-pound dog. So . . ."

"So?"

I try to process this as quickly as I can—and then she explains.

"I was just worried about you. That it would be heavy. That it would upset you. I've been so worried about how it would feel for you to hold that bag."

Jess is crying a little now, and before I know it, I'm hugging her. She's been worried about me for days, and she's so vulnerable right now, and we are having a moment that is just ours.

For the first time, I feel like she is my friend too. Not just someone I inherited.

I open the fridge, take out one of the containers of scallion pancakes she just put in there, and start eating one cold. I groan a little because it tastes so good.

Jessica grins.

"I made those," she says.

"They're magic, as usual," I say, and swallow another bite. "Thank you.

"The thing is," I continue, needing to make this point out loud so I can breathe easier about the second box, "we asked the funeral home for four boxes. So one box at a time isn't so heavy."

This time she blows her bangs up with relief.

"That makes sense," she says. "Four boxes makes it better."

"I think so," I say, and in this moment I want to hug her again. I know it was hard work for her to tell me all this.

"Lori?" she asks. "Will you have to move?"

"I think so," I say. Jessica's frowns, and I nod at her reaction. "I don't want to leave. This is the only place that's ever felt like home."

"I like having you here," she says. "I love our group."

We have a group, and I've never really understood how important that is.

"And I'm worried about Chris," she adds.

"I'm more worried about me," I admit. "Me without Chris."

"Why do you think you guys have never tried to be together?" she asks.

She's never been as blunt with me about this, which is kind of weird.

I tell her what I've already told Seth.

"We would never risk the friendship," I say.

"I'm risking it with Jason," she tells me. "I know that and I don't care."

"This is better," I tell her. "It's less messy. In fact, it's time for me to get used to needing him less. I'm going to try to wean off. See him one or two fewer hours a day, to start preparing."

"I guess I get it," Jessica says. She doesn't seem to get it at all, but it's okay.

"Anyway, he should be here soon, so I should probably get ready," I tell her. "But thanks, you know, for the food and for checking in on me."

"Sure," she says, and she gives me a quick hug and leaves.

The doorbell rings a few minutes later, and I know it's him, as if he knows that I don't really want to have to let go of him at all.

❧

It's already easier without Mom and Bill. We need only one car for the three of us, and the ride feels upbeat. Less like we're going to a funeral.

I keep glancing at the rearview mirror so I can watch Chris, who is sleeping in the back seat. Occasionally his lids flutter, and I know he's dreaming. He can fall asleep anywhere.

Seth has been asking me all about school and about my friends—where I want to go to college and why kids like to watch *Friends* on Netflix even though it's old (I do not watch that show, I tell him, but I do like older shows like *The Office*)—and I realize that he is more interested in me than Mom ever has been. The actual me, not just the parts of me on her "I'm not the worst mother in the world" checklist.

She asks about grades and about what I'm eating and whether I'm meditating with the app she sent me, like I ever would, but she doesn't ask about things that matter. Sometimes she calls and asks a question but doesn't pay attention to the answer. Like I could just say random syllables and she'd say, "Okay, good, honey."

Seth actually cares who I am.

He has been extra interested on this trip, maybe because I'm more grown up. I'm becoming a peer. We shared a life-and-death experience together that will bond us forever.

"Like, what happens with kids and prom these days," he asked at the start of the ride. "Is that whole promposal thing real? Do people still rent tuxes, or are we finally beyond that?"

I told him about the controversial promposal last year, when this guy, Nick Luster, convinced his history teacher, Mrs. Holmes, to help him ask Sloane Green to prom. Basically, it was this whole thing where Mrs. Holmes asked Sloane to read aloud from her textbook some passage that was supposed to be about the industrial revolution. Unbeknownst to Sloane, Nick had taped a note to the page Mrs. Holmes asked her to read. It said, "Sloane, will you make history and go to prom with me?—Nick." He'd made the text the same size, so that it perfectly lined up with the book.

"So what happened?" Uncle Seth asked.

"Well, Mrs. Holmes was apparently like, 'Sloane, will you open your textbook and read from page 168, or whatever, and Sloane was like, sure, and then she opens the page and starts reading. She reads the entire sentence out loud and then realizes what she's said, and she stops. Freezes. And the whole room is waiting for this romantic moment where she's going to be like, 'Oh Nick, yes, take me to prom!'"

"And?"

"And she closes the book, puts it down on her desk, and tells Mrs. Holmes that she needs to be excused."

"Oh my god," Seth says. "She didn't want to go with him."

"It was terrible. She basically ran out. And Nick was apparently just sitting there, stunned."

I explained that the whole thing led to a massive school debate. People were mad at Sloane for embarrassing Nick, but the smarter people were mad at Nick for assuming that Sloane —whom he *wasn't even dating*—would say yes. He totally put her on the spot.

"It does seem like a major risk," Seth said. "Public proposals are always a bad idea."

"Yeah, but I think Nick did mean well. There are always some real dicks at any school I've been to, but Nick didn't seem like one of them. When he realized what he did wrong, how much he'd put her on the spot, he felt really bad. He actually apologized.

"But anyway, after that, Mrs. Holmes got in trouble for aiding and abetting a promposal gone wrong — like she should have thought about the public humiliation factor and how Sloane might want to say no — and now there's this policy that you can't do a promposal on school grounds."

Seth looked at me as if I'd just told a riveting story, and then he paused.

"Have you been to prom?" he asked.

"No, but, like, I think of it as a senior thing."

"So you'd go this year," he said.

"I would if I lived here," I say, glancing in the rearview mirror again. "Maybe."

After that, Seth changed the subject, telling me how he went to senior prom with this girl named Michelle, how lovely she was, and how they're still friends on social media and how he can't believe her kids are already in college.

I was quiet. I didn't want him to stop talking. The conversation was as effortless as it was with Grandma, but with Seth, there were no boundaries.

Almost an hour later, he's talking to me about authors I should read, and I'm trying to memorize every name. Even though I read more than everyone at my school, I feel dreadfully unschooled in modern fantasy books when I'm sitting next to Seth. He's not very into sci-fi, but he knows all the good writers.

"She writes magical stories like you, but it's all very feminist and deeply rooted in horror," he says, after emphasizing each syllable of an author's last name. "I'll get you a copy of her latest."

An hour and a half ride to Rhode Island feels like a blip.

We reach the address, and Seth is confused because the sign out front says GREEN ANIMALS.

"I thought this was Brayton House or Estate, or whatever," he says.

Then I pull down a driveway that leads to an expansive property that was once a very rich person's house. I've done a lot of googling about it this morning.

I drive over a big rock in the parking lot, and Chris snaps awake in the back seat.

"We're here already?" he asks, groggy.

"Not already. We've been driving for an hour and a half," Seth says. "You had quite a nap."

"He can sleep anywhere," I tell Seth. "On a bus. Sitting in a chair in school. It's a superpower."

Chris wipes his eyes and blinks rapidly, waking himself up, and then he notices the Chico's bag next to him. We've decided to continue to use it; Seth put the second box in it this morning.

There's a seat belt around the bag, like it's a person, and I guess it sort of is. It's a morbid scene.

"She never mentioned this place?" Seth asks.

"Not once," I say. "The Garden Girls told me they went here once and she liked the view. But when I was texting with them this morning, they seemed a little surprised by the choice."

"I wonder why," he says.

We park at the top of the lot, and then Seth understands why even a person who loves gardens might not want their cremains scattered here for all eternity. This beautiful lush property is popular with families who have little kids. For a reason.

Seth takes the Chico's bag from the back seat and holds it at his side. Chris exits the other door, his backpack on, and he's already sweating under the sweltering sun.

I take my phone out to pull up the website and explain.

"It's the Brayton Estate, but only technically," I say. "According to the site, the place was owned by a really cool writer, Alice Brayton, who never got married and basically had parties here on her own."

"Sounds like someone Mom would have admired," Seth says.

"Indeed. But the cool thing is that the estate had this gardener who watched over the property for, like, forty years, and he's the one who made the decision to make it all topiary."

"Topiary," Chris says. "Like shapes."

"Right. Then, after the gardener died, his daughter and her

husband watched over the property, and eventually it was taken over by some historical society, but it's technically the oldest topiary garden in the country. But now it's called Green Animals."

Seth gets us tickets, and we follow him through the gate, and the first thing I see is a giant—like maybe fourteen feet tall—teddy bear made out of shrubbery. There's a smaller bear next to it. In the distance I can see hedges cut into the shapes of giraffes, elephants, and dogs. Children run nearby, some being forced to pose for pictures taken by parents. The animals are all oversize and creepy. There's one kid crying in front of a topiary fox, and it looks like he just realized that the Turkish delight he took from a witch is not as good as he'd hoped.

"I think topiary might be extremely my brand," I say, and Chris lets out a laugh.

"Why does that not surprise me?" he says.

"You've seen *Edward Scissorhands,* right?" Seth asks. "This makes me remember Edward Scissorhands . . .

"Sexually," he adds after a beat.

Chris and I gape at him.

"Have you seen the movie?" Seth asks.

"I know what it is," I say. "I've seen pictures. It is not a sexy movie, from what I know. It's about a man who has scissors for hands, right?"

"Listen, there are two types of people in the world," Seth says matter-of-factly. "There are the people who want to have sex with Edward Scissorhands, like, as a character, and the people who don't. You two should watch the movie and find out what kind of people you are."

We hear an "excuse me" and see a woman a few feet away from us. She gives Seth an angry look, and he responds with a saccharine grin.

"We should probably watch our language," Chris says, nervous. "There are a lot of kids here."

"They deserve to know my truth," Seth says, and I love it.

"Which kind of person are you, Uncle Seth?" I ask. "When it comes to Edward Scissorhands?"

"Isn't it obvious?"

"I guess it is," I say.

Chris's shakes his head and smiles.

"He has scissors for hands," Chris whispers. "Why would anybody want that?"

"Well, now we know what kind of person you are," Seth tells Chris, and he makes it sound like an insult.

A one-note laugh explodes from my body. "I guess I need to see it," I say.

"Later," Seth says. "Come on. It's a hundred degrees. Let's find a resting place and make this happen." He marches in, and Seth and I fall in line behind him.

●

The Green Animals Topiary Garden is laid out in big squares that remind me of rooms. Hedges serve as borders. In one area, there is a standard garden—no shrubs carved into weird shapes, just plants and pretty flowers. In another section it's all topiary shapes, and some remind me of chess pieces. A few are geometric and modern.

Most of the topiary is animal-shaped, which I guess is why it's called Green Animals.

"I would think that if Grandma Sheryl went to the trouble of putting this garden on the list, she'd want to be near the actual topiary, right?" I ask. "That's what makes the place special."

We walk around a large topiary giraffe that towers over the property.

"But how can we put anything here?" Chris whispers. "I mean, look down."

Seth and I follow his command and see the problem. Everything beneath the topiary shrubs is dark brown mulch. One can't just sprinkle a gray and white substance on the ground and expect it to go unnoticed.

"Seth, what do we do?"

"Well, we don't put it here," he says. "All these animals feel like a joke anyway. We will not put my mother under a giraffe. I'm going to look around the periphery of the place."

He starts to explore the property, and I see that Chris is making his way to a corner of the garden that has more shade.

"I'm gonna sit for a bit, if that's okay," he calls back to me. "I want to draw some of this."

"I'll come," I say.

I follow him, and we both relax under a tree.

"We might have to wait until some of these families clear out," Chris says as he removes colored pencils from his backpack. "It'll probably be a little easier not to get caught then."

He finds the green pencil and begins sketching the giraffe.

"If you wind up picking an animal for this, I liked the elephant," Chris says. "You could put her in the little border around him. I think Sheryl would appreciate Mr. Elephant."

I go to answer him, to tell him I also like the elephant, but what comes out of my mouth is not that.

"Why didn't you want me to move in with your family for the year?"

The words are out of my mouth before I've understood them. I guess I've been holding them in for twenty-four hours, but they have escaped without my permission, and I slap my hand over my lips.

Chris's hand freezes at the same time; the tip of his pencil is stuck on the center of the neck of the giraffe. His head doesn't move, but he glances up at me ever so slightly. He doesn't speak.

"I saw you," I say, because I have to. "I was asking your mom, and you were in the hallway. I saw your face. She turned me down, and you could not have looked more thrilled."

His head snaps up. "I wasn't thrilled, Lori."

"Fine. Relieved, then."

"I was not—look. Relieved is a strong word. But it's complicated."

I have to look away from him to keep from showing how hurt I am. Not far in front of us, a little kid is weeping and screaming at his mother, and he keeps yelling, "I don't want it!" and I envy his freedom to wail without shame.

I feel my own tears coming on. Chris catches it.

"Lor," he starts. "Lor, please don't cry about this. Cry if you need to, but not about this."

"Forget it," I say. "I'm not."

"Do you actually want to live in my house?" he asks in a more challenging voice than I'm used to. "Live with men who put up shelves and take over the television? Do you want to follow my mom's rules about cleaning and church and community service?"

Chris and his brother have to do five hours of giving back every month. It can be volunteering for a charity; sometimes Chris and his dad spend an afternoon organizing bags at the food bank.

"I love doing stuff with your church! I love helping your mom! You know that."

"But watching what you say? Dealing with Adam twenty-four-seven? Look, I love my house, but it's not like Sheryl's. The two of you were like roommates, with no rules and plenty of space. And for me . . . for us . . . we'd be right down the hall from each other at night and . . . that could get awkward."

He scratches behind his ear. He doesn't say more.

"Okay," I say, mostly to stop him.

Sometimes I feel that my friendship with Chris would be easier if we'd met before high school. He and Jessica have thousands of stories from when they were kids—camping in a tent in the back of Chris's yard, birthday parties with scary clowns, or, after Jason came to town in seventh grade, trips into Boston to see Red Sox games with Jason's dad, who used to play for a minor-league team.

I know that Jess is not in love with Chris, and I wonder if it's because she's known him forever.

I wish I'd had the chance to know him forever.

"It seemed like an impossible idea," Chris finally says. "If I looked relieved, it's only because my mom said it well—that it just wasn't going to happen. But . . . are you really mad?"

"No," I say. "Not anymore."

I am relieved that he was conflicted.

I guess I am consoled that he also thought about how it would feel for me to be down the hall at night—how that might be difficult, knowing our boundaries.

I stand up. "I'm going to find Seth."

"Should I come?"

"No. I'll text you when we find a spot for Grandma."

I push the conversation with Chris from my mind when I spot Seth kneeling in front of the big topiary teddy bear, looking up at it like it's a deity.

"Honestly, I don't know what Mom was thinking."

"Wait," I say, and find my phone. "Let's find out."

I pull up the Garden Girls text chain. There have been a few messages since the arboretum; mostly Lenny sending facts about the Explorers Garden near where we left Grandma Sheryl, and a few emojis from Rochelle (she likes the two pink hearts).

"We're at the topiary garden," I message the group, and before I can write more, their responses start coming in fast.

"How lovely," Jill says.

"Beautiful," Kevin says.

"Isn't it cute?" Deb says.

The pink hearts emoji from Rochelle.

And so on.

"The thing is," I write back, "the ground is very dark under the topiaries here. I don't know that I can put ashes at the bottom of any of these plants. It'd be too obvious. Also, would Sheryl really want to be buried under a bush in the shape of a giraffe?"

Kevin responds first. "Oh, no. That's not what she'd want."

"Have you walked down to the water?" Jill writes.

"Good memory, Jill!" Kevin writes.

"Go to the water," says a message from Deb that comes in at the same time as Kevin's.

Before I can ask, Jill is calling me.

"Sweetie," she says when I pick up, "it's the water. You have to take her down to the water. The beauty of the Brayton Estate is the view of Narragansett Bay. You can see all the way over to Prudence Island. The Girls, all of us, once took a bus trip down to the Newport mansions. We stopped at the Brayton Estate because of its history. We didn't intend to stop for long — topiary isn't necessarily our thing — but then Sheryl wandered off with her book, and after hunting for her, we found her at the edge of the property, looking out at the bay, deep in thought. I know that's where she'd want to be, down by the water with that gorgeous view."

"So not under a massive topiary teddy bear," I say.

"I wouldn't think so, no," Jill says, and laughs.

"Thank God, honestly," I say.

"Take some pictures of whatever spot you choose, will you?" Jill asks.

"Of course. I'll send them to the group."

I thank her and hang up.

"Come on," I tell Seth, and he gets up to follow me. I can see a strip of water beyond the house, so I follow it. We walk slowly down the hill until we get a better look.

A much better look.

"Oh wow," Seth says.

The bay is blue and calm and gorgeous. The border of the property is covered with grass and small plants — the perfect kind of growing things that will cover Grandma's ashes. The spot won't be trampled on by crying kids. It's the place where I know Grandma probably sat, where she would have read her book and wanted to stay all day.

"This is it, then," Seth says, and he sits. I join him.

He opens the Chico's bag. At this point we're committed to it as the official carrying case of Grandma.

"Do you want to call for Chris?"

I don't have to, because I see him coming down the hill.

"I thought you guys left me," he says.

"The Garden Girls told me this was Grandma Sheryl's favorite spot," I tell him.

Chris has his hands on his waist, his backpack on his back, as he looks out at the bay. "She had good taste, as usual. Do you guys want to be alone? I don't need to third wheel this every time."

"No," I say. "Sit. We need the drawing of the spot."

He settles himself cross-legged, and the three of us make a small triangle by the water. I pull the Dorothy Parker book out of my bag.

"Did you pick another reading?" Seth says.

"I think this one short poem will do. Do you want to do the craisins this time?"

Seth nods and takes the box out of the Chico's bag. Then he removes the bag of cremains and sprinkles them carefully around the row of plants in front of us. He blends them with the dirt with his hands. It's much simpler this time.

Chris illustrates the landscape as fast as he can. I can't see his notebook, but I assume he's focusing on the water and the island we can see across it. The way the lawn just drops off and then suddenly it's the bay, and then another shore, maybe with people looking back at us.

The whole experience is less intense this time, probably because we're not shocked to see what the cremains look like. Also, Seth pulls a small bottle of hand sanitizer out of his jeans pocket, which makes the act feel less sacred and more practical.

"Read," he says when he's made it through the bag.

I open to the dog-eared page.

"This is 'Sanctuary,' by Dorothy Parker," I begin.

My land is bare of chattering folk;
The clouds are low along the ridges.
And sweet's the air with curly smoke
From all my burning bridges.

There is a pause. That moment of silence that I now recognize is part of a Dorothy Parker one-liner sinking in.

Then Seth gives me a slow clap.

"God, she was good."

"She was probably the best kind of jerk," I say. "Like the person you'd want to be in a corner with at a party." Like Grandma Sheryl and Seth.

We're quiet for a while, looking at the water. Then I find my phone and take a picture of the view and send it to the Garden Girls.

"How perfect," Kevin writes back.

Jill says, "Well done."

The rest of them respond with thumbs-ups and hearts. Rochelle adds a shooting star. That's a new one for her.

We don't wait long before we decide to return home. Chris doesn't sleep on the ride back, but he doesn't talk either. Seth looks deep in thought, and I am too.

❦

Back at home, Seth goes outside to make a call to Ethan while I heat up lasagna. I put a big tin tray of it in the oven and then watch Seth pace around the front lawn while he talks, Devin Coogan bouncing up and down in the distance.

Later, we watch *Edward Scissorhands,* and I learn what kind of person I am.

Edward's skin is soft and pale around his scars, and his hair is wild and black, and when he smiles, it is the most earnest kind of happiness, which reminds me of Chris.

"So?" Seth says. "Forget who plays him, and the real world, and the practicalities of the scissors, and ask yourself, 'Would I?'"

"I would," I tell Seth because I know it will win me points —and it does.

"Damn right you would," he says.

This is the new plan, the one I want to make happen. Maybe it is possible.

It could be like this every night if he stayed. I could avoid moving my entire life to live with a parent who is probably somewhere clutching a crystal, coaching someone on their life instead of improving her own. I could have something like what I've had with Grandma Sheryl—a home where I can be myself, an adult who gets me.

As the movie credits roll, we both fall asleep on the couch. I wake us both up at, like, three a.m., and we shuffle, exhausted, to our rooms. I hope he is comfortable.

Chapter 8

My mom has been a lot of things. The first job I remember her having was as an office manager in a doctor's office. That's when we lived in New Jersey the first time. Already she was into meditation and self-help books, and she loved one book called *The Secret,* which basically says that if you are confident that you should get something, it will come to you. But you have to be really sure about it. No doubts. You have to be like, "I *will* get a puppy," and then you're bound to get one. A puppy will be thrust upon you because you made it so.

Mom's wish was for a career and a partner, she said at the time. I guess that's why she kept moving in with boyfriends and quitting jobs to take new ones. She would make those things materialize, but they were never quite right. The minute I left and moved in with Grandma, Mom settled down a little, which makes me wonder what she was really running from. I try not to think about that.

It was after I moved out that she started going to school to be a life coach. She trained in this program to help others manage their lives. Which is big-time irony, the most frustrating kind if you're her daughter.

Seth told me one Christmas that people who have careers helping others often can't help themselves.

"I've known so many therapists who are messes," he told me. "It makes *perfect sense* that your mom is becoming a life coach."

I'm in the middle of imagining her in a session with someone, grabbing her geode necklace while telling them what to do, when my phone starts ringing. It's FaceTime, and it's her.

Maybe I accidentally did *The Secret*.

I sit up and answer so she won't bother me for the rest of the day.

"Hey, Mom," I say.

She's not looking into the camera. Her face is to the side, and she looks pale, with no makeup on. She's not wearing her necklaces.

"What's up?" I ask, getting worried.

"Look!" she says, and then moves the phone to what's behind her, which is a white wall.

"I see nothing."

"Oh, shoot," she says, fiddling with the technology. "Maybe if I turn it this way."

She's walking the perimeter of the room, and then I get it. This room will be mine.

There is some construction debris on the floor. Pieces of wood.

"Is the ceiling falling down?" I ask.

"What? Oh! Oh, no, Lori," she says. "Bill is making you a desk!"

That is so nice. That makes what I'm about to say so much worse.

"Mom," I say in my kindest voice, which is also a fake-sounding voice, "I have an idea. What if Seth moved in with me here for the year. Like, he could go back and forth and see Ethan. He teaches most of his classes remotely anyway . . ."

Silence.

"You want to live with Seth?" she asks after an eternity.

"It's not about wanting him instead of you," I say. "I just want to stay here, you know? I mean, that's not news."

Mom's face deflates—literally sags—like a bouncy house that's taken on too much weight and is sinking to the ground with a bunch of tumbling bodies inside.

"You don't see anything positive about living with me," she says.

"It's not that," I tell her. "I just told you that wasn't the case."

"He lives in New York," she says.

"It's one year. Ethan could visit, and I think Seth could do a lot of writing here. I keep seeing him inspired, making notes. Also, we get along so well and have so much in common. And he's doing a really good job of watching me."

Now I'm being honest. He's better at this than she is.

"You think he's parenting you well," she says, and her voice is bitter. "Like you thought *my* mother was a better parent than I could ever be. You think that's the truth."

I don't say anything for a bit, but then I decide to be honest.

"I'm not sure everyone is cut out for parenting," I tell her. "Grandma Sheryl was a teacher. She didn't mind sitting at home all night and focusing on someone else. You have other stuff to do. Boyfriends to move in with. That's okay, it's just not great for me."

Mom looks directly into the phone and becomes an entirely different person—the one I like and rarely see. She's so woo-woo usually. She talks with this high voice that's all light and airy and feel-good and blissed-out—too confident about her positivity—even when things are miserable.

But every now and then her voice drops an octave and she sounds like some person I'd want to know. Usually that voice came out when she was fighting with Grandma Sheryl on the phone, or when she's telling an old story about my dad.

It's been forever since I've heard her sound this way.

"You think there's only good and bad. That your grandma was a good parent and I'm a bad one, and that Seth is wonderful and I'm terrible."

I don't want to have to confirm this, so I say nothing and look away.

"Your grandma was a great parent because she got a second chance."

"What is that supposed to mean?"

Mom hesitates.

"She wasn't so perfect with me," she says, her voice even lower. "Mom ignored Seth and me for, I don't know, most of our childhoods. Dad died, and then all Mom did was work and tutor into the night. She did it in the house, so she'd be in the living room patiently working with kids on their homework. Perfecting their college essays. Meanwhile, Seth and I would be in our rooms upstairs, fending for ourselves. The house felt like a business. We felt like burdens just by being there."

"But she loved kids," I say.

"Other people's kids!" Mom says.

I want to defend Grandma Sheryl. She worked nights to support her kids *because* she loved them. There's no way she ignored her own.

"She and Seth were so close," I argue. "I know she didn't ignore him."

"Because my brilliant brother figured it out," Mom says. "He took on Mom's interests. He loved reading, so he didn't have to fake anything. But he realized that if he read all her favorite books, she'd pay attention, and she did. They functioned that way ever since. By the end of high school, he was helping her tutor other students. They were like partners, more like twins than he and I could be.

"I'm not a reader, Lor. You know that. I wasn't an anything, really. She didn't help me figure out what *I* liked, what *I* might be good at. She and Seth had their little club, and I wasn't part of it."

I can't imagine Grandma Sheryl ignoring anyone on purpose. But . . . I also always liked what she liked, just like Seth. We could always talk about books. But what if I hadn't been interested, I ask myself for a second. What if I'd been a kid who loved sports? Would she have invited me to live with her?

"I know you love your uncle Seth," Mom continues. "I love him, too. But he has never been responsible for watching over anyone, including himself. He does what he wants. There's no way he supports himself financially—that's Ethan's territory. Seth has never had to be the person giving the final answer. It wouldn't be what you think."

Of course he does what he wants, I think. He's an adult.

"Could we try?" I ask.

She exhales.

"I don't know, Lor. I can talk to him. I just—I need time to think about whether it's a good idea."

I nod. I don't want to break the silence in a way that will change her mind. Inside, I'm squealing. Even this much commitment feels like progress.

"Listen, honey, I'm going to go talk to Bill. Forget what I said about Grandma. It's complicated grown-up stuff, and your memories of her don't have to match mine. It's been a tough week, and I'm trying to process it all. I shouldn't be putting it on you."

This is the most my mother has ever said about why she is the way she is. I wish she was like this more often.

"Okay," I say, not wanting to push her.

She hangs up, and all I can focus on is the news—she will talk to Seth about staying.

I find myself walking into the spare room, her old room. There is no desk. There are no bookshelves. Just Seth's stuff. For the first time, I notice that there is no evidence that my mother was ever here.

Chapter 9

We walk down a side street in the South End, a swank neighborhood in Boston, and Seth nods his approval of our surroundings. It's a cooler day, finally, so I'm in my red dress with the yellow collar that I found at the secondhand clothing store near the movie theater in Somerville. Chris always says the appropriate accessory for this dress would be a massive knife. That's the ultimate compliment.

But Chris is not here today. I told him that Seth and I could do this third box alone.

This is part of my backup plan, the one that involves me having to move. I want to see Chris a little less this week, to maybe get used to not turning to him for everything, to figure out how to enjoy him from afar, if that's what has to happen. I don't need him near me every second. I can survive without him.

Also, I want him to have some space for himself. I know this week has been a lot. I am usually better at thinking about him first. This whole thing has turned me into the neediest person and I hate it. He should have a minute to draw on his own, or play with Adam. Or sort clothes with his mom.

God, if I have to move I'll miss Mrs. Burke so much.

But if my plan A works, it won't have to come to that.

I let out some stress by kicking a cobblestone.

"I know I always say I would never live in Boston, but I could live on this street," Seth says, looking around. "I could see myself here."

"Oh, really? You could imagine yourself being happy on *this* street?"

I'm being sarcastic because literally *anyone* could see themselves here. We are in one of the richest neighborhoods in Boston, the kind of Boston you'd see on a television show, with pretty brownstones and manicured trees. The South End is lined with French restaurants, people who walk dogs that wear clothing, and a craft market Grandma Sheryl used to take me to before Hanukkah. Last year we stopped for hot chocolate and walked from booth to booth until we found handmade worry dolls and bought some for Mom and Seth. We got some for me, too. I wonder where I put them. Because I am worried.

This could be the last time I'm in the South End for a long time, so I take it in. I try to see it through Grandma Sheryl's eyes, now that I have had more time touring gardens with the botanic bible that I've found myself reading before bed every night. There are azaleas in front of the row of brownstones next to us. There are pink and yellow mums. There are some wilting dahlias—or at least that's what I think they are—which might be my favorite. I can't believe I know this.

"Are we going in the right direction?" Seth asks.

I grab my phone from my dress pocket and type in the location again.

"My GPS says we're forty feet away," I respond, confused. We should be right there.

Seth looks around to the brownstones on either side of us. "But there's no garden."

"There must be. It says Tapestry Garden is right here."

"What's the address we're looking for?"

"One eighty-one."

Seth squints to see a plaque on the browwnstone in front of him.

"This is one eighty-nine, so it must be on this block . . ."

We wander side by side until we see the gorgeous home between 179 and 183.

"*This* is one eighty-one?" Seth mutters.

The building is so beautiful, I gasp. It is a very tall brownstone with fancy marble stairs and tiny gargoyles on each side of the landing. A man with a bow tie should live here. Or a very fancy widow.

There is large brass plate on the front door. It says COFFIN.

"What the fuck," Seth says. "Why does it say coffin?"

I let out a sharp laugh. "I have no idea."

"I'm googling it," Seth says, taking his phone from his bag.

I don't wait. I hit the buzzer.

"Lori, what are you doing?" Seth asks.

"It says coffin," I say. "It's a sign that we're supposed to be here. Literally."

"What the hell, Lor—"

Before Seth can finish, the door swings open, and on the other side is a man. An adult, younger than Seth by some years. He has peachy skin, with a beach tan and floppy blond hair. He wears skinny jeans and a black T-shirt that says SIMPLE in all caps. He's painted his nails dark blue, and I decide he must be interesting.

"Can I help you?" he asks, running his eyes over us. He takes a long look at my dress and my hair, but I can't tell if he likes my look. I stand taller.

"I hope so," Seth answers from behind me, and with that one phrase, I can tell that Seth wants to climb all over this man, which is fair, because he is Uncle Seth's type and objectively cute. I mean, this SIMPLE man is everybody's type, I think. He radiates the entitlement and confidence of a Jake or a Tyler.

"What can I do for you?" the man says to help move us along.

"Um . . ." I say. Seth is legit just staring at him. "We're actually looking for something called Tapestry Garden. Google says it's at this address, but maybe it's wrong. Have you heard of it? Is there a garden nearby?"

The man smiles, showing straight white teeth. His eyes are so blue.

"It's here. It's my mother's garden."

Seth and I show our confusion.

"It's a private garden," the man clarifies. "It's called Tapestry Garden — by the family. Technically, it's just our backyard."

"But it's in Google Maps," I say.

"I mean, it is a designated society garden," the man says. "I suppose it's on a map. But it's not a public garden or run by the Parks Department or anything. It's only on a map because the home is historic."

"Shit," Seth and I whisper at the same time. This is a setback we did not expect. We glance at each other — and then at my backpack — which has the Chico's bag inside of it, and we're both a little baffled about what happens next.

"I'm Seth Seltzer," Seth says, climbing the last step to the door and sticking out his hand for the man to shake. "This is my niece, Lori."

"Hi," I say sheepishly, and wave.

"Liam," the man says, shaking Seth's hand. "Liam Coffin."

"Your last name is Coffin!" I say, stating the obvious, based on Seth's expression. "That's why it's on the door."

"Yes," he says. "We're not *the* Coffins, but we're distantly related. I suppose every Coffin is technically one of *the* Coffins."

I nod, even though I have no idea who *the* Coffins might be.

"Would you like to come in?"

We must look very lost or very unthreatening, because we are one hundred percent strangers and this man is letting us into his house. We follow him down a long hallway that has wide built-in bookshelves Grandma Sheryl would have killed for, into a living room that has pristine white walls and dark blue velvet furniture. There are very old-looking paintings on the walls, and I doubt they're replicas. One is of a miserable-looking woman staring out a window.

"If you're interested in the garden, my mother can tell you all about it," Liam says, still standing as Seth and I sit on a leather love seat. "I'll grab her," he adds, and disappears.

"What is the plan here?" I whisper to Seth because we are in a private, very expensive and scary home.

"Shhh," he responds.

We're silent until he says, barely audibly, "My god, there is so much Wedgwood."

"What's Wedgwood?" I whisper.

"Those little bowls," he says, eyeing the light blue one next to me.

I reach for it, but he slaps my hand and shakes his head in a way that makes me think this bowl could pay for my college education.

*

I imagine that Liam's mother, Mrs. Coffin, will look like British royalty—like pictures I've seen of the queen. I assume that she wears pearls. But the woman who descends the staircase looks much younger and stylish. Her skin is pulled back tight, though.

Somehow there are no lines around her eyes, and her lashes are so long they remind me of whiskers.

We stand when she enters the room, and then we all sit down again. It seems like the thing you do in the presence of a woman who looks like this. She's in a loose-fitting, silky long-sleeved dress that, with the right accessories, could be formalwear. But she's just wearing it around the house.

"Please sit," she says, and gives us a thin, glossy smile.

Liam enters the room again behind her and gives us an encouraging nod.

"This is Seth and—"

"Lori," I finish for him.

"Right," Liam says. "They were looking for Tapestry Garden. I explained it's just the yard."

Liam's mom looks surprised—at least I think that's what her face is trying to show.

"I'm sorry to bother you," Seth says. "It's just that we're here because my mother died last week."

As soon as the words are out of his mouth, it seems like they've taken up the whole room. Liam's mom puts her hand on her heart.

"I'm so sorry," Liam says.

"How awful," Mrs. Coffin says.

"Thank you," Seth continues. "It feels odd to say that out loud. I need to work on my delivery."

"Don't even think about it," Liam says, and Seth smiles.

"My mother was a lover of gardens. It was her passion," Seth says, and he is in full sales-pitch mode. I love when he talks like this, when he talks about his books. "We're not having a formal funeral, but Lori and I wanted to visit her favorite gardens together, and to read passages from her favorite books in each spot.

"She left us a list, and this one, Tapestry Garden, was on it. We hoped to see it and to say a few words there. Honestly, we had no idea it was a private space. It's so nice of you to let us in, but we'll be happy to get out of your hair. We wouldn't have come if we'd known it was a family's home."

"I wonder how she would have even known about a private garden," I add.

"Did she attend the annual neighborhood garden tour?" Liam's mother asks. "We're on the open house tour every other year. That's how most people know about us."

"Yes!" I exclaim. "She totally did."

I decide I have to start whispering because everything I say sounds like a shout in this library-like room. I'm going to have to write a story about this place. There are definitely ghosts here. And the last name of the ghosts is Coffin, which is a bit on the nose, but I love it.

"She must have really connected with this place," Seth says, and even though he's told these people we'll get out of their hair, he's not going anywhere.

"We don't do many private tours," Liam's mother says, and now it's awkward.

"I'm sorry," I say, although I'm not sure what I'm apologizing for.

"Mom," Liam says, getting Seth's hint. "What if I show them the garden. It'd be nice to let them honor their mom for a few moments. I can take them out there myself, and they can do a little reading. You know, for their loved one."

Mrs. Coffin takes a beat and then nods. She's not afraid to let us know she's unsure about this, but now it's too late; her son has decided to be hospitable, so she's stuck with us unless she's willing to look like a jerk. "I'll come with you," she says, and once she stands, we all follow.

We trail her in a line—Liam, Seth, then me—through a narrow hallway that has more books and art, hundreds of books on more of those shelves, and I wonder if any of the books have been read. Their spines, whether they're old and leather-bound or new, are all pristine. Some are novels. Others are about home design.

We walk past a kitchen where two older women, who appear to be staff of some kind, are shuffling around in a panic.

"We're hosting a dinner for the French Cultural Center in a few hours," Mrs. Coffin says, explaining the trays of food on the counters. I spy tiny mushrooms filled with something creamy. There are little French flags sticking out of them. "The guests will arrive by six."

It must be about four by now. She's giving us a deadline. This family has fancy things to do tonight.

We arrive at a stained-glass door.

"This is the garden," Mrs. Coffin says, and ushers us outside.

I have never seen anything like this place in real life.

I feel better when Seth's gasp is louder than mine.

*

I did not like reading much before I found horror, fantasy, and some science fiction. The first book I loved was *Pet Sematary* by Stephen King, and I pretty much still read it once a year.

It's the reason I usually spell *cemetery* wrong. Stephen King ruined me.

But of all of the regular, non-magic books I had to read growing up—the depressing required fiction like *A Separate Peace*, which made me feel nothing, and the big books like *East of Eden*, which Seth says is amazing but I think was just fine—I most enjoyed *The Secret Garden*.

At least, I liked the part of it that was actually about the garden. There's something cool about the idea of a place that no one knows is there—a place that, once discovered, becomes totally yours. I didn't care much about the characters and the illnesses and everything that happened in the house, but I liked the part where the girl gets to go into the garden. When she brings someone new there for the first time, it's as if the place is making them feel better. I think of the book now because of what's in front of me. The garden is small and square and much wilder than I thought it would be, based on the rest of the house. Ivy snakes up the back of the brownstone, and the grass springing from the walking path looks lush and untamed.

I wish Chris were here to draw it.

"It's best in spring," Mrs. Coffin says, as if she has something to be embarrassed about. "The perennials have long peaked."

"Not those," I say, pointing to a patch of flowers. "Are those calla lilies?"

Mrs. Coffin is impressed by my quick ID. So am I.

"I love my calla lilies," she says, beaming. "I only get to see them for a few weeks, but when they're here, they're good company."

I love that she talks about flowers as if they're people. Grandma Sheryl did that too. Maybe it's just a garden person kind of thing.

I find myself wondering whether Mrs. Coffin has ever had a job or if she's been to the Natick Mall. I wonder if her son lives here full-time, who her husband is, and if she is lonely.

I am drawn to a patch of pink flowers that remind me of starfish.

"Toad lilies," Mrs. Coffin says, answering my unspoken question.

"How'd they get that name?"

"They're bumpy," she says, and nods her permission for me to touch their weird freckles.

Next to them are a patch of bright petals that are easy to ID because there are so many of them in Grandma's field guide.

"Nice begonias!" I say too loud, and Seth lets out a snort. To my surprise, Mrs. Coffin gets why he's laughing.

"Many men have told me so," she says.

"Mother!" Liam says, and he's delighted. Suddenly we're all friends, and Mrs. Coffin no longer looks like she's desperate to push a button to send us through a trapdoor.

"The garden tours can be difficult for homeowners," she tells me, as if she understands that she needs to explain why she's been so unfriendly. "We want to make our private gardens available for garden clubs, and we love the concept of an open house, but it's an entire afternoon of people coming through our private quarters. That's why we offer Tapestry tours every *other* year. I wonder when your grandmother visited."

I wonder, too.

"I've only lived with her for three years or so, so I don't know," I say. "I didn't always pay attention to where she went with her garden club. Now I wish I had."

"Well, I only ask because I'd like to think I met her," Mrs. Coffin says, and then pauses. "You said you're not having a funeral. Have you laid her to rest?"

It's a spooky and personal question, and before I can stammer out an answer, Seth steps between us.

"She was buried at a Jewish cemetery in Framingham," he says with so much confidence that I forget for a split second that a quarter of Grandma Sheryl is in my backpack.

"Lovely," Mrs. Coffin says, and clears her throat. "Liam, let's give them some privacy to do their reading and have whatever moment they need."

"Sure," he says, following her to the back door. "If you need us, we'll be just inside," Mrs. Coffin says, and Liam smiles again.

"Come on," Seth whispers, and swings me around to pull the backpack off my body. "We have to be really fast with this."

"Wait," I say, pulling away from him, my arms flailing like I'm a turtle. The backpack falls to the brick path beneath us in the garden. "We can't actually do this. It's a private garden, Seth."

I turn around, and we stare at each other, both of us confused.

"It was on the list. This is Box Three," Seth says.

I am trying to figure out if he is kidding. We cannot put Grandma Sheryl here. It's the house of a real person, not the estate of a long-dead family that's willed the property to a trust for public tours.

"This is no longer Box Three," I tell him. "She clearly didn't mean for us to bring her craisins to this house. She must have confused the name of this garden with another. Or maybe she forgot where she saw it. Or maybe—I don't know. She wouldn't want us to dump her body in someone else's backyard without them knowing."

An annoying thing about having a loved one die is that they're not around to answer practical questions. What *was* she thinking?

"Wait," I say, and pull out my phone. Seth remains impatient.

"EMERGENCY," I text to the Garden Girls. "Tapestry Garden is private! Like in someone's house!"

Kevin is the first to respond. "Yes," he says.

"???" I write back.

"She really, really loved that garden," Jill says.

"I'm sure she did," I write. "Who wouldn't? But it's private!"

"Have you asked for permission?" Rochelle writes.

"I did think it was curious that it was on the list, TBH," Lenny says.

"We're in the garden," I say. "They let us in so we could see it, but they would not want us dropping ashes back here."

"I would let someone put ashes in my garden," Jill says. "I would be honored."

"That's because you're a doll, Jill," Deb writes. "Lori, what's blooming?" she asks in a second message.

I mutter a profanity and put the phone away. The Garden Girls really do have one-track minds, and at the moment, they do not understand the weight of my problems.

I don't have time to take pictures or search my book to ID all the blooming things in front of me.

"Stop asking permission. This isn't that big of a deal. Think about all the birds that shit on this garden. Or their friends who spill wine here. It's *outside*," Seth says, and he's already pulled out the Chico's bag and the box inside. "Pick a spot, fast."

I grab his arms. "Seth, this is weird!"

"It's all earth," he whispers. "What's the difference between putting tiny stones here or putting stones by the water on a property that *used* to be owned by rich people?"

My mother's words from last night, the ones about Seth doing what he wants, scroll through my head, but I push them out. Seth is just emotional and committed and, at the moment, eyeing this garden as if it's a bank he's ready to rob.

Maybe he's right. Maybe this is fine, and no one will know. It is not that much of anything. Just rocks.

I feel short of breath, and I want to rip my dress collar off. I know he won't be stopped, so timing is most important. We can't get caught. I turn in a circle and think about where I want Grandma Sheryl to have a home.

"There," I say, pointing to a patch of swaying black-eyed Susans.

"They're a little weedlike," Seth says, scratching under his chin.

"Grandma Sheryl liked them. We passed a field of them once near this strawberry-picking farm and she pulled the car over and just stared at it awhile."

It was last summer. The weather was steamy that day, the way it's been for the past week. I'd gone for my phone to take a pic of the never-ending field of brown and yellow flowers, and she stopped me.

"I want to show Chris," I had said, taking my phone out to capture the scene.

"No," Grandma Sheryl said. "How would you describe it? You're a writer. How would you put it in a book?"

"I wouldn't have to describe it that much, because he'd illustrate it. That's why it's good to know an illustrator."

"Illustrations shouldn't make you a lazy writer."

I looked at the field of bright yellow black-eyed Susans that day, thousands upon thousands of them bobbing their heads in the same circle, their centers making them look like friendly Cyclopes, and I told Grandma Sheryl, "They look like August. They look like the last moments of summer when you're about to go back to school. They look ripe. Does that make sense?"

"It does," she said. "Well put. You might just be a writer."

That's why I know this flower so well. I have no pictures of that field of flowers, but I'll remember them forever.

I snap out of the moment, and Seth is already squatting by the patch, looking sinister, as if he's about to bury a body, and then I realize that's exactly what he's about to do.

I glance at the back door to keep watch. This feels so wrong.

"Cover me," he says as he peels off the gold Walsh's sticker from the box and removes the bag inside. I position myself on my knees behind him, fully shielding him.

He moves fast, and I clench my fists when I see the bagful of craisins, not because they are human remains—the pieces of bone no longer upset me—but because I know this is wrong. No matter how I spin it, it's a violation.

If Chris were here, he would not allow it. I'd have someone on my side.

With his free hand Seth digs a small hole in the soil between the flowers.

"Here," he says. "Get down here fast and help."

I use two fingers to tunnel through the dirt.

He lifts the bag and shakes it.

"It's all stuck together," he says.

He's jostling the bag, which is so disturbing.

"Stop doing that," I hiss.

I pull the book from my backpack, the Dorothy Parker, but he bats it down.

"Lori, there is no actual time for that. We can read it when we're outside, maybe in front of the place."

We both look at the size of the bag compared with the small patch we have to put it in.

"We can't put this whole bag here," I say.

"We'll just put in as much as we can and bring the rest to the next stop," Seth says.

His eyes are wild, and for maybe the first time in my life I wish my mom were here. She would not allow this either. She'd talk about bad karma or something and force Seth out of this place.

"Seth, this isn't . . . this doesn't feel right," I tell him.

"Lori, let it go. This is for my mother," he says, and he begins to pour.

Just as the craisins begin to flow into the dirt and the dark brown mulch, the pieces looking way too white to belong there, the back door slams open and Mrs. Coffin is there, Liam behind her, and she's shouting, "No, no, NO!" Seth quickly moves the bag behind his back and stands, moving his body in front of what he's just done.

"Wait, it's not what it looks like—" I stammer.

"Don't move," Mrs. Coffin says. "Please stop doing what I know you're doing."

Her voice is shaky. She is furious, and she might also be afraid of us. I don't blame her.

"Really, it's not what it looks like," I say again, although I literally have no idea what it looks like. Whatever it is, we are terrible.

"We're not stealing anything," Seth says, and the rest of us look bewildered.

"I didn't think you were stealing," Mrs. Coffin says. "It looks like the two of you are scattering your loved one's ashes in my garden."

Liam shoots a look at Seth, his face a mix of empathy and betrayal. He lobbied for us to get back here, and now we're putting my grandma in a secret garden that belongs to his mother.

Seth pauses, maybe trying to think of a lie, but we've been caught, and at this point I just want to get out of here.

"Please don't call the police," I say.

"The police?" Seth says. "They wouldn't call the police, Lori." He looks over at Liam Coffin. "Wait . . . you'd call the police?"

"I don't see why I shouldn't," Mrs. Coffin says. "Please. Please go."

I notice how much her voice is trembling and that she's crying.

Tears aren't quite escaping from her eyes, but they're there. My heart sinks into my stomach.

"We're so sorry," I say. I grab the bag of Grandma from Seth, kneel down, and cup my hands to scoop the cremains from the soil and put them back into the bag. It's a messy process; I can't pick up all the white pieces without taking a lot of soil with them. Seth isn't helping. He's sort of frozen.

He's never had to be the grownup.

"This is so disrespectful," Mrs. Coffin says in Seth's direction. "You told us you were visiting the garden, that you were doing a reading. I knew it, though. I knew you were up to something. That's why I asked—and then you said she was buried in Framingham? You lied."

"We didn't mean to upset you. It's just rocks, basically," I tell her. "It's basically fertilizer. It decomposes. My grandma loved it so much here. We wanted to honor her. I'm so sorry."

"My husband is back here!" Mrs. Coffin says, and that's when what we've done sinks in for Seth, as if he's seeing the world around him for the first time today. He drops to his knees and tries to help me, but I push his hands away. For the first time in my life, I am mad at him.

"Why doesn't everyone just calm down," Liam says. "Mom, they're grieving. Give them a second to get their things and get out of here. They're not criminals."

"Aren't they? It's criminal—putting a stranger's ashes, without permission, near your father!"

Liam gives Seth an empathetic, apologetic glance.

"Stop looking at him like that!" Mrs. Coffin says, which makes Liam's face turn red.

"Mrs. Coffin," Seth says, his voice smooth again, his regret suddenly clear, "and you too, Liam, I'm so sorry. This was . . . well, I'm an adult, and this was disrespectful. Please don't blame Lori. I should be setting some sort of example. Why my mother put this garden on the list is a mystery, but I should have turned around as soon as we realized it was in a private home.

"The truth is . . . her death doesn't feel real. These ashes don't seem real. Never in a million years did I think I'd be in someone's backyard doing what I'm doing. But this was her wish, and I wanted to do it right."

It's kind of a lie. Grandma never mandated that we go to all four gardens. It was a list of options. Tapestry Garden was never essential.

"I'm sorry. I just can't allow it," Mrs. Coffin says.

"Of course," I say.

She wipes her teary, less angry eyes, and Seth nods. She doesn't forgive us, but she no longer looks like she wants to bring us to trial. The mulch under the flowers is a little messy now, but the ashes have fully been removed. Our bag holds a mix of soil and cremains.

"We'll leave," Seth says.

"Do you mind my asking where your husband is?" I say to

Mrs. Coffin. I don't know why I want to know; maybe I want to see how the Coffins did it.

She points to the exact place where we were putting Grandma Sheryl.

"I see. Popular spot," I say, but she doesn't smile.

"It gets some lovely light," she finally responds, although she's stiff about it.

We sigh, and Seth has started to walk to the door, so I follow.

"Do you want to do your reading?" Mrs. Coffin says. She hasn't moved.

We turn around and find her looking less scary, less furious.

"You're here," she says directly to me. I think she'd like to make Seth disappear, but she doesn't seem to hate me. "You might as well read your passage, assuming you were telling the truth about that part of your story."

"That's really kind of you," Seth says.

She doesn't acknowledge him, but tells me, "Come sit," and we all find a place on the two benches in Tapestry Garden.

"You won't mind if we stay to supervise," she adds.

I smile. Of course we are not trusted to be alone. And I don't want to be alone with Seth right now.

I reach into my backpack and take out the Dorothy Parker anthology.

"That's not what I expected," Mrs. Coffin says.

"What did you expect?" Liam asks.

"A prayer? A Jewish reading?" she says.

I smile.

"My grandma was an English teacher, and she was a big Dorothy Parker fan," I say. "There's actually some nice stuff about death in here."

"I'd love to hear," she says.

I decide that today is not the day for one of Dorothy Parker's sassy sarcastic poems. This needs to be something classy. Mrs. Coffin deserves that much.

I flip to a poem called "Little Words."

"'When you are gone,'" I read, "'there is no bloom nor leaf, Nor singing sea at night, nor silver birds; And I can only stare, and shape my grief. In little words.'"

The poem goes on.

It's sad and thoughtful. There's a line about having a "weary pen" that I totally understand.

Grandma Sheryl has died, but the world is blooming everywhere. I am tired, and the family is unraveling. All I have are little words.

"I should read more Dorothy Parker," Mrs. Coffin says, dabbing her eyes.

"I should, too," I say. "What do you like to read, Mrs. Coffin?"

"Oh, you know, whatever's popular these days," she says. "I'm in a book club that just read — oh, what was it . . . HBO made a show about it."

Seth makes a face, and I kick his foot.

"Well, anyway—" she says.

We all stand and walk to the door and then back through the house.

"Where will you take her?" Mrs. Coffin asks when we reach the front of the house.

"The Mount," Seth says. "That's another location on her list, so we'll try there."

Mrs. Coffin hasn't heard of it.

"It's Edith Wharton's home in Western Mass, Mom," Liam says, and Seth looks impressed.

"Do you have *Edith's* permission?" Mrs. Coffin asks. I think she's joking, but it's hard to tell.

"Again, we're so sorry," I say.

She nods.

"Don't worry about it," Liam whispers after his mother has turned away. "She'll recover by tonight's party. Good luck," he says, giving us a smile as he closes the door.

Before we go, Seth takes a piece of paper from his wallet, writes something on it, and leaves it in the mailbox.

"What was that?" I ask.

"Just a thank-you, with my number," he says. "I'm making friends."

"You don't need friends," I say. "You don't even live here."

"Don't I?" Seth asks.

I pause.

"Your mom talked to me this morning," he tells me. "She told me you'd like me to stay."

"Oh," I say, my brain too busy to say more.

My bag feels heavier now than it did when we walked in, mostly because I thought it would be lighter on our way out.

We find the lot where we parked the car, and that's when we really talk.

"I'd consider it," he says. "I guess I *am* considering it. It would give us more time to deal with the house. I could get so much writing done, away from city distractions. Also, it means a lot that you want me here. I know it's more that you want to stay around Chris and your high school, but . . . it means plenty that we'd be able to spend time together."

"Right," I say, but it doesn't come out with as much confidence as I'd like, so I say it again, trying for conviction. "That's what I want."

It is, but after today, the picture looks different.

Chapter 10

The sun has started setting a little bit earlier. The light flashes stripes across the kitchen wall as I eat more of Jess's mom's noodles at the kitchen counter.

I check my phone, and there's nothing on it. This is the most silent it's ever been. Chris hasn't messaged, nor has my mom. It feels weird.

Up until today, Mom had been messaging and calling all day, like any usual week. She'd sent a link to the high school I'd go to if I moved in with her and Bill. That was before I asked her if I could live with Seth.

Seth has been upstairs showering and on the phone, probably with Ethan. I wonder if he told him the real story about our afternoon.

Then he runs downstairs and is energetic and smiley—as if we didn't just have a horrible experience where we got caught dumping Grandma Sheryl's ashes on private property. He opens the refrigerator door, takes out the container of scallion pancakes, and eats one in a few bites.

"Yum," he says, and I don't know why, but the word annoys me.

"What about Mount Auburn Cemetery?" he says.

"For what?" I ask.

"We're down a garden. We'll go to The Mount, but what about a new fourth place? I was googling gardens near Boston, and Mount Auburn Cemetery kept coming up."

That's when I notice what he is wearing.

It's a shirt the Garden Girls bought Grandma for one of her birthdays. It was a joke gift, because she'd never actually wear it. It is a bright orange tee that says I WET MY PLANTS.

"You're supposed to be donating that stuff, not taking it," I say.

"This T-shirt is *mine*," he says, grinning.

It fits him well, like it was meant to be worn by an aging New York hipster writer.

"Oliver Wendell Holmes is apparently buried at Mount Auburn Cemetery. It's a beautiful place."

"It's not a garden, though."

"Yes it is," Seth responds. "I went on like forty school field trips there. The whole thing is a big garden. There's shit growing everywhere."

"Yeah—but I don't know. It's still a place of death. Like, *for* death. I think she wanted to be in a place that's all about life. She basically told us *not* to put her in a cemetery."

"Fair," Seth said. "We'll keep thinking."

Then it's clear he's going out. His wallet is in his back pocket. He has his keys.

"You're leaving?" I ask. "In that shirt?'

He looks down. "I think it's appropriate enough for the Big Whale."

"Ah," I say, and smile. I guess this is good. If he's reacquainting himself with the local sites, he's really thinking about staying. That's what I want, I remind myself.

"What if you get there and you don't know anyone?" I ask.

"Then I'll get an IPA and do people watching," he says.

Seth is comfortable anywhere.

It'll be good for him to see Ethan tomorrow. Maybe they'll talk about how a year in two cities might work. And Seth must need him by now. My mom has Bill, and I have Chris, but Seth has gone through the loss of his mom—and taking care of me —on his own. Maybe that's why he was so messy today. He's lost his compass. Ethan will remind him of how he's supposed to be.

The front door shuts behind him.

I'm restless, walking around the living room and then the kitchen—wrestling with what Grandma Sheryl would call a bad case of *shpilkes,* which I believe is the Yiddish word for not being able to sit still. That's when I hear the faint murmurs of conversation.

I lift the kitchen shade and see them in the backyard. Jill, Kevin, Deb, Rochelle, Lenny. They're standing in a circle, sort of like it's a séance.

I grab my flower book and head out the back door to join them.

Jill notices me first.

"There she is," she announces.

"The beautiful Lori," Kevin says, which is hilarious because I'm in pajamas again and I know I look wrecked.

I find a space to stand between Rochelle and Lenny, and I see that they are all holding a small piece of a purple flower that's in bloom. I guess I see that the plant, which is like a wave of color all around the backyard, has been there for a while. How could I have missed it?

"What plant is this?"

"Consult your book," Deb challenges.

"It's hard to go page by page," I say, flipping through it. "You know what would be a good app? Something like the one where you lift your phone up so it can hear a song and then tells you what it is. Someone could do that with plants—like, you could take a picture of a flower and the app would spit back its name."

"Good business idea!" Rochelle tells me. Most of the Garden Girls are in shorts and dirty T-shirts for working in the soil, but Rochelle is dressed like a celebrity on an island vacation. She's in a simple sundress and espadrilles, but she's just so elegant.

"What ended up happening today?" Kevin asks.

I take a deep breath. I could give them the short version— that it didn't work at Tapestry Garden—but I decide to go long. I tell them about Seth and the ashes and the horror of being caught.

At one point Lenny covers her mouth with her hand, embarrassed on my behalf, and that makes me ashamed all over again.

"Seth was weird," I say. "He couldn't read the room; there was no way it was okay to leave the ashes there. Not even Mom would have done what he did. It was clear we were trespassing from the start, and he was so . . ."

"Entitled," Deb says.

That's it. That's the word I'm looking for.

After some awkward silence, I say what I'm surprised to admit. "He doesn't always think of others like most adults do."

Rochelle places her hand on my back.

"It's a complicated time," she says. "He's just lost his mom."

"He adores you," Jill says. "Just like your grandma did."

I feel a little better.

My eyes are back on the book, and the Girls are watching me. Finally I see a page with a flower that matches what's in their hands.

"New England aster?" I guess, and they nod. "So it's local."

"Sheryl'd always come out right about now," Lenny says, her voice thick with feeling. "A brilliant purple."

"I hope you don't mind," Kevin says, "in light of the talk about trespassing. We've made some cuttings so we can plant them at our own homes. It was Lenny's idea—that we'll propagate the plant in our own yards."

"I love that idea," I tell them.

"If you wind up moving," Jill says, "you can take it with you, too."

That's a nice thought, but I'm not ready to compromise yet.

"I still might stay," I say. "Seth . . . I think he and I could do well here together, you know?"

They nod, just as hopeful.

I will try to stay hopeful too.

Not long after they've gone and I'm back indoors, I wander into the spare room, once my mom's room, and open the closet. That's where there's evidence that my mom did have a life here. There's a poster for the old boy band New Kids on the Block still taped to the wall inside. Next to it is a poster of some kind of goth band I don't know. My mom never could decide who she wanted to be.

Maybe there's some truth to what she told me about what it was like for her growing up, but I know my grandma didn't mean to leave her out. I don't mean to do that either. It's not my fault that Seth and I have interests that my mom doesn't share.

The Garden Girls have made me feel a little better about him and what happened today. He hasn't had much space to grieve.

I wish Grandma could see Seth and me like this. Him in this house, taking me everywhere. Him wearing her ridiculous shirt. The two of us googling houseplants so we can keep them alive. I want to tell her everything that happened at Tapestry Garden. I know we didn't succeed in our mission, but she'd want to hear all about it—about who lives there. I want to ask where she'd send us instead.

Chapter 11

I can't sleep. My inner clock is all messed up, and it doesn't help that Seth keeps the house at negative degrees. It makes me get up to pee a lot.

I went to bed early, after a little bit of *Poldark*—which somehow I'm starting to like—but now it's just after eleven and I am all-caps awake. Also, I'm alone. Seth hasn't returned.

I will not text Chris. I want to prove to myself that I can make it one full day without communicating with him. Just in case.

I can't text Jessica and Jason. They are not late-night-texts-about-nothing kind of people. They get up early to run before it's too hot.

I didn't think Seth would find anything interesting at the Big Whale, but he's still out, so he must have found some sort of high school person. This is good. I do want him to want to stay, and maybe he will if he has a good time.

And today was just a blip.

I put my hand over my eyes, remembering the look on Mrs. Coffin's face as we defiled the soil where she'd already put her husband. It must have been horrifying for her.

I decide to use this insomnia time to look at Grandma's things. Mainly, I want to make a record of her bookshelves; I know they belong to Seth now, and I guess he'll take them to New York eventually. Grandma has the titles arranged in such a specific way, and I never want to forget what it looks like, so I figure the best thing to do is to take pictures of every shelf.

Maybe one day I'll read all the titles one by one. A book club curriculum designed by Grandma. I could do it with Seth.

The titles and names are familiar because I've been staring at them for so many years, even before I moved in. She always separated the books by gender and in alphabetical order, which is kind of weird but makes sense. She was always so concerned about ratio. On the women's side, there's a lot of Toni Morrison. Tillie Olson. Nadine Gordimer. Ntozake Shange. Gertrude Stein. There's something called *The Pagan Rabbi* that, when I was young, I always misread as *The Pagan Rabbit*. I notice that there's an Alice Walker book called *In Search of Our Mothers' Gardens*.

I wish she'd lived long enough for me to be published, so that I could be put on these shelves. I'd have had a place in the *S*'s, just after Alice Sebold. Just before Mary Shelley.

I belong next to Mary Shelley, I think. What a dream spot.

I walk to the men's shelves — there are only two — pull Seth's first novel down, and smile at how much it's been loved. The pages spread open like meat falling off a bone. Grandma has dog-eared the pages and circled paragraphs with a pencil. It makes me jealous of him.

That makes me want to be nosy.

I go back upstairs.

Seth has left his writer's journal on top of his laptop in the spare room. I can see that he's drawn a little flower on the front of it, which makes me smile.

I flip it open, just to the first page, not to spy, but to see how he takes notes. That's all.

On the first page he's written the names of the gardens on our list and some of the plants we've seen. We'll both be amateur botanists by the end of this journey.

I also see that next to the notebook is a printout of one of my own stories, one that Grandma was reading before she died. It had been near her bed, but it looks as if Seth has taken it for himself.

Grandma would have given me a critique (all positive; her notes were too nice). She would have talked about Chris's illustrations and how beautifully he brought my words to life. She was my best fan.

I have not considered what it means to no longer have her as an editor. By the end, she was all things to me, but that was a big part of our relationship.

I think that maybe Seth could take Grandma's place. If he stayed with me, even for a few months, we could talk more about our work.

I know it's a violation, but I flip to the next page in his notebook. I tell myself it's because I want to learn whether he writes his notes in full paragraphs or in phrases that look like poetry. I want to know if I take after him as a writer.

Turns out, whereas I'm a paragraph girl, he's a phrases kind of guy. There are three- and four-word half sentences around the page. The shorthand probably means something to him. All I know is that I like his handwriting.

I flip to another page.

Then I see what he's writing, and I can't breathe.

He's written things about me. Things that I've said, like recently, during the trip today.

Things about school and my mom and Grandma and Chris.

At first I'm excited, in the way that anyone gets when they see their own name and stuff written about them. It's cool and flattering, and I'm thinking that he's trying to remember this important week, the way I am.

But then, as I read more, the tone feels different. It's not a diary entry or anything like that. It's . . . something else. Not all of it is nice.

He's described my eyeliner. "She doesn't wash it off, and it's uneven, one cat eye stretching further than the other," it says.

Instinctively I run to the mirror in the spare room. He is right. I am an uneven cat.

What else? I wonder. What else is he writing?

The notebook has only random phrases, but I know there's more to this.

At night this past week, when I've gone to bed, he's told me he'll be working for a few hours. He's been on his laptop late into the night. When he wakes up, he's in bed with it.

I open his laptop, and when it asks for a password, I type "Ethan." What else could it be? And with that, I'm in.

I open "recent documents" and see one called "Scattered."

There are ten thousand words that are all about a girl.

I read them all, and my body gives out like it's a wet shopping bag. I slump over the laptop.

This is a story I know, but it's like reality has been warped in a haunted fun-house mirror at a carnival.

I want to slam the laptop closed, but I have to force myself to keep reading, to know how furious to be.

❦

This is the second time I've left the house at night in my pajamas and flip-flops. This time, at least, I've brought my phone and my wallet.

I am not trying to escape to the mall. This time I'm on a hunt. I take the car.

The Big Whale is in a strip mall in Framingham, one town over — but a quick Uber ride for Seth. It looks like the relic it is, an aging suburban bar with a blinking sign, in a building that will probably be torn down to make room for something better as soon as the ever-expanding mall is ready to swallow it.

I park the car all crooked because every car in the lot looks that way. It's drizzling, and the small drops that fall on my shoulders make me shiver.

I take one breath for bravery before I open the door, and then I take stock of what I see.

I don't think I've ever used the word *saloon,* but this would count as one. Everything is dark and made of gnarled wood, and there are blinking neon signs on the walls that say the names of beers. The one that says GANSETT is the brightest.

There aren't many people here, only a few tables of two. The place smells like Buffalo chicken wings.

I spot Seth at a back table, seated across from another man. I am on my way to confront him, but am stopped by a server who comes out of nowhere.

"Can I help you?" the woman says as she looks me up and down. I'd taken a minute to put on a real bra, at least, but I'm still in full pajamas. My white tank top sort of looks like something you could wear during the day, but the thin white pants with rainbows on them, less so.

"Just looking for someone," I say.

"We're twenty-one-plus after six," the woman says. She's wearing a Red Sox shirt and a jean skirt.

"Lori."

I see Seth's mouth form the word when he spots my entrance. The server nods her permission for me to go talk to him.

"What are you doing here?" he asks, concerned, as I approach his table. "Is everything okay at home?"

"Fuck you, Seth," I say.

It's not the most creative sentiment, but it's all I've got at the moment. Chris would flinch if he heard me say something like that in public. I push the thought of him aside.

Seth is embarrassed by my unfriendly hello. He looks across the table at the man he's with and says, "Give me a second to talk to my niece."

But before he stands up, I lean over him so he can't move. I am feeling wild and angry, and my only weapon is to embarrass him the way he's embarrassed me.

"I opened your laptop," I say.

I'm standing and he's still sitting, and I feel ten feet tall. "I know what you're doing—why you've wanted to spend time with me. Why you're thinking about staying in Natick with me."

Seth's mouth makes a thin line. He pushes his chair out, forcing me to take a step back. Now we're the same height. He walks past me toward the front door of the bar.

"Where are you going?" I yell to him.

"Outside," he barks without turning around.

It's the first time I've heard him sound angry.

I look to the man at the table for a second, and I freeze. He's around Seth's age, and he's the prettiest man I've ever seen, even counting famous actors. He takes a sip of his beer as if there isn't a conflict happening right in front of him. He smiles at me like he's Captain America.

"Is your name Jake?" I have to ask.

"How'd you know?" he says.

"Of course!" I say to the ceiling of the bar and then walk outside to meet Seth.

I'm barely out there when he yells first.

"What gives you the right to go through my things?" Seth asks. "How'd you get into my laptop?"

"Your password is *Ethan*," I say. "I didn't have to crack some code or hack you or anything. Anyway, I'm not the one who should be getting yelled at here. I only went into your laptop because I looked at your notebook. Maybe I shouldn't have . . . but I was curious. I wanted to see how you took notes, as a writer. Then I saw you were writing things about me. And the file — is that what you think of me? What you said about my problems. My clothes. My room!"

"It's a compliment! She's a character! I'm writing about you because you're a remarkable character!"

"I'm not a character!"

"It's just some ideas, Lori," he says. "It's not anything to be concerned about. Writers write things all the time. It's an exercise. It's a *process*."

"It's ten thousand words! You've been acting like you want to support me, to know me, and it's for a book!"

"Lori," Seth says, softer this time.

"You put in little details that I gave you, that are real. The story about the promposal at my high school. All of it."

He's looking at me like he doesn't understand the problem.

"Seth, my stories are mine! The way I feel about Chris, that's all mine, too."

That's the worst part, how he documented what I told him about how I feel about Chris, the most important person in my life. My face burns thinking about it.

"First of all," he says, "can you lower your voice? Can we just calm down?"

There are two guys outside the bar, smoking cigarettes and watching us, and one is laughing, maybe at what they're hearing, but I don't care.

"Lori, you have to get home. It's late and it's raining," Seth says.

It is more than drizzling now, and I'm shivering a little, but that could be because of my rage.

"No," I say, crossing my arms in front of my chest. "I think I'll stand here and yell. Wouldn't that be good for the book? Maybe if you're lucky, I'll get my period while I do it. Maybe my eyeliner will run down my face."

"Lor," he says in a softer voice. "You're overreacting."

"How do you figure?"

"I'm a writer!" he says.

"So am I!"

"That means you should know that inspiration can come from many places. Yes, I've been very inspired by the death of my mother and being here with you. It is totally normal that a writer would put those thoughts to paper. It's been very healing for me this week."

"You said you'd consider staying to help me. You wanted to take Grandma Sheryl's ashes to beautiful gardens with me. You said you wanted to get to know me better because you cared. You wanted . . . material? Is that it?"

"I have every right to take notes on this trip. I have every right to write about it," Seth says. "You take notes and write about a lot of things in your life!"

"I write fantasy stories and turn living people into zombies. I don't ask my niece about her hopes and fears and dreams and then use everything she says for some book she doesn't know anything about."

"You should be honored!" Seth says, and I reel back, stunned. "Lori, you are drenched, and it's freezing."

He sees our car behind me.

"That's your parking job? Get in the car and go home."

I *am* freezing now, and there is nothing else to say, so I turn and walk to the car. I won't give him any more inspiration.

I look back, thinking that he'll watch me leave, that I'll see a look of remorse on his face, or maybe that he'll follow me, but the bar door is already swinging shut. He's back inside.

We'll get through this week, I think, and then that's it. He will not replace Grandma. No one could. I'd rather live in Maryland with Bill and know that it's Seth's fault. What I saw at Tapestry Garden wasn't a lapse in judgment; it was any other day, maybe.

Back in the house, I open his laptop again and return to the file. I hit control A and then the delete button. The screen goes blank.

Almost immediately I am nauseous. I hit control Z, undoing what I've just done, and scream. As angry as I am, that is too big of a betrayal.

❧

It's late, almost one in the morning, but I call Chris. Like, really call instead of text.

"Lor? You okay?"

"I love you," I tell him, and it feels big to me, but it doesn't sound big. Because I've told him before that I love him. I mean, of course we love each other. He doesn't know that I mean it in a different way right now. I know this because he responds, "I love you, too," without missing a beat.

"Things have been weird," I tell him.

"I know," he says. "We didn't talk all day. The vibes have been . . . off."

"Will you still come tomorrow? To The Mount?"

"Of course," Chris says, his voice all soft and scratchy and perfect.

"Can you sleep?" he asks.

"I don't think so."

"Why?"

Then I tell him what I found. How Seth and I fought. Why I'm hurt.

And Chris reinforces what I know, which is that he's my best friend. He validates and comforts me and promises me things will be okay. He listens without pretending that he knows the answers. He tells me I don't even have to try to sleep.

"How was your day?" I ask him.

"We finished the shelves," Chris says. "Big shelving day over here."

"That's good," I say, trying to keep it light, but I can't. "I'm sorry I might leave you. I'm sorry I need so much."

"Lori," he says, his voice sleepy. "Stop."

I'll miss this when I move to Maryland. But I know there's no way for me to stay now.

"How about you write for a bit?" he says. "Give me some-thing to draw."

I sigh. It's a good plan.

"Okay," I tell him, and hang up.

I go back to my room and open my own laptop. The story I write is about a girl who wakes up in a town where everyone over twenty-one has disappeared.

It's a little bit obvious, but I don't care.

Chapter 12

The car is silent and cold. Literally and emotionally cold.

I have the air conditioning on blast because I'm exhausted. I've pointed the vents right at my face to keep me awake. There are low voices coming from the stereo. I've been listening to a podcast about horror films, and the hosts are ranking the adaptations of Stephen King books. It's keeping me focused.

These guys love *Christine,* but they have complicated feelings about whether *It* should have ever been adapted at all.

Sometimes I have to look in the rearview mirror, and when I do, I see Seth. We accidentally make eye contact, and then I look away. He's been angry with me all morning, but I will not let him make me feel bad when I know I'm right.

"What *is* this?" Seth asks angrily from the back seat, startling me.

"It's called *Evil Clowns,*" I say. "It's a horror podcast."

I glance up and see him roll his eyes.

"It's very academic," I say angrily. "It's often about gender and queer themes in horror."

"I'm sure it is," Seth says, and he sounds like such a jerk that I am a little bit stunned. I have never seen him so dismissive. Never experienced an adult being so petty. He has decided to play this like he's mad at me for appropriate reasons. I can't deal.

I look in the mirror after a minute and see that he's actually listening to the podcast, which makes me feel smug.

Seth and I did manage to say about twenty civil words to each other this morning. We spoke just long enough for him to tell me that Ethan would be meeting us at The Mount and that he'd be treating us to some nice rooms near the property for the night so we don't have to drive more than four hours in one day. I'd grunted, "fine," in response.

I am excited to see Uncle Ethan, though. He is so wonderful, and he gets me a fancy pen for Hanukkah every year. I mean, I mostly write on my laptop and take notes with a basic Bic throw-away pen, but it's a cool thing to have all these fancy writing instruments on my desk. Sometimes Chris uses them.

I'd texted Ethan, "Thanks for the hotel rooms! Looking forward to seeing you," and he responded with a thumbs-up emoji. I wanted to get in a thank-you before Seth complained about me to him and spun our whole conflict to make it look like I was angry about nothing.

Mom had also checked in again.

"You okay?" she'd asked. "How is this process going for you? How is Seth holding up?"

"Fine," I'd said because I didn't want to give anything away.

I don't want to think about Mom, or Seth's betrayal, or my rootlessness. Today I am thinking about Edith Wharton.

Grandma Sheryl loved Edith Wharton. She has all her books, or a lot of them anyway. She also reread them a lot, the way I always go back to Stephen King's *The Stand,* which I read out of order, in different sections, because it's so crazy long.

I do not like Edith Wharton. Grandma thought I'd like *Ethan Frome*—she'd recommended it when I moved in—but I couldn't get through the first fifty pages. I know from the back cover that it's about a guy named Ethan who can't date the woman he wants, and his life is a super bummer, and that's all I can pretty much tell you, because it was quite clear that nothing was going to happen in that book.

Still, I appreciate that a woman wrote it and that Grandma liked it.

I did not know it was written at The Mount, but apparently it was. So that's something.

The Mount is Edith Wharton's home in Lenox, a town in the Berkshires, which is where people go in Massachusetts to see pretty trees, buy homemade jam, and experience cultural activities like outdoor symphonies. It is two and a half or three hours away from Natick, which means we should be there soon.

The road is getting smaller and narrower. The fields next to the car are bigger, with more cows. I've spotted signs for pottery shops and fresh produce. There are also little street signs that have grapes on them, because out here, there are wineries.

Just as the podcast hosts begin debating the merits of adaptations of *The Stand,* a topic on which I have many opinions, I see a sign that says THE MOUNT. I pull into the driveway and feel Chris shuffle to life in the passenger seat.

"Ethan just messaged. He's pulling up," Seth says after clearing his throat. The second I turn off the engine, he bolts from the car and stands next to it, not hiding his need to have a door and lots of space between us.

"Wow," Chris says. "That was an icy ride."

"I can't apologize," I say.

"Even just for reading his private stuff? Maybe if you start with that, he'll listen and apologize back."

"I can't," I say.

He nods. He gets it.

I exit the car, and I see Ethan at the far side of the dirt and gravel parking lot. It's a relief because Seth and I need a new buffer. Any calm person who can separate us from each other.

He's walking to us from his white rental car, and Seth is already by his side. They hug and kiss hello. Then Ethan sees me and smiles.

The last time I saw Ethan was Memorial Day. I had taken the train down to New York, and we went to get Chinese food and saw a Chris Evans movie. The next day he and Seth took me to a show. I don't love musicals, but it was cool to be there.

Ethan is wearing dark purple shorts, a peach top, and sunglasses with spotted frames. He has shaved his beard for summer.

"Lori, it's been too long," he says, and pulls me in for a hug.

He smells like spearmint gum. Then he shakes Chris's hand. "Hello, Christian."

Chris blushes. I think it's Ethan's English accent.

Ethan gives me a long look. "How are you faring, my girl?"

"Bad," I say without looking at Seth.

"Your grandmother was a wonderful, brilliant soul," Ethan says. "And what a lovely tribute, to bring her here."

Now everything is a little bit better. Uncle Ethan always knows what he's doing.

"Has everyone been here before?" Ethan asks. "It looks quite scenic, I must say. I'm embarrassed that I had no idea Edith Wharton's house was an attraction in the Berkshires."

"We've never been," I respond, "but I'm excited."

"Lori doesn't read Edith Wharton," Seth says, stepping in front of me ever so slightly. He's trying to make me feel stupid, but Ethan doesn't pick up on this.

"I should probably whisper this, considering where we are at the moment, but I found *Ethan Frome* to be very boring," Ethan says. "I'm an *Age of Innocence* man myself."

"Grandma Sheryl liked both," I answer.

"Lori, I'm surprised you're not interested in Edith Wharton's ghost stories," Ethan says.

"She wrote ghost stories?" I ask him, but my eyes are on Seth, who looks into the distance as if he can't hear us. I wonder if he knew that.

"Yes," Ethan says. "Those I enjoyed. Ghosts in libraries, and haunted things happening in creepy meadows. I imagine an old house in the middle of nowhere gave her some good inspiration. The dead are everywhere here."

As soon as he says those last words in a spooky voice, he regrets them. His face falls as he remembers that we're here to scatter ashes.

"How tasteless," he says, but before he can apologize, I stop him.

"It's okay," I say, giving him a warm smile. "Please. The more death jokes, the better."

❧

The four of us follow the other tourists from the parking lot to the entry booth to buy tickets, and Ethan pays for all of us. That's the kind of thing he does. Then we make our way down a long driveway shaded by tall trees. If we walked off the path, we'd venture into cavernous woods covered in green plants. It's peaceful and quiet, even though I know there are lots of visitors here. The sound travels up and disappears.

Had I known the property was like this, I would have come here with Grandma.

We turn a corner and see a huge, castle-like gate. Behind it is *the house,* The Mount, and the second it enters our sightline, we are transported back in time.

Edith Wharton knew how to live. Her home is huge, and there are many windows.

Seth takes out his phone for a picture, and even though I'm annoyed with how much he's been on his phone while we've been avoiding each other, I can't blame him. I hate pictures of myself, but even I want to stand in front of it and pose.

This is the kind of home where an old-timey writer in a bonnet carries a parasol and has dinner parties that have many courses. If I lived here, I'd be Lady Seltzer.

The property around the house is covered with beautiful flowers—there are so many things growing here. We could put Grandma anywhere, really; the whole place is in bloom. As we drove in, I could see the outline of the gardens in the back. I know they'll be square and well-manicured—and maybe a rabbit will dart by and tell us to follow him because he's late.

A bunch of other visitors are loitering near the main gate, and in front of them is a woman. Her name tag says MARGE. She looks like a Marge, and that is a compliment.

"Hello . . ." Marge calls out to us, greeting all the visitors. Most of the tourists here are older men in pairs or women with cool glasses. They all look cool—like they're the kind of people who own antique typewriters at home. Three of them are hold-ing the exact same *New Yorker* tote bag.

I notice that there are no little kids, which makes sense. Even though there's a ton of open space on this property, it's not the kind of place where you'd want anyone to run around and play. Chris and I are the youngest by far.

"Welcome to The Mount," Marge continues. "I'll be starting the next tour now, so please line up if you'd like a guided walk through the house. You're more than welcome to navigate the property on your own, of course."

Ethan turns to us. "We're doing the tour, yes? Before we . . . find the gardens?"

As much as I always get super bored during official tours, I nod. We should know more about this place that made it onto Grandma's list.

Seth's sunglasses are on, so I can't read his mood.

We line up with Marge's followers, ready to be educated.

"One of the first things you'll notice about The Mount is symmetry," Marge begins. "Take a moment to look at the windows on the building."

I see them. Rows of dark green shutters that stand out against the bright white paint.

"Some of those windows are not actually windows," Marge says. "Edith liked everything in her home to be symmetrical, so she added false shutters for balance."

I look closer and see that indeed, some windows are not actually windows.

Edith Wharton was apparently particular and weird. This makes me like her.

"If you'll all stay in line and follow me, we'll see more of that symmetry inside."

The house looks like any rich person's old house should. There are a lot of rust-spotted antique mirrors, and furniture with shiny fabric upholstery.

When we get to a sitting room, we learn the basics. Edith was the first woman to win a Pulitzer Prize for fiction. Edith had some weird marital stuff, like a complicated husband and some other guy later. Edith died in France. Edith loved dogs.

Marge also tells us about Edith Wharton's interest in design —how much she loved writing about architecture and houses— and I start thinking about how horrible it is that Seth always has a snarky thing to say about any writing that isn't literary. *Everybody* has to be working on some sort of sad family novel, or it's not real writing. But Edith Wharton—who won a Pulitzer!—devoted her entire first book to decorating houses.

"Her great love was design," Marge says.

If Edith Wharton were alive today, I think, she'd probably be a really big Instagram influencer, taking pictures of all her symmetrical rooms.

And Seth would probably write her off as useless.

I crack my knuckles and follow the group into the dining room.

"What do you notice about the lighting in these rooms?" Marge asks.

The fifteen or so people on the tour look around, dumb-founded.

"Look up," Marge hints, and then gives it away. "You'll notice that there are no chandeliers with lights in any of these rooms. No lights on ceilings. Edith believed that overhead lighting was bad for complexions — unflattering to everyone. She avoided it completely."

"Well," one of the women with a *New Yorker* tote whispers to the woman next to her, "now I'm going to have to rip out all the fixtures I just put in my kitchen."

Marge smiles and continues.

"We've put place settings on the table to show you who would have been dining in Edith Wharton's company," she says. "Edith liked small groups; she preferred an inner circle of friends."

The tiny cards on the fine china show familiar names, although I don't quite know who they are. Henry James is the only one I've heard of.

I think about who *I'd* put at this intimate, circular table if it were my own. Chris, obviously. Jessica and Jason. It's been too long since I've seen them, but really, it's been only a few days. Where there's a placard for Edith Wharton's husband, I imagine Jason in sweatpants, eating a hamburger.

I could live here.

"Now, to her bedroom," Marge says, and we follow her down the hall into a simple, modest bedroom with a white knit bedspread. There are handwritten letters strewn across the bed as part of the display.

"These are Edith's real letters," Marge whispers, and I'm surprised they don't put everything under a glass case.

"In every official portrait of Edith as a writer, she's shown at a desk," Marge says. "But she actually did most of her writing in bed, in the mornings. She'd awaken, a lady's maid would bring her breakfast, and then she'd write for five hours every day. She wrote a book a year—twenty-six in all, not counting the short stories."

"Must be easy to just write all day when you have a lady's maid," Seth says to Ethan, and his tone gives away too much. He's jealous of Edith Wharton.

"Are you really getting competitive with Edith Wharton right now?" Ethan whispers, reading my mind.

"Don't do that," Seth whispers back, and I'm not sure what "that" is, but I am smug because he is being called out on something by someone other than me.

"All I'm saying is that it's easier to work when you can sit in a country house and write all day."

"Right. It would have been much harder for her if she'd been living your strenuous life," Ethan says.

Everyone hears that, and we're all silent. I am shocked. Chris looks like he wants to run. Then Ethan looks ashamed. The tops of his cheeks are red, and he wipes his forehead.

Marge clears her throat and breaks the silence. "There's some private space in the room down the hall," she offers.

An older couple flashes a look of concern in our direction. Seth storms out of the room. Ethan follows, sighing.

"Sorry," I say to the group. "My grandma just died. We're all going through some stuff. But she loved Edith Wharton, so . . . anyway, it's nice to be here!"

It's an overshare, with too much enthusiasm, but the tour group looks sympathetic.

Marge nods. "Well then, let's move on."

"What was that?" Chris whispers as we head back into the hallway.

"No idea," I say.

Eventually we exit through the gift shop—which sells lots of books and magnets with Edith Wharton's face on them—and we find Seth and Ethan standing outside, wearing smiles.

"Sorry about that," Ethan says, his voice too bright. "I think the heat was getting to us." Ethan holds up a bag. "I got you some of those ghost stories."

He is so thoughtful.

Seth's expression is sort of blank, and then he shields himself with his sunglasses again.

"Well, I guess it's time," he says, and it is.

During the tour, Marge had told us that there are two main gardens in back of The Mount. One is French in style, the other Italian. There's a path lined with big trees that connects one to the other.

It's difficult for Seth and me to decide which garden to visit first when we're barely talking to each other.

"Shall we start with French?" I ask him, but I'm looking at his neck.

"Sure," he says, and his voice is even enough for me to assume we're calling a temporary truce.

I can ID the French garden from where I stand. Marge said it was colorful and open, whereas the Italian one has more overhead trees and stones, as if it's a hideaway.

I lead our group down the tree-lined path until we come to the entrance of the square, large garden that we've heard is known for its tulips, which are greens by August. There's a rectangular pool in the middle.

The pool of water is boxed in by circular plots of bright green grass that are also lined with flowers. If Grandma wanted to be around "things that grow," this is it.

"Well, isn't this lovely," Ethan says, and I turn around to see him place his hand on Seth's back. Seth is looking around, scowling, and I think I know why.

As much as this garden is all in bloom, the mood doesn't seem right for Grandma Sheryl. It's scorching again today, maybe over a hundred degrees. In this French garden there's no shade, and the sun is beating down on us so hard, it's difficult to imagine anyone wanting to be here for eternity.

Also, there's no privacy for what we need to do. The space

is open, and people are loitering everywhere. There's a couple —two of the women from our tour with Marge—posing for a photograph in front of a bed of lilies. Tourists keep wandering into the shot, and the photographer, a hired professional carrying bags of equipment, is trying to be nice to passersby, but he's getting annoyed.

"Um, can you excuse us?" he says. "These are engagement photos. If you could just give us some room."

He lifts his old-school camera to take another photo, but when the women pose, their faces close, an old man with a cane wanders into the frame.

The photographer sighs, and I shoot him a sympathetic look.

"It's our fault for coming in the afternoon," he tells me. "We should have done this first thing, before the tourists."

I blink. I don't even know what time it is. Every day since Grandma died has felt like we're stuck in some never-ending summer Thursday. I wake up whenever and go to bed a few hours after it gets dark.

I look at my phone to check the actual date. August 28, which means school starts in less than a week. In Natick, at least.

Grandma hasn't even been gone a week. That seems unreal. Shocking, actually.

"This garden is a crowded mess," Seth says.

"It's kind of funny," Chris says. "Based on what Marge told us, Edith Wharton would have been miserable in this kind of public environment. It's an introvert's nightmare."

"Her ghost must wait until night to come outside. Then she can hang out by herself," I say, and Ethan smiles.

Chris stares into the distance for a second, and I know his silence means he will be drawing Edith Wharton's introverted ghost later, maybe hiding in one of the closets until the crowd gives her some space each night.

"Let's go to garden two," I say. "It looks like less of a party over there."

We walk in pairs, Seth with Chris, me with Ethan, back down the path, until we enter the parallel square that is the Italian garden.

Inside, it is something else. This one is perfection.

"Even more gorgeous," Ethan whispers.

It's much cooler here because it's under the shade of the woods next to it. It's also walled in, which makes it feel magical. Those walls are covered with greens that snake up the rocks. I pull my phone from my dress pocket, take a picture of the walls, and send it to the Garden Girls. It feels like a betrayal, like I shouldn't even have a phone in this place.

"Beautiful porticos," Ethan says.

I don't know what a portico is, but everything in here is pretty, so I nod in agreement. I like that I can enjoy this garden without having to squint. I kneel down to get a better look at the square fountain in the center. Water bubbles up from a sculpture that's basically a pile of rocks on top of one another.

There are other people milling about, but they are quiet and slow. There's one man sitting near the fountain, reading a book. I can make out that it's *Ethan Frome*. He probably just bought it in the gift shop.

"Lor, come look," Chris says, and he's taking my hand.

He leads me to the side of the garden and points to the ground.

"There," he says, and his eyes are watery, which makes me skip a breath. "Read it."

There is a plaque next to our feet. It is a quote from Edith Wharton: "In spite of illness, in spite even of the archenemy sorrow, one can remain alive long past the usual date of disintegration if one is unafraid of change, insatiable in intellectual curiosity, interested in big things, and happy in small ways."

I read it again and then feel Seth and Ethan come up behind me. They're reading too.

"Well, that seems relevant," I say, trying to make a joke, but my voice cracks.

I look around and see the view of The Mount from where we stand.

All this beauty, and I am so grateful that Grandma saw it. That she took trips with the Garden Girls.

I wonder if she visited during spring or in late summer, like we are now. What was blooming? I take out my phone and text them.

"Thank you," I say to these women—and Kevin—who brought her to beautiful places when I wasn't really paying attention. "Thank you for bringing her to this perfect garden." I take a picture of the plaque and send it along.

I can see they're responding, the messages and emojis — tiny pink hearts from Rochelle and prayer hands from Deb — pop up fast, but I put my phone away. I need to be present now.

I sink to the ground next to Edith's words.

Seth starts to cry, and Ethan puts his arm around him.

I tug on the bottom of Seth's shirt, and he understands. He reaches into the backpack and pulls out the plastic Chico's bag. He brings out the third box again, the one that was already opened during our failed stop at Tapestry Garden, and then he's unsealing the bag of remains.

Chris stands at our backs, facing out, trying to be a human shield. He'll let us know if anyone is coming. There aren't many people in the garden anymore, and no employees from what I've seen, but we do need cover.

"Are you sure this is okay?" Ethan whispers. "It's a historic property."

"They'll be fast," Chris tells him over his shoulder.

"Where exactly do we put her?" Seth asks.

I look around.

"It's all perfect. Every inch of this garden is perfect," I say.

"You're right," Seth says. "Let's not pick one spot. Let's crop-dust."

"What?"

"Let's just fucking crop-dust this one," Seth says again. "It's all too perfect."

Still confused, I whisper, "Crop-dust?"

At that, he shoves his hand into the bag, takes out a big scoop of Grandma Sheryl's remains, and bends over some big flowers I think are hydrangeas. Pretending to admire them and leaning in farther, he sprinkles the remains around them. It's almost unnoticeable. He walks to the next bed of flowers, and with every step, he drops more.

He is sprinkling Grandma like salt on a steak. A little bit all around.

I stand up. "I'll do some."

I take the bag, which is on the ground at Chris's feet, and shove my hand in. This is the first time I've touched the cremains with great comfort. It's a little like the rocky sand on the beach once you get close to the water. With a full fist, I walk to the openings on the border of the garden and sprinkle Grandma at their base.

I come back and tell Chris, "You can help. No pressure or anything. But . . . you loved her, too."

He nods, honored, and puts his hand into the bag. He ducks through one of the openings in the garden wall and brings Grandma to a patch of wildflowers just outside its border.

I stand behind him as he lets go.

"It's a nice view back here," he says. "I want her to be able to see this too."

I keep thinking, or hoping in my heart, that Edith Wharton would love what we've done today. If she is a ghost here, if she does wander the hallways of her grand estate, Grandma Sheryl will be very good company.

As Ethan takes the last handful in the bag and brings it to a pristine patch of flowers with little pompom heads, I imagine Edith and Grandma in beach chairs, reading good novels, living long past disintegration, happily here forever.

Chapter 13

Earlier this week, when we realized we'd probably want to stay overnight at The Mount because it is hours away, I imagined a situation out of a romantic comedy, and I don't even like romantic comedies.

I fantasized that we'd bring the ashes to The Mount property —like we just did—and then drive to a quaint bed-and-breakfast, the kind with tiny bedrooms with mismatched quilts on the mattresses. The kind with a cat.

In my fantasy, we'd all get to this small inn—run, of course, by a gray-haired couple who would greet us with freshly baked chocolate cookies—and we'd realize that Chris and I would have to share a room, and that the room would only have one bed. Oh no!

In my fantasy, the temperature would drop at night, and Chris and I would be forced to cuddle under a blanket for warmth, until eventually it became clear that we were going to kiss. Then we would.

I forced myself to delete that story from my brain, to push it into a tiny box or, at the very least, replace the Chris in the fantasy with anyone else. That kind of thinking is dangerous.

But it kept sneaking into my subconscious, especially after we left the property in separate cars and Chris and I were alone.

We'd driven to a place called the Friendly Table, where the whole experience was anything but. Whatever truce Seth and I came to at The Mount evaporated as soon as we left the grounds. I got a salad and picked the chicken off it in silence. I was too preoccupied by all the remaining questions about my life, and the shrinking timeline to answer them.

I didn't know what Seth was thinking about—if he'd decided to rescind his offer to stay in Massachusetts—but he seemed preoccupied too, checking his phone a lot, ignoring his salmon.

Ethan looked confused by the vibe at the table, but he didn't ask.

The only person who consumed his dinner without looking miserable was Chris, who inhaled a massive bowl of gnocchi.

"You okay?" Ethan had whispered to Seth when he noticed him staring blankly at the wall of the restaurant, which was covered with pink floral wallpaper that made me feel like we were at a fancy tea party.

"It's been a week," Seth said.

Then he exhaled, and it was so dramatic that I dropped my fork to the table and rolled my eyes.

I tried not to make direct eye contact with Seth at dinner, partly because I wanted to stay mad. Yes, we'd had a meaningful day at The Mount, but that didn't undo what he'd taken from me without asking. The way he'd pretended to care about getting to know me when he was just digging for material. I know I said shitty things to him in front of that bar, but they were absolutely true, so I shouldn't have to feel bad.

Ethan paid for dinner, and now I'm following his rental car in my car, and I see that the hotel he booked is right down the street from The Mount. We'd passed it on the way in, but I never imagined I'd stay here. It looks expensive. Historic and massive. Another long driveway.

I have stayed in a bunch of hotels, but never without my mother. We used to stay in them whenever we moved—she'd send our belongings to the next city, and after the U-Hauls left, we'd go to a hotel before driving to the next place. Sleeping at a Marriott and listening to my mother snore meant that I was about to start over. Find my way around a new school. Reinvent myself for three days until I fell back into who I was, because I couldn't be anyone else.

That means my hotel stays involved existential dread.

This is different. It is now a road trip with Chris.

When we get closer to the building, I see that it is quite old —everything in this area is old, I guess. The exterior is white, with brown shutters, and it's just as symmetrical as Edith's house. It is on a sprawling property, the hills literally rolling and green.

I still do not know what a portico is, but I'm sure this building has a bunch of them.

I am no expert on historic things, but I imagine that Edith

Wharton's rich friends could have lived here. Like maybe she would tell her husband, "Don't wait up, I'm going over to the Whistlesnitchers for dinner! They'll be making lamb stew!" — or whatever rich people liked to eat in the early 1900s. Then she'd go over, and they'd play backgammon and drink tiny glasses of wine and she'd talk about her latest book idea.

It was probably quite a party.

Inside, the hotel is just as classy, although Edith would not approve of the overhead lights. It makes me wonder about my complexion. Ethan stops at the front desk. I try to keep my expression neutral when he pulls a line straight from my fantasies.

"Oh, blast," Ethan says, sounding especially English. "I only got two rooms. I wasn't even thinking about Chris . . ."

Ethan turns to the clerk.

"I have reserved two rooms for tonight. Is there a third available?"

"We're completely booked," the woman at the desk answers, and I hold my breath.

"Lori and Chris can share, right?" Seth says, and raises his eyebrows like a challenge. "Right, Lori?"

"It's fine," I say, narrowing my eyes at Seth. "Chris, it's fine with you, right?"

"Sure," Chris says. "I'm used to sharing rooms with siblings. It's not a big deal."

My breath hitches when I hear him use the horrible S-word, and Seth has the decency to wince on my behalf. I take a big breath and remind myself that Chris is just being polite. He's not implying that I'm like a sibling, only that he's used to sharing a room. Maybe he's trying to make me comfortable.

"Also," Chris adds in his awkward voice, "I can help pay for the room . . . my mom gave me some money . . . I feel like I've been mooching off you guys all week."

"Don't think of it," Ethan says. "We so appreciate you being here for Lori. She's lucky to have such a great friend."

Chris looks away and taps his foot, embarrassed. Ethan's delivery is so kind, and for a mean second I wish he was the uncle I'm really related to instead of Seth. He's a better person and a better guardian.

"Thank you, Ethan," I say, and then I mumble, "Thank you, Seth."

"Cool," Chris says, and smiles at me.

"Well, let's all get some rest then," Ethan says after the clerk checks us in, and we follow him toward the elevator, our rolling bags grinding their path along the ancient but regal-looking creaky wood at our feet.

Both rooms are on the third floor, but Seth and Ethan's is on the opposite end of the hallway, so they turn left where we bear right.

"We'll meet at ten tomorrow, Lori," Seth says without turning around.

"Got it," I say.

⁂

Chris has the key, and as he fiddles with it, failing a few times to make it work, I find myself praying, although I'm not sure what for.

I mean, I am praying to all relevant higher powers—the Jewish ones, Chris's, even Franken-Jesus—that there will be two beds. Six beds. Anything to make my life easier right now.

I am supposed to be preparing to live without him. To disconnect so that when faraway calls, texts, and writing in a shared Google Doc are our only options for communication, I'll be okay.

"You okay?" Chris asks, echoing my thoughts, and I realize how weird I must look with my eyes shut tight.

"Yeah. I'm just tired."

He swings the door open, and my body sags with relief— and maybe a little subconscious disappointment.

"It's huge!" Chris says with absolute delight, and I thank the ghost of Edith Wharton for the fact that there are two beds.

The room has antique floral prints all over it, but it's mostly modern, with a massive television and outlets everywhere. The beds are bigger than mine at home, and there's also a small sitting room with a couch that a tall person could easily sleep on.

This is good. This is safe.

Chris drops his backpack on the bed closest to the door and falls face-down on the white bedspread, his arms and legs flailing. "This is luxurious," he moans into the duvet, and I have to smile. At his house, he can't take up too much space. He's always moving to the side to make room for his parents and his brother. There's never privacy. It's a real family there, and everybody's running around, active.

Even when Grandma Sheryl and I were both at home, we were always sitting and calm. It's the opposite at the Burkes'.

"I am beat," he says after flipping onto his back and propping his head on the pillows. He does look super exhausted, and we've been in the heat all day. His lids are heavy, and he has sweat stains under his sleeves. He's showing the look of someone who has been steamrolled by the Seltzers with a week of profound decisions about death, long drives, late nights, and today's journey, which involved three hours in the car and an entire afternoon under the blazing sun. Not to mention the emotional toll of two passive-aggressive people in the car.

He pulls water out of the backpack next to him and finds his pills for anxiety that he always takes before bed. They predate my meeting him. I asked him years ago how and why he got on them, and he shrugged and said the world can be scary and terrible sometimes, and I know that it can, so I'm happy this helps.

"I should call my mom before I pass out," he says.

"Tell her hey," I say, and then I grab my pajamas and face wash and head for the bathroom. I get into the shower because I am gross, and I shave my legs, although I don't know why.

When I'm out, I look at my face close up in the mirror. I am a different person without eyeliner on. My naked face is without disguise.

My cheeks are flushed, and my hair is doing a cool curly thing because of the humidity. Somehow, the purple and blond look like an intentional pairing instead of an absolute mistake.

"Ombre," I whisper in the mirror, impressed that I have achieved it.

I don't want to put makeup back on. I want Chris to see my whole face.

I put on this weird silky pajama set — short shorts and a top with a collar and buttons on it. It is sky blue and has random embroidered letters on one side.

Grandma bought it for me for Hanukkah last year, and I asked, "What am I supposed to do with this?"

"Wear it," she said. "All your pajamas have holes in them." I balled it up in my underwear drawer, where it lived until I packed it this morning, aggressively pulling off the tag. I told myself it was because all my other pajamas were gross and dirty and I didn't feel like doing laundry. But somewhere deep down I knew that I wanted Chris, if we were in the same room, to see me in something nice.

I had ignored these pajamas for six months because they're

so dainty looking, but now that they're on, I realize I'm an idiot. These might be the most comfortable items of clothing I've ever had on my body. I should have been wearing silky Target pajamas this whole time.

I can be the kind of girl who wears nice, new matching pajamas. They will not take away from who I am.

I return to the room holding my breath and find Chris still on his back, his head on the pillows. He's holding the book of Edith Wharton's ghost stories that we got from the gift shop, covering his face. He's changed out of his day clothes too and is in his dark gray track pants and a white T-shirt. His legs are crossed at the ankle.

"This is really good," he says without looking up. "I had my doubts, which makes me feel bad—because Edith Wharton is *Edith Wharton*—but her haunted stuff is supercool. It reminds me of Edgar Allen Poe—like old-school literary, but scary."

"Edgar Allen Poe isn't actually scary, he's just depressing," I say, leaning against the bathroom doorframe, trying to look natural. "'The Raven' is like the least scary horror story I've ever read. It's literally just a bird."

Chris pulls the book away from his face and looks at me, one brow arched. He takes a big breath and sits up straighter before continuing. He doesn't even seem to notice the pajamas.

"If a raven flew over to you, opened his beak, and said, 'Hey

Lori . . . wanna know what's up? *Nevermore,*' you'd freak out. You'd be scared to death."

"No I wouldn't," I say, hands on my hips. "Because it's a bird. It's not even *thousands* of birds like in the movie *The Birds*. It's just one bird, which is not scary."

"One bird is scary when it says 'Nevermore'! Birds do not speak."

"Parrots speak."

"Fine, except for parrots. If a raven spoketh to you, Lori, you'd lose your mind."

"'Nevermore' is not even a scary word. If the raven said, 'I'm going to come murder you by pecking your face to pieces in the middle of the night,' I might be scared, but 'nevermore' doesn't really say horror to me. And now I can't even remember why he says it."

Chris scratches behind his ear as he tries to recall the story.

"Because he's lost his love, Lenore. She died, and the narrator wonders if he'll ever be with her again, and the raven is just like . . . you're stuck with your grief. Nevermore, man."

"Not scary. Not even *emotionally* scary," I say. "Get over Lenore, dude. Plenty of women out there."

"We'll have to agree to disagree," he says.

"Nevermore," I answer.

"Whatever," he says. "Maybe 'The Raven' isn't that scary, but 'The Tell-Tale Heart' is badass."

This is what I will miss most, I think. We could banter about Poe all night.

I look at the clock. Eight forty-five. I can get through a night in a hotel with this person without it being weird.

He folds the page of the book, drops it onto the bed, and shuffles to the edge, his legs hanging over.

"Lori, come here," he says.

"Why?" I ask, and my voice is panicked.

"Just come here."

I walk to the bed and sit on the edge of it, next to him.

"Wow. Your face."

"No makeup," I say. "Naked face."

He swallows, and it makes my mouth dry.

"Your eyes look nice without eyeliner. Not that I don't — I would never tell you how to look. You always look great. You're just . . . you look pretty."

My eyes find the wall.

"Jess thinks I should wear less makeup," I say.

"No one should tell you what to do," Chris responds. "It's just nice to know what you look like without anything on."

Oh god.

"I didn't mean that the way it sounded. I'm sorry, I'm just tired."

"It's fine," I say, and stare at him. There is no hair on his face. I have to ask.

"Do you shave?"

"What?" he asks, grinning.

"Sometimes you have a little bit of stubble and like—" I stop, losing my ability to form words that make sense. "It doesn't look bad, it looks good." I need to stop talking. "But then it's gone, but you never talk about shaving, and sometimes the hair isn't there for like weeks." What am I saying?

"You're asking me when I shave? If I shave?"

"I guess," I admit.

"I shave like once a week. Sometimes less," he says with a curious face. "I don't have to shave that much, if that's what you're asking."

He looks amused by me, but I'm embarrassed.

"I don't know why I asked. We've never been in a hotel room, and I just shaved my legs, so it made me think of it . . ."

His eyebrows spike. Why am I mentioning my leg hair?

"Anyway—" I say, like it's going to reset the conversation.

Then I run around the room, turning off all the lights, and climb onto the other mattress.

A minute passes before Chris starts laughing.

"What?" I ask.

"It's barely nine," he says. "You're going to sleep now?"

"Oh," I say, and I laugh, too. "I figured we were tired. I don't know."

"We are," he says, "but there's no way I can actually sleep at nine." Then I hear his body sliding off the mattress, which makes me hold my breath. He pads across the carpet.

"Slide over," he says.

I slide to the far edge of the bed, and he lies down on top of the covers.

This would be normal in my bed at home. We would never be like this at his house, but at mine, we've literally spent hours in bed, staring at the ceiling, coming up with stories. Usually we start on the bed together until he slides to the floor and draws while I'm still talking. Then I grab my laptop to work.

But we are in a hotel, and the lights are off, and I might be moving away for good in a few days, and my legs are shaved.

"I don't want you to move away," Chris whispers. I can see him wipe his hand down his face.

"Duh," I say, because it is the first thing that comes to mind.

He kicks my foot.

"I mean it. I want you to understand that. Because maybe you don't, after the whole thing with my mom. Had she told you yes, that she'd let you move in, I would have been excited. I swear I would have come around. I would rather have you there, sharing my bathroom — me having to sleep on Adam's floor — than have you move somewhere else."

It means a lot to hear that, so I tell him.

I turn on my side to face him.

"Maybe it's good for me to try being with my mom. I don't know. Seth isn't . . . who he's supposed to be."

Chris turns on his side to face me, too.

"I know why you have issues with your mom, but I've always liked her. And she wants you with her, you know?"

"I guess," I say. "Plus, it's only a year. If she and Bill break up and she moves again, it probably won't happen until the end of the year, and then I'll be in college anyway."

"Then we'll be at the same college," Chris says.

"I hope so," I say.

Our breath mingles. Chris smells like dried apricot. He had a snack pack.

"Lori," he says, pulling me to him and putting his arm around my back. We're hugging, but horizontally, and I recognize this as a potential cause of actual death. I could write a story about a girl who is so desperate for someone, so in *like* but also so in *love,* so good at keeping all her feelings in a little box in her soul, that when the object of her affection gets into bed with her and pulls her close, she explodes into confetti.

I don't want to turn into confetti, so I start to move away, but when I do, I'm awkward about it because he's holding on tight, and then our bodies are very close. So close that I notice his whole body.

"Oh my god," I say, and I roll away and hop to my feet at the end of the bed.

Chris scrambles up, too. "Lori! I'm sorry, Lori!"

"I'm not mad," I say, and I know he's panicking about basic biology and what I felt on my leg, but I can't deal with it right now. "It's fine! It's not anything!" I hope that's enough to make this less weird.

I turn on a light on the wall, which only makes this moment worse because it is now unsettlingly bright. He understands this and turns around. I still can't look at him, but I see my slip-on shoes and I run to them and grab the room key on the desk by the door.

"I'm going for a walk!" I yell.

The door slams behind me, and I am shuffling down the hallway as if it's a fire drill.

I will take a walk, and he will be asleep by the time I get back. We won't have to talk about it.

Things are going to be so busy tomorrow anyway, and really, what is there to discuss?

I make it halfway down the hall and let out a string of very bad words, only to look up to find an older couple staring at me as they come out of the elevator.

"Sorry," I say.

I make it to the lobby and see a bathroom—thank god it's a one-stall—and then I feel safe. I stay seated on the toilet long after I've used it.

I will not give in to temptation and go back upstairs before I am ready.

There is a poster on the wall that shows a bunch of pictures of different styles of New England barns, and I read them over and over.

Yankee Barn. Three-bay Barn. Connecticut Barn.

Barns are soothing.

I am going to tell my mother that I am excited to move to Maryland. Seth can go back to New York and see how he fares without his muse in front of him. Chris and I will forget what just happened, and we will benefit from having Rhode Island and Pennsylvania and Delaware and a bunch of other states between us. We'll share a Google Doc for stories, and we won't ruin what we have.

I wonder, for a second, whether I could spend the entire night in this bathroom, sleeping with my head against the wall, but I know I can't. I will have to go back to the room.

I wash my hands and exit. Maybe there's a computer down here where I can email my mom now—just to tell her I'm all in —but I stop short because I see Ethan in the reading room off the lobby. He's on the couch by himself, wearing pajamas not unlike mine. They're silky, and the top and bottom match, but instead of short shorts, his are full pants with a matching button-down top. His initials, EF, are on the pocket. Classier than the M on mine for whatever brand they sell at Target.

This style of pajamas looks so much more natural on a well-groomed Englishman who has a cool accent and says *chips* instead of *french fries*.

It's when I wave to him and he doesn't respond that I know that something is wrong. He's staring at the wall, lost in thought, even after I wave a second time, so I clear my throat and say, "Hey, Ethan."

"Oh, hello, Lori," he says, as if he's waking from a zombie coma. His eyes are unnaturally bright now, his smile big and fake. "Do you need something? Is the room okay?"

I sit across from him, on the opposing leather love seat. The room is decorated with old leathery books. Old leathery everything. I notice, looking closer at Ethan, that his beard is coming in. He's tired.

"The room is great. Thanks for putting us up; it's super generous," I say. "I just needed to escape my room for a few minutes. Or hours."

Ethan looks concerned, and I realize that what I've said—especially the word *escape*—might have implied that there's been a conflict. I don't want him to worry, and I can't think of a lie that will serve as a good explanation, so I tell the truth.

"I needed some air. And I had to poop," I confess, because that did just happen.

"I see," Ethan says, and smiles again, but his expression is flat. I know this kind of meaningless smile. I've been showing it to people a lot this week. To Chris's mom. To the Garden Girls. To Ethan, probably right now.

"What about you? What brings you to Ye Olde Library?" I

ask, gesturing to the sturdy decor. I'm trying to lighten the mood here. "I assume you are not here for the same reason."

"What? No," he says. "Oh, no."

I notice the clear tumbler in his hand. It's filled with brown liquor, maybe something like bourbon or whiskey. Chris's dad drinks something similar every New Year's Eve and at midnight says, "Here's to another one, my sweet," and kisses his wife.

When I look up again, Ethan's eyes are super glassy. Then I look down and see that he's wearing socks that have tiny dogs printed on them. He has wandered down here without shoes on. That seems out of character.

I'm not wearing shoes either, but I am seventeen and my hair is purple.

I think, for a second, that in the story Seth is writing, I'm the exact kind of girl who wanders around in a hotel not wearing shoes. That makes me scowl.

But Ethan is not messy like this.

"Ethan, are you okay?" I ask. "You forgot shoes."

"Of course, yes," he says, and he sounds miles away.

I don't believe him, obviously, and I don't have anywhere else I want to be, so I pick up a magazine on the table and flip through it. It's a glossy guide to the area, and there's a family on the cover who look like they're living their best lives in this part of Massachusetts. There are pictures of them doing different things. In one, the parents and their two kids are running through one of those corn mazes that are all over New England every fall. They cut the corn into some shape. Like it's a field of corn with paths cut into the shape of a ghost if you were looking from above. I went to one with Chris's family once. The Maize Maze. It's a whole thing.

In another picture in this magazine, the parents are having a romantic dinner at a winery. Both blond and pale, they look like siblings. In the third picture, the kids are wide-eyed at a children's museum of some kind. In the fourth, it's summer, and the family is eating cotton candy.

The magazine is called *Berkshires Now!*, and all I can do is imagine a different issue with my family on the cover — my mom, Seth, me, and Ethan and Bill — and in every picture we'd be looking more and more confused and miserable. Or maybe our pictures would show us in gardens, illegally dumping bags of ashes all over the place.

"Your uncle and I are just — we're just going through it."

I look up, and Ethan's eyes are on his socks.

I consider his words and try to make eye contact, but he's more interested in the floor. It's also clear to me now that he might be drunk. He's holding the tumbler at an angle. He's a little shaky. And if it wasn't mostly empty, it would have spilled. He hiccups.

"Going through what?" I ask.

I've seen drunk people my age, and I guess I've seen older people drunk too, like the time at the Cheesecake Factory when a bunch of guys watching hockey at the bar were yelling so loud they got kicked out. But I don't think I've ever in my life seen an adult get really, really wasted. My mom doesn't drink; it taints her energy, she says.

But Ethan is fully smashed, and now I know I'm not going to leave him.

". . . just some troubles," he mutters.

"You're having troubles with Seth?" I ask.

"That's probably an understatement," he says.

"Oh."

He looks up at me and waits for me to say more.

"Are you guys in a fight?" I ask.

Ethan laughs, and it sounds angry and mean.

"Lori, we ended things three months ago."

I cover my mouth with my hand.

"No," I say.

"Technically, six months ago," he says, and he drags out the word *technically* so it sounds like five syllables. "At first it was a trial breakup. We'd open ourselves up for a bit. But it was never about that. We'd ceased to be romantic partners in all ways."

I nod. I don't know what else to do. I mean, I've never even had a boyfriend—I was with Frankie the lacrosse player for a few weeks, and it was mostly just making out in his car—so I have no idea what it means to be a partner.

All I know is that Seth and Ethan are my example for that kind of relationship. I've known them together my whole life. Ethan is my uncle by marriage, even though they're not married. They always told me they already shared real estate and other important paperwork, and didn't need the wedding gifts. They're a unit.

"But you're here with us," I say. "And you and Seth still live together."

"Oh, you noticed that, did you?" Ethan says, and stands up. He walks to the other side of the room, where there's a small bar with water glasses and a wicker basket full of tiny packs of pretzels — the same brand they had at Walsh's Funeral Home, a place that I feel like I visited a thousand years ago, as opposed to last week.

Ethan picks up an empty water glass, pours about two inches of alcohol into it, and slides it over to me.

"Really?" I ask.

Seth gave me wine just days ago, but this looks more serious.

"Where I'm from, we let young people learn to drink alcohol so they can do it more responsibly when they become adults. Americans — it's all depravation and then excess. It's not a good way to teach self-control."

This is a good point, but it's a little meaningless coming from someone who's slurring his words and can't stop hiccuping.

"Yes, I know I'm one to talk, in my cups," he says, reading my mind.

I love that he says things like "in my cups."

For the record, I also like drunk Ethan. He has no filter, and he's clearly fed up, and hearing this from him makes me feel older than I've ever felt in my life. But I want to assume that whatever's happening with Seth is just a fight. I can't imagine that it's actually over.

I take a sip of what's in the glass. It burns going down my throat, in a good way. Based on the way it clears my sinuses, this could do a number on me quickly, so I have to take little sips. I try not to pucker my whole face every time I taste it.

"If you guys really broke up, why are you still together? Why are you here with us? Why are you acting like things are normal?"

"Because we built a home together, and that's a pretty complicated thing to split up. We are two separate people who have agreed to move on, and we both know it's time, but I also know that when I get out of the shower in the morning at home, there will be a coffee cup on the counter made just how I like it, with two teaspoons of milk and one of honey. Our routines continue because we are roommates and friends, even when we're not partners. We know we've fallen out of love. But there's still love there."

"Oh," I say.

"And I'm here because of that love for him, for all of you. Because Seth's mother died, and I lost my mother years ago, and I know how it feels. I know that even if he is functional this week, this loss is going to wreck him once it sinks in. Our breakup doesn't change that.

"He's still the love of my life. I wouldn't be anywhere else right now. But . . . it doesn't make it easy.

"Being in this gorgeous place in a hotel room that is designed for romance is not easy for either of us. You have these memories of the attraction and the patterns you can fall into that would . . . in our case, it would confuse things. At home, it's easy to sleep in the same bed without even thinking about . . . *intimacy,* but what is it about hotels?"

Indeed, I think.

He adds, "I'm down here so I don't make mistakes up there. There's a temptation to pretend we can mend things that are supposed to stay broken."

He surprises me by adding, "We should have gotten married."

"Why?"

"Because this loss is monumental. I don't want to call him an ex. He's an ex-husband."

"Ex-partner," I offer.

"That sounds a bit better, I suppose. It still doesn't scratch the surface."

I take another sip of alcohol, and I'm really starting to feel it now. The whiskey is warm, making my brain tingly. His words are sinking in. My chest gets tight as I realize that I'm losing someone else. It sounds like Ethan and Seth are really over, and I don't want this incredible man to be out of my life.

He's disclosed all this to me as if I'm a peer or a friend, so I do the same.

"That's why I'm down here too," I say. "I didn't want to make a mistake up there."

"Really," Ethan says, his smile twitching, and he looks relieved to be talking about anything else.

"I . . . it got weird."

"You and Christian are just friends?"

"Best friends," I say.

"You don't have romantic feelings for him?" Ethan says.

"Oh, I do. I have every romantic feeling for him. But I need him for the long haul, you know? I can ignore the love stuff. I need his friendship and our creative partnership more than anything else."

Ethan nods.

"I never had to worry about it, because he's fine with it. We had a small talk about it when we met, but we're friends. We hook up with other people. And I've always thought that if anything, it's been harder for *me* to keep the boundaries. But then, upstairs . . ."

Whatever I'm saying is sobering Ethan up. He's got his concerned-dad face on.

"Do you want to come back to our room? We have the pull-out. No one should be uncomfortable tonight."

I hesitate for a second. "No. I feel like I owe him an apology," I say finally, "because I ran out when things got too close. He looked . . . stung. Like rejected and then confused. But it's complicated."

"It sounds like you care about him quite a bit," Ethan says.

"I do," I say.

"Lori." Ethan leans forward. "Sometimes the best way to make something less awkward is to acknowledge it. Maybe you should let him know why you ran out."

"Is that how you and Seth communicate?" I ask, and I don't mean to be rude, but it sounds as if there's a lot unsaid in that relationship.

He leans back and finishes the last sips of his beverage.

"We're doing our best. Once one of us finally said what he was really thinking, once *he* had the courage to say that he wanted to move on, the path became clear. Now it's just logistics — the practicalities of letting go."

I think about Chris, and how I ran out without telling him why. That I count on him to be indifferent about me because I'm constantly thinking about getting closer to him. That the moment I realized he wasn't, that his body wasn't indifferent at all, I had to depend on myself to make sure we stayed safe from anything more.

I sink into the couch.

"What I have with Chris can't be temporary," I whisper. "I need to tell him that's the problem."

"Everything is temporary, technically, Lori," Ethan says. "That doesn't mean it's not worth experiencing."

"He's probably so confused."

"You sound pretty confused too. Maybe you can help each other."

With the empty tumbler in his hand, Ethan gazes through the bay doors that lead out to the back of the hotel. He stands up and walks to them, and I follow.

"I guess he didn't want to stay in that room either."

I move close to the door to see what Ethan is looking at, and it turns out that it's Chris. My best friend—if that's what he still is—is on the hotel's lawn. He's circling the oversize chessboard that sits on the ground. We'd passed it on the way in.

I don't know what he plans to do on that board. Like me, he does not know how to play chess. Somehow his dad taught his brother how to be a chess whiz, but Chris stopped at checkers.

Maybe he left the room to look for me. Or to avoid my return.

"Go out there and be honest," Ethan says.

I nod.

Ethan takes my arm and turns me toward him. The skin around his tired eyes look crinkly, like paper. As if it could fall off his face and turn to dust, like craisins. Everything is dissolving.

I look at my uncle's big brown eyes and kind smile, and I want to tell him that he is such a cool person, that since I was a kid, everything about him has made me feel happy and safe. He is better than Seth. He speaks before I can.

"Lori," he says, "if I can pass on one adult lesson—one I learned too late—it's that sometimes having an awkward conversation makes life so much better in the long run. I should have had *many* awkward conversations with Seth. Maybe if we'd had them long ago, we wouldn't have spent the last few months in misery, having to unearth all these things we'd been compartmentalizing for years."

I nod and smile, letting him know I understand, which I guess I do, despite the fact that he slurred all his words during that whole bit of advice.

"Ethan," I say.

"Yes, dear?"

"What happens to us? If Seth moves out and you guys are broken up, will I still get to see you? Are we allowed to stay in touch? You're my family. At the moment, actually, you're my favorite uncle."

Ethan pulls me in for a hug. "That doesn't change, my dear. Romantic relationships end, but family is family."

"Good," I say. "You've always been an honorary Seltzer."

"Thank you," he says. "Meanwhile, on that note, can you try to forgive your uncle?"

This shocks me. He knows what happened. He's giving me a look that suggests he isn't on my side.

"You think I'm wrong to be angry?"

"No," he says, taking a beat to think. "Although I don't know that I can condone your digging into your uncle's notes without permission. It's hard for me to be objective, I have to be honest. Seth told me that this is the first time he's been inspired to write this much, this quickly, in years. I'm happy he's unblocked. As someone who cares about him, I have to celebrate that on some level . . . I do know he has a great deal of respect for you, Lori."

I nod, even though I don't believe that.

"You'll go upstairs now?" I ask.

"Yes," he says. "I suppose it's time for bed."

"Will you be able to handle the awkward?"

"It's what we do," he says, his hands up and out like the shrug emoji.

After a glance at the side door again, he says, "Good luck out there.

"Oh—and Lori," he adds, "it's nice to see your eyes. Quite lovely, my dear."

I smile and watch him walk away, not quite in a straight line.

—◆—

I turn back to the glass door and press my nose against it and see that Chris has made his way to the center of the chessboard. He is standing there, under a light in the back of the property, moving one big piece to an open square and then another.

I could let him have his privacy. To cool down and let him join me upstairs when he's ready. Really, it's probably easiest for me to go back to our room and fall asleep so he can return without having to acknowledge me at all.

But I don't want to let this go, and Ethan's right—it won't go away in the morning.

I swing open the back door, close it behind me, and walk to meet him. He doesn't notice my approach until I'm steps away. He raises his eyes enough to acknowledge me, but there's no smile. Then his eyes are back to the board, and he stares at it like he's thinking of his next move, like he's actually playing a game. He's wearing jeans again.

"What are you playing? Because it can't be chess."

He moves another piece, but doesn't answer me.

"I'm just getting some air," he says in a too-cool voice, and then asks, "Are you okay?"

"Of course, but . . . Ethan and Seth broke up."

"What?" he asks, concerned, his head snapping up to meet mine. "Just now? Because of the fight at The Mount?"

Chris has transformed into my best friend again. His voice is back to normal, and he's super concerned.

"No, not just now. Months ago, apparently. I ran into Ethan in the hotel lobby, and he told me everything. They're figuring out how to separate things, like a divorce without the divorce. Ethan's here to be supportive."

Chris places his hand on the horse-shaped chess piece. "That's too bad. I like Ethan."

"He promises he'll still be my uncle."

"Of course he will," Chris says. "You know I still see Papa Dale."

Papa Dale is Chris's dead grandmother's second husband. She'd been divorced from him long before she died, and he's not related to anyone by blood or marriage anymore, but he's at all the Burkes' holidays. He is also a riot and makes incredible seven-layer dip.

The example of Papa Dale gives me hope. Maybe Ethan can be around like that forever.

"I feel so gross and bad about upstairs," Chris says suddenly, and he pushes another chess piece to the open space in front of it. "I'm freaking out thinking I made you uncomfortable."

"Oh my god, no," I say, and walk to Chris and take his hands. "It is not your fault, and you were not alone in feeling whatever you were feeling. Like if I had the same body parts, I would have been in the same boat."

He looks down and squeezes his eyes shut. I've embarrassed him. I don't want that.

"I was surprised," I said. "That's never happened with us before."

He lets go of my hands and walks to the other side of the board.

"I'm not usually alone in a hotel room with you," he says. "Hugging in the same bed. Again, my fault."

"Listen," I say. "I didn't run out because I didn't reciprocate, I ran out because I *did*. I *do,* like all the time."

"Come on, Lor," he says in disbelief.

The fact that he doesn't understand how much this is true is both tragic and hilarious. I know he's thinking back to *the talk*— the one we had years ago, just to confirm that it was a friendship and nothing else. That was two full years ago, and we were fifteen.

"Your clavicle," I say.

"My clavicle?" I see the outline of Chris's hands on his hips.

His stance is so unnatural, and I realize he doesn't look like himself without his pen or a pad or his backpack holding a bunch of art supplies. His arms are usually full.

"If I could draw for one day, if I could borrow your talent for twenty-four hours, I would spend the entire time drawing your clavicle from memory. The way it sticks through your stupid soft T-shirts. The way it moves when you laugh. God, I hate it so much because I am so desperate for it."

I groan, annoyed just thinking about it. Chris and his stupid clavicle.

I look over at him, no longer embarrassed by any of this. Now that I've confessed my deepest, darkest secret — the clavicle problem — I feel better. I remember that we're two friends negotiating a story the way we always do. This time it just happens to be our own.

"You're the first person who's ever stuck around, and you're the person I know and love most, not counting family. Or actually — go ahead and count family, now that Grandma's dead. Mom and Seth are . . . I don't know who I can count on anymore . . . But I can live with it, you know? Those feelings? That's what we decided. That's how it is."

There's silence, and then, "We decided that a long time ago."

"Yeah," I say.

"But your feelings have changed," he says.

The stillness of Chris's body tells me he is annoyed; I don't even have to see his facial expression to know it.

"You should have told me," he says.

"No. Because I didn't want it. I didn't want to change us at all. The clavicle thoughts were private, for me. I'm only telling you so you don't feel bad about being a totally normal human person with an erection in a hotel room."

"Lori," Chris says.

"What? Is that word too much for your sensitive ears?"

"No. It's just humiliating," he says.

Chris puts both hands on his head, his elbows out. He walks to another chess piece, the one that looks like a tiny castle, and pushes it with his foot. "I'm thinking about 'Vampiresplainer,'" he says.

"What about him?"

Chris smiles.

"Vampiresplainer" was the title of a short story we wrote about a very sexy vampire named William who moves to a new town and enrolls in a high school—one much like ours—to hide from a new rising force of vampire hunters.

Although William looks eighteen, he is more than six hundred years old and therefore has seen a lot. Basically, over centuries, he's observed wars, the building and destruction of cities. He's earned multiple degrees. Degrees on top of degrees.

He's a prolific knitter. His culinary skills are unparalleled.

His expertise in all things has made luring victims very easy. All he has to do is seduce a woman with his knowledge, and she's in. For anything, including biting. Women hear him speak of history and poets, then they look at his sexy hair, and the combination of it all makes them fall to pieces.

Except not anymore.

William gets to this new school ready to find young women to charm, but he seems to have lost his touch. Girls seem super annoyed with him. He can't even get a prom date.

After one epic fail with a classmate named Daphne, William says to her, "Daphne, what gives? Why are you so put off by me? Why does every young girl at this school behave as though I'm covered in garlic?"

So she gives it to him straight.

"William," Daphne says, "I'm going to be honest with you for the sake of humanity and every girl at this high school. You, my friend, are the worst mansplainer."

William runs his fingers through his glorious hair and sputters, not understanding her. In six centuries, he has never heard this word. "What does it mean to be . . . a mansplainer?"

He clenches his retracted fangs.

"You don't know?" Daphne asks with mock surprise.

Chris's illustration showed a vampire with sexy, bouncy hair. Above it, in a chat bubble, he had the vampire saying, "Well, actually . . ."

It was so fun to write. It's one of my favorites.

"I always thought it was weird," Chris says. "You gave him a sexy clavicle. That's what you wrote."

Yikes.

"I did?"

"Yeah, and at first I thought it was some autocorrect thing, because who makes note of a clavicle, but you said it was the word you chose, so I just drew what you said. I figured it was a girl thing to notice about a guy."

"I guess I had real-life inspiration," I say.

"That's one of my favorite stories," Chris says. "We should finally put it in *N-Files*. If you stay."

"Sure," I say. "Or you could publish it without me."

It must be late. The temperature is dropping, and I'm starting to hear new chirps and noises from the woods. The hotel's window lights are starting to go out.

"We should go to bed," I say.

"But what if it turns out you *are* moving for sure?" Chris asks, taking a step toward me.

I don't get it.

"What if you were leaving for good in just a few days, and you knew we wouldn't be together all the time. If you knew this was going turn into a long-distance friendship, and we only had a few nights together, and we went upstairs, and what happened . . . happened again. Would you still leave the room?"

"I mean, I probably *am* moving," I say. "It's not about that.

I'm trying to keep us *us,* no matter where we live. If we hook up, it'll still be in our memories when I move. It'll be there — like *out there.*"

I wave my hand around to signify that I mean the ether. If I hook up with Chris, I will not be able to forget it, no matter what it's like, no matter where we live.

"Okay," he says. "Right."

He leads us up the lawn to the back door, but it's locked now. We have to work our way around the building to the front.

The desk clerk flashes us a knowing look as we walk in, but we both smile and head to the elevator.

Inside the room, Chris takes off his jeans, but not in a sexy way, and walks to the mirror on the wall. Then he pulls down his shirt collar a few inches, checking himself out. "I guess it is kind of majestic."

I burst out laughing, so grateful that he just made everything normal yet again. That's all I want.

We get into our separate beds, but I can still smell him a little on my pillow, and it makes me sad. But we are fine now, at least. Every adult in my life is a mess, but the people in this room are good.

To punctuate that, Chris begins to snore.

I let my eyes adjust, and I turn and watch him in the dark.

Chapter 14

I am still awake when light begins to sneak through the blinds. I've tried every position, I have tried counting down from a thousand, I've tried to read books on my phone, but I am wired and stuck on a hamster wheel of anxious thoughts, some about the decisions that will be made in the next few days, but mostly about how I will now have to live with the memory of what it felt like to be waist to waist with Chris.

I am still thinking about those few seconds of possibility.

Based on the way his body looks, he's thinking of something interesting at the moment. His long lashes twitch on his face as he dreams. He sleeps on his back, mouth slightly parted; it's almost a smile. He's still snoring a bit, and there is dried drool next to his mouth, but I am totally into it. I need to get out of this hotel, which is somehow cursed with hormones and possibility.

I edge out from under my covers and slide my feet into my slip-on sneakers. I put on a bra and grab my room key and phone and decide to take a quick walk. It doesn't seem like an unsafe thing to do. We are in antique-market cow country. No one is around, and if they are, they're inside their historic, precious bed-and-breakfasts. I make my way through the front door, past the same sleepy desk clerk, and I'm greeted by pleasant, cool air.

I consider walking to the chessboard to relive whatever happened last night, but I see the driveway in front of me and feel a tug. Like I need to be somewhere else. It's very Edgar Allen Poe, as if I'm some character being called by a bird or a heartbeat under the floor.

And then I remember.

"We didn't do the reading," I say out loud to no one. "We didn't do the stupid reading!"

Yesterday, when we crop-dusted Grandma all over Edith Wharton's perfect garden, we didn't read Dorothy Parker. We just left and went to the restaurant. I suppose we read the Edith Wharton quote on the stone beneath us, but I'm not sure that counts.

I don't want to be superstitious—or religious—but now that I'm outside, I feel like that's one of the reasons I'm up this early. This nagging feeling is about unfinished business. I'm supposed to go back to The Mount and get the reading done.

I can use my phone to find some Dorothy Parker quotes online.

I walk down the driveway; my phone tells me The Mount is only a half mile away. The journey seems foreboding, I have to admit, because the sky is overcast and still kind of dark, and I'm in flip-flopping shoes and my Target pajamas.

But when I get to The Mount, it seems safe. It's early enough that I can walk right past the ticket booth; it'll be hours before anyone shows up to man it. Once I make it past that checkpoint, I walk down the gravel driveway and see the shape of the white mansion. It looks more impressive and frozen in time than it did yesterday, probably because no one is here.

I make it down the winding paved driveway; the greens on either side of it look shimmery, like they're magic, but I know it's just the morning dew. The huge gates, which were open yesterday, are now closed, but there are a few cars and trucks in the parking lot. I tread lightly, walking around the side of the house to make it to the back gardens without being noticed, and that's when I see the creepy thing we missed yesterday.

Up on a hill, on the far left side of the property, there are tiny gravestones coming out of the dirt. They look very old. I need to go up there.

Up close, it is way more interesting than I expected. It is Edith Wharton's pet cemetery. How did we miss it?

"*Pet Sematary,*" I whisper to myself.

"Excuse me—"

I hear a woman's voice yell from down the hill, and I duck, as if I can hide from her, even if there is nothing to shield me.

I turn around then and see the woman coming down the lawn toward me.

"Excuse me—" she yells again. "Can I help you?"

I am tempted to run, but on this wet soil in these flimsy sneakers I'd probably wipe out big time. Also, I'll look more mischievous if I bolt, and I am not here to dig up a grave or steal something.

I put up my hands and place them palms out so she knows I mean no harm, and when she gets closer, I recognize her.

"Marge!" I say.

She stops a foot away from me, confused.

"I'm sorry, do I know you?"

"Yes! I mean, no," I tell her. "I was on one of the tours yesterday. You did an awesome job. You were an exceptional tour guide, really. But I'm sure you toured a ton of people yesterday, so don't worry—I'm not offended that you don't remember me."

Marge has reached the bottom of the hill, which means she's close enough to give me a once-over, and she's clearly trying to decide why I'm in my pajamas and sneakers on this hill.

"I'm not here to cause trouble," I tell her. "I'm staying up the street at the inn. I was just out taking an early-morning walk and thought I'd come back to the property."

"I'm sorry," Marge says, looking less friendly and more disheveled than she did fourteen hours ago. "The Mount grounds are technically always open for walks, but we have a very big event happening today. There's a lot of commotion on the grounds. I think it'd be best if you came back much later. With an adult."

"Sure, it get it," I say, trying to think of what might calm her down. She looks like I might ruin her day, and it's barely started. "I didn't mean to come here . . . like this. In pajamas. I mentioned it yesterday . . . my family is here because my grandma just died, and she really loved the gardens at The Mount, so I wanted to check it out one more time. But I can come back another day."

Marge's shoulders relax. Invoking my dead grandmother was a good move, and it is not a lie. Now she looks concerned about me instead of *because* of me. "I'm so sorry, dear," she says. "Was your grandmother a patron of The Mount?"

"I know she came here a few times, but I don't think she had a membership or anything. She was really big into reading and gardens, so this was a perfect spot to bring her."

Ugh, I don't know why I said that part.

Marge gives me a quizzical look, and her glance flies to my hands, as if I might be scattering ashes as we speak.

"I mean, we didn't bring her ashes here or anything," I lie. "We just wanted to visit her favorite places."

"I see," she says, not believing me.

I think she'll let it go.

I don't want to make Marge work right now, but she's the expert on this place and I have questions.

"I didn't see the pet cemetery yesterday."

"Oh, Edith loved her dogs. She buried four of them up here. The other two gravestones were placed here by subsequent owners. But Edith's dogs were her children."

"She didn't have kids?"

"She did not. I suppose it speaks to her prolificacy as a writer."

I think of what Grandma told me many times; she had no regrets about having kids, but if she hadn't, she might have written a book herself. "It's possible to do it all," she'd say, "but it's not easy."

I have to ask.

"Is it against the rules to scatter someone's ashes here?"

Marge doesn't seem surprised or grossed out by the question.

"I suppose it is against the rules," Marge says. "To be honest, I'm sure many people have brought their family members' ashes to The Mount without asking. If I saw someone doing that, I'm not sure I'd stop them. Ashes are everywhere."

"They're all over Fenway Park, apparently."

She pauses. "Really? That's disturbing. I'm not sure where you'd put ashes in a ballpark. Everything is steel and concrete. But I always assume they're on beaches, in the water, beneath our feet. It's rather comforting, if you think about it. We're surrounded by so many people's loved ones. Back into the earth they go."

There's some noise behind Marge then, and I see that closer to the estate house there are men carrying large tables from the driveway to the lawn.

"What are they doing?" I ask.

"We have an afternoon wedding," she says. "That means it's a very early morning. I'm here for the caterers so they can set up. We'll be transformed by noon."

"It must be really romantic to get married here," I say. "It's so regal and old."

"Indeed," she says. "Which reminds me, I do have to get to work. The weddings here are memorable, but they take quite a bit of oversight. This particular affair involves three hundred chairs and a chocolate fountain."

"Seems kind of weird," I say. "You say Edith Wharton liked small gatherings."

Marge considers this and smiles. "It's true. Sometimes I see a great crowd enjoying the property and think about how Edith built this place as an escape, to get away from just such a mob."

"I like that you call her Edith," I tell Marge.

"What else would I call her?"

"Edith Wharton. I like how you call her by her first name, like you know her."

"In many ways, it feels like I do," she tells me. "I hate to say this," she says, "but I think you really should go now. I'm sorry to rush you out."

"Do you mind if I do a quick reading? I've been trying to read my Grandma's favorite author at her favorite gardens, and we forgot yesterday. That's why I came back, really — to read a passage."

"And her favorite author is Edith," Marge says, smiling.

Yikes.

"Actually, no," I say, trying to sound apologetic. "Her favorite writer is Dorothy Parker. Is that weird?"

Marge starts laughing.

"I mean, she also loved Edith Wharton, but her favorite was Dorothy."

"Your grandmother had great taste," Marge says. "Regardless, if you want to read, go right ahead."

"Sure," I say, pulling out my phone to find the passage. Then I stop.

Marge seems like someone who has thoughtful things to say about death, and I want to talk to her about it. I know she has a wedding to prepare for, but she's the first impartial adult I've been able to talk to since Grandma died.

"Marge," I ask, "was Edith Wharton cremated?"

"Her body was buried in Versailles, in France."

"Oh," I say. "Just out of curiosity, would *you* want to be cremated?"

"Pardon me?" Marge asks.

"I'm sorry. I know that's a weirdly personal question, but my family is Jewish, and I guess Jewish people aren't supposed to be cremated. And this whole thing with my grandma . . . I keep worrying that we did the wrong thing."

"By cremating her?"

"Well . . ." I brace myself. What I'm about to admit is so, so stupid, but if I'm honest, I've been thinking it ever since I first saw the craisins. "I know Grandma Sheryl asked to be cremated, and we were just following her wishes. But as a writer, I love supernatural stories and horror. Zombies, magic, sci-fi, demons—all that stuff. I know in stories it's all just metaphor—like vampire stories are about fear of 'the other,' and zombies are about consumerism or something like that . . ."

Marge looks baffled, but I continue.

"My point is, I know that supernatural stories are about the real world. They're just metaphors. But in all these tales, the vampire ones specifically, when people die and come back to life, they crawl out of a grave. Like, you see a grave, and the actual reanimated body comes out of the grave."

"I see," Marge says, but she doesn't. "I think I'm missing the question here."

"Let me try it this way," I say, and exhale before embarrassing myself. "My uncle Seth and I cremated her, so now she's just tiny pieces. I keep thinking that's all she is now, so she'll never crawl out of a grave. She'll never reanimate like the dead people do on my shows or in my stories. Like, that's it. She's gravel. She's craisins."

"You mean cremains?"

"You know that word?"

"It's what they call ashes."

"Right," I say. "Sorry. I know this sounds so ridiculous."

But she isn't looking at me like I'm saying anything ridiculous.

Even though I have just confessed to Marge, a stranger, that I'm upset because I cremated my grandma, which means she won't be able to come back to life as a vampire or zombie, she's looking at me as if I've said a really meaningful thing.

"You seem like a pretty macabre person . . . what did you say your name was?"

"It's Lori," I say.

"Lori," she continues, "I'm just going to give it to you straight."

"Absolutely, yes," I tell Marge.

"My cousin Steven is a medical examiner, and from him I

know that bodies are almost fully decomposed within a month. Like liquid, without preservation."

"Jesus," I say, shocked to hear these words coming out of this woman's mouth. "Marge, that's so gross."

"I know," she says. "I'm telling you this for a reason—so you know that the body doesn't sit there preserved forever. Maybe your vampire stories allow you to believe that bodies are frozen in time, ready to come back to life, but it's dust to dust, in pieces, no matter how you play it.

"I'm Catholic," she continues, "and most of my family has been cremated at this point. But we don't scatter the cremains. You still bury your loved ones in a sacred place, like a church. I also had trouble with the idea of burning a family member's body—it seemed disrespectful and a bit violent to me. But then I learned that in some religions, it's believed that burning the body is part of letting the soul free. It's an essential part of the process. There are many ways to honor the dead, and I'd like to think that none of us are accidentally doing it wrong. Your grandmother asked for this, and you honored her choice."

"Wow," I say, and I'm crying because Marge is amazing. "I mean, her soul is almost free. There's still some of her that's trapped in a Chico's bag."

Marge lets out a snort. "Lori, you are by far the most interesting person I have met in a very long time. I do hope you'll return. A friend of Edith, for certain."

I start to walk. I know she has to get moving.

"I should mention—" she adds. "I have a friend in New York, a fellow historical guide, who claims that the Algonquin Hotel is haunted by Dorothy Parker. And Dorothy was cremated, so there you go."

Wait.

"Dorothy Parker was cremated?"

"Oh yes! It's actually a fascinating literary story. I'm sure your grandmother knew it, as a fan."

I wait for her to say more. There's no way I'm leaving now.

"Okay, I'll tell you, but then it's time to go. And I have to be quick about it."

"For sure, Marge," I tell her.

"When Dorothy Parker died, she left her entire estate to Martin Luther King, Jr.—whom she'd never met. Dorothy Parker was a vocal supporter of the civil rights movement, and she wanted all her resources to be left to the cause. But Martin Luther King, as her beneficiary, died only a year later, and Dorothy Parker's estate—including her remains—became property of the NAACP, based on the terms of her will."

"That's so awesome and random," I say, because it is. "So where is she now? Where is Dorothy?"

"Still with the NAACP—at its headquarters. I believe it's in Baltimore. Her ashes are in a small garden there."

A garden.

In this moment I know that Grandma Sheryl directed me to Marge for this information.

This is a sign. This is where I have to go. I have to bring her to Dorothy.

"Thank you so much, Marge," I say. "You should get to work, and I should go."

"You didn't do your reading," she says.

"Oh!"

I pull up the phone again and read the quote I'd planned to deliver yesterday: "'Wherever she went, including here, it was against her better judgment.'"

I explain. "Apparently Dorothy Parker once said that was what she'd want on her tombstone."

Marge grins. "What a brilliant woman she was."

"Thanks," I say before I realize that she's talking about Dorothy Parker, not my grandma.

Now I do have to leave.

"Thank you so much, Marge. You're the best," I say, and I'm basically sliding down the hill that holds Edith Wharton's pet cemetery. The path out of The Mount looks so gorgeous at this hour that I'm a little upset I can't stop to smell the flowers, which, by now, I can identify—hydrangeas and geraniums everywhere. Then I'm running down the street to the inn, where my family and Chris are probably all still asleep.

I run inside, make my way up the elevator, and knock on Seth and Ethan's door, like, six hundred times until Ethan opens it.

He's wearing his pajama pants and a T-shirt I recognize as

Seth's, and my heart breaks for him. Seeing him—and Seth sleeping in the big bed behind him—they look so perfect that you'd have no idea it's over.

"Lori, what's wrong?" he asks, noticing my breathlessness.

"I'm fine. I was just running, and I'm not used to that," I tell him. "But we have to go."

"What? Where?" he asks, looking around.

I move past him and jump onto the bed and begin shaking Seth.

"What, Lori? Jeez!"

"Wake up. I know where we're taking the last box of craisins!" I yell.

He sits up and wipes his eyes. "I'm going to kill you. What time is it?"

"Dorothy Parker was cremated."

Now he's listening.

"And her ashes are in one place."

"Continue," Seth says.

"In a garden."

"Really."

"In Maryland."

"Maryland?"

"Less than six hours away. I googled it."

"Are you saying we should drive to Maryland right now?"

"I'm demanding," I say.

He looks at the clock, which tells us it's almost eight.

"The Realtor's coming to do the house appraisal tomorrow," he says.

"Push it off a day," I say. "Seth, it's Dorothy Parker."

"Your mom is coming back up—from Maryland—on Friday. That's tomorrow." he says.

I stare him down.

He nods. "You're right. Just give me an hour, okay? I need coffee and a shower. I need to think."

"We're going," I say.

"I just said that," Seth says.

I'm standing by the bed, worried he'll change his mind.

"Go, Lori!' Seth says. "I'm in, okay?"

I grin.

On the other side of the door, I call my mother.

"Sweetie!" she says, sounding relieved. I haven't responded to three phone calls and four texts, all of which she's sent since yesterday. I've heard her on the phone with Seth, but I haven't had the brain bandwidth to deal with her.

"Do you like a hard or a soft mattress?" she asks. "Bill and I are setting up your room—no matter where you live, I want you to be comfortable here—and anyway, Bill has a friend in the mattress business who can get us a deal on something nice."

"Forget about that," I say.

"Lori," she says, disappointed. "I'm trying to be understanding here. Flexible."

"No, Mom. I don't mean to be rude. It's just that we're coming down to Maryland. We're going to drive to you now."

"What?"

"We have one more box of craisins, and we're bringing it there," I say.

There's a long pause.

"I thought you didn't want to bring the ashes to Maryland."

"I didn't want to bring her somewhere random that wasn't on her list," I say. "But we're not. We're bringing her to Dorothy Parker."

"Lori, you're confusing me."

"Dorothy Parker is buried in Baltimore!" I tell her.

"She is?" My mom's question is brimming with excitement, and I'm relieved. She gets it.

"She is! Or maybe not buried there, but that's where her ashes are. We're going to drive down there today. We can meet you at the site."

"Bill—" I hear my mom shout. "Honey, there's been a change of plans."

"Well, this feels like destiny, doesn't it?" Mom says. "Maryland. You and Mom are both coming to Maryland. You're coming to *me*."

"Sure," I tell her, because I guess we are.

"Just tell me where to meet you."

"I'll text," I say.

"And sweetie," she says, and it sounds like she's crying a little, "thank you for including me."

Before I can tell her I wouldn't have done this without her, she hangs up.

Chapter 15

Ethan can't extend his trip because he has a grown-up job in finance. Plus, his car is a rental. He's out for the rest of the trip.

At least those are the reasons he gives. I get it if he needs to tap out on this journey.

The good news is that Chris's mother has given us her blessing to take Chris with us. Mrs. Burke demanded to speak to Seth and my mother first, because it would require him being away from home for one more night, and she wanted to know that he's safe and where he'll be staying. I could hear Seth assuring her that Chris and I will stay with my mom and Bill, and that there will be no "walking around new cities by ourselves."

The goodbye between Seth and Ethan in front of the hotel makes it seem like they're still a couple.

"When do you think you'll be home?" Ethan asks Seth.

"End of week?"

I don't know if that means he's no longer thinking about staying. I don't ask.

"I'll make a plan with Becca when we get down to Maryland," Seth tells him.

"Check in later," Ethan responds, and then they give each other a quick kiss on the cheek.

I remind myself that this breakup isn't new to them and that they still love each other. They have a routine. I'm sure it's hard to break from it.

"Do you think they can work it out?" Chris whispers to me as he walks to the driver's seat. I'm so tired, and it's safer if he takes the keys.

"No," I say. "And I don't want them to. At least I don't think I do."

At Chris's puzzled expression, I explain, "I want them both to be happy."

Chris nods. "I get that."

Then he gives me a long look, which makes me wonder what he's thinking.

The moment is interrupted as Seth slides into the back seat with his luggage. I think he's going to talk about what's happening, maybe tell us that he and Ethan are done. I'm not even sure whether he knows that I know.

Instead he says, "Baltimore is only six hours away?"

"Five hours, thirty-five minutes," Chris says, eyeing the GPS on the dashboard.

I send Mom a text with the address and our estimated time of arrival.

"I'm looking at hotel apps," Seth says. "I am absolutely not staying with your mother."

"I thought you said I should be happy living with her," I say. "You can't stay with her and Bill for a night?"

"It's different when it's your sibling," he says.

Chris's eyes are on the road. Finally I close my eyes and give in to sleep.

After what feels like only a few minutes, Chris wakes me. I must have been sleeping like the dead.

"We're not far," he says, tapping my shoulder with a free hand.

I wipe my eyes and hear Seth spring to life in the back seat.

"Where are we?" he asks.

"I don't really know," Chris says. "It's telling me to get off at the next exit."

The GPS voice instructs us to make a turn off the highway and go down a winding road that leads to what looks like an office park.

"This can't be right," Seth says.

But then we see the sign for the NAACP headquarters. The building is brick and big, and people are coming out, and for a second I'm reminded that while we've been dealing with this family drama for the past week, other humans have been going to their jobs, as if life is normal. As if somebody didn't just die. As if the world doesn't know that Chris and I almost made out last night.

We park the car and stand in front of the building, confused about where we're supposed to be.

I look over at Chris. He's standing there, jaw dropped.

"What?" I say.

"It's just . . . a lot of Black people," he says, and then I notice that yes, there are people coming in and out of the building, some holding lunch bags, some walking to their cars. They are all Black.

Chris is smiling, his eyes huge.

"So many people," he whispers.

I am reminded that where we live, he is always outnumbered, unless he is at church.

"Sorry," he says, shaking his head. "It's a little shocking. In a good way."

I nod. I hope college looks more like this. That it can be even half of what this is for him right now.

"The building isn't as—I don't know—as majestic as I thought it'd be," Chris adds, looking up. "I thought it'd be, like . . . a tower."

I nod in agreement. I didn't expect an office park.

"This doesn't look like the kind of place that would have gardens," Seth says from behind us.

"I'll google it again," I say, and pull up the part of Dorothy Parker's Wikipedia page that tells me her ashes are somewhere here.

There is a young woman, maybe not much older than I am, standing outside the building. She has braids and is wearing a pretty blue dress and is maybe waiting for a ride, checking her phone.

"Excuse me," Seth says to the girl. "Do you work here?"

"I do," she says, smiling nervously as she eyes the Chico's bag in Seth's hand, which he is clutching too tightly. "Summer intern," she adds.

"We're looking for Dorothy Parker," I say. I am impatient.

"I don't know a Dorothy Parker," she says. "But I've only been here for two months."

"No. We're looking for the Dorothy Parker who's dead," Seth says, and now this young woman looks truly concerned.

Seth scowls, frustrated with himself. "Sorry. I haven't slept much, and it's been a long week."

Chris moves to stand in front of us. "I apologize," he tells her. "It's hard to explain, but—"

He's cut off by a tall older man nearby who's been talking to a group of people on the walkway. "Excuse me, did you say you were looking for Dorothy Parker?" He smiles through his white beard.

"Yes," I say, speaking for the group now. "We're looking for the grave of the writer Dorothy Parker. We've heard it's on this property."

"You heard right," the man says. "It's quite a strange story. I'm happy to take you around back."

We follow him around the side of the building as the man, who is probably someone important in this building, retells the story I heard from Marge and tried to repeat for Seth, Ethan, and Chris. This man explains it better, with more details.

"I'll admit that I worked here for three years before learning the full story, with all the details, of Dorothy Parker's estate," he says as we approach the area in the back. "She never even got to meet Martin Luther King. They say he was shocked when he was told she left him all of her money. She knew who would do right by it."

We're all listening with rapt attention. Seth looks like he's in pain, and I know why; I can't believe Grandma Sheryl won't get to know that we're here. I can't believe she won't get to come here herself.

"There's a move planned," the man tells us. "I assume we'll wind up in Washington D.C., although it's up for debate. I do hope we move Dorothy with us."

The one side of the building looked pretty basic and boring, but as we turn a corner, following our leader, we see that the property has a lovely patch of green. I wouldn't call it a garden, but there are ornamental grasses and plants, and it is all scenic. If I worked here, I'd bring my laptop outside. I take a few quick pictures and send them to the Garden Girls.

"What do you think of this place?" I ask them.

As usual, they respond within seconds.

"Gorg," Kevin writes, meaning *"gorgeous."*

"Where are you?" Jill says next.

"Maryland," I write back.

"Why!?" Jill asks.

"Dorothy Parker is here," I respond.

"!!" Deb says.

Rochelle sends her favorite pink hearts.

The man who led us here clears his throat.

"Well, here we are," he says, and it's his polite way of asking if we need any more of his help.

"Is Dorothy in . . . a specific place?" Seth asks.

The man starts to answer, but he's interrupted by a familiar voice.

"Lor?" Mom says. "Oh, there you are."

Mom is wearing a tan linen tank dress that extends to her feet. She's also sporting a turquoise necklace that is actually normal necklace size.

"Who knew the NAACP was here?" Mom says, and I imagine, based on the look on the man's face, that a lot of people know. But he is being polite.

Behind Mom is Bill, who's in jeans and a Ravens T-shirt. His suit from the arboretum would have been more appropriate for this visit. He walks over to the man who works here.

"I'm Bill," Bill says.

"Ben," the man says, and noticing the shirt, he adds, "Season already looking good."

"I'll take it," Bill says.

Bill is so weirdly disarming. The man who's helping us — Ben — already loves him.

"Honey," Mom says, and hugs me.

"Christian," she says next, to Chris.

"Hi, Mrs. Seltzer," he says while I give my mom look of appreciation for getting his name right.

"Please, call me Becca," she says. "Or Brenda. At this point, I deserve it."

Chris shakes Bill's hand.

"So," Mom continues, looking right to left. "What is our plan here?"

"Dorothy is here, somewhere," Seth says, and looks to Ben, our new friend.

"A plaque in her honor is here, and somewhere beneath it an urn with her remains," Ben says, walking in front of the benches, pointing down, and looking at the space below him with reverence.

"Thank you," Seth says, and Ben nods.

"I have to head out for a meeting, but enjoy the property," he tells us. "Lovely to meet you all."

"Thank you, sir," Chris tells him, and they shake hands too.

The rest of us say a collective thank-you, and I kind of want to hug him, but I hold back because that would be weird.

Once Ben is out of sight, we gather around a bronze memorial for Dorothy Parker that's on the ground in front of us. The plaque is about two feet across, and it's circular—sort of like a giant coin.

"This is the spot," I say.

"Sure is," Seth agrees.

I drop to the ground so I can see it better. Then I read aloud as everyone crowds around me.

"Here lie the ashes of Dorothy Parker . . . Humorist, writer, critic, defender of human and civil rights. For her epitaph she suggested 'Excuse my dust.' This memorial garden is dedicated to her noble spirit, which celebrated the oneness of human kind, and to the bonds of everlasting friendship between Black and Jewish people."

We all breathe in at the same time, as if the words have knocked the wind out of us. This group of people has never been so quiet.

I trace the words on the plaque with my fingers.

"Excuse my fucking dust," Seth says in amazement. I look up at him, and he's crying, and I am a little bit, too. "What a good line."

"This is so beautiful," Mom says, looking behind her at the wave of grass swaying in the mildest of breezes.

"She'd love that we're here," Seth says, and I'm thinking the same thing.

Of all of the places, this is the most meaningful spot. It wasn't on her list, but it's just right.

"This is unfair," I say. I am so desperate to tell her how all this worked out. How we got here. In the past week, we have all done everything in service of Grandma Sheryl, and she's not around to enjoy it.

"Dorothy Parker has a monument at the NAACP headquarters," I say to the sky. "And there is an amazing quote on her grave. And Grandma doesn't know."

"Honey," Mom says, wanting to console me.

I'm starting to ugly-cry, so I use my last clean dress — the yellow tank dress I'd brought to The Mount — to wipe my eyes and nose. I've had some small to medium cries since this all happened, but now it seems that every emotion I've stored up is clearing out of my body, and it feels euphoric.

I bend over next to the plaque and put my head on the ground, needing a minute to breathe.

Then I feel arms around my waist, and I look up to see that they belong to Chris. His chin is on my shoulder.

"Lor, you okay?" he whispers. "You appear to be having a meltdown."

"I just need a minute," I whisper, breathing into my folded knees.

His body is shaking, and after a moment I realize that Chris is laughing.

"What?" I ask.

"We're really showing off the everlasting friendship between Jews and Black people right now," he says.

I smile, imaging what we look like, hunched over in back of the NAACP headquarters, holding each other over this quote.

"We could be on a pamphlet," I whisper.

"Sheryl would approve."

He lets me go, and I sit up.

"I'm okay," I promise everyone. "Let's do this."

I rearrange myself so I'm sitting crossed-legged in front of the plaque, and Mom, Bill, Seth, and Chris lower themselves to the ground too, making a circle around the memorial.

"Where do we do it?" Seth asks. "We can't dump them on the plaque, so maybe around these flowers? Or the trees?"

"Anywhere," I say.

We move a few feet away to something that could be flowers, but they might also be weeds. It doesn't matter what they are. The grass is soft around them. Seth digs to make some small holes for Grandma. Then he opens the Chico's bag, takes out the box, and goes for the craisins.

I am so used to seeing them, watching someone touch them, but it's still kind of new to Mom, days later, and I see her flinch, so I talk her down.

"It gets less weird," I tell her.

"Really? I can't imagine it ever would."

"I've touched them a bunch of times, and it's not really Grandma," I say. "I mean, it's her, but it's also not. It's just her bones."

My mom makes an unhappy face, and for the first time ever, she reminds me of Grandma. It's the scowl Grandma would give me after she tasted something unpleasant. I know that, as a spiritual person, Mom doesn't want to think about bones.

I remember what Marge told me about some religions believing that cremation sets you free.

"When I think of remains now," I tell my mom, "like what it means to look at someone's remains after they die—I can't think of someone's body. It doesn't really remain, no matter how you try to preserve it. Like, the stuff that remains is people. *We're* Grandma's remains."

"That was really lovely, Lori," Mom says, and I notice Seth paying attention.

"That just came to me," I say, and then I look at him and smirk. "Quick, you better take notes. Need a pen to write it down?"

"Touché," he says, but he actually looks contrite, and I appreciate it.

Seth reaches into the bag to grab more of the remains. He gets more of the bigger pieces, as you can't always get to the tiny ones.

I know that there will always be a little bit left, the pieces that get stuck to the plastic bag.

I know that when we throw the bag into a nearby garbage can, it will feel like there's a little of Grandma in there, too. That freaked me out after our first stop—I tried to forget the image of Seth tossing the not-quite-clean bag into a public garbage can —but I have let go of the importance of the actual body. The important thing has been the honoring of it, and the reading, and the letting go.

I know that Dorothy Parker is right—it is just dust.

I know that Edith Wharton buried her dogs on her weird little pet cemetery hill, not for them, but for her, because it was important for her to visit them. I know that even though her body is in France, her spirit is probably with those dogs, or maybe with her inner circle of friends. I imagine that wherever Heaven is for Edith Wharton, there is no overhead lighting, parties are always small and intimate, and everyone sleeps over and hangs out in pajamas talking about literature.

I know that even though Grandma did not choose this particular office park for her ashes, she would be happy with it because things are growing here.

I am growing by the minute. By the millisecond.

Seth hands the bag to me, still half full. I'm less precious with the goods this time around. I put my fingers straight into the bag and take a handful. I close my eyes and imagine writing about the way this feels. Like glass. Like pebbles. Like seashells. Like dust.

I put some of the dust in the holes carved out by Seth, but then I move past them, standing up and bringing a handful to a pretty patch of ornamental green. I bring some more to a big tree nearby.

Then I take the bag to my mother.

"I don't think I can," she says, and her graying curls bounce as she shakes her head.

"You'll be happy you did it," I say.

She dips her hand into the bag, closes her eyes, and feels. She takes a small handful and sprinkles it around the grass in front of her. Her shoulders relax.

"Thank you," she tells me when she's done.

Then she does something really great; she hands the bag to Chris.

"Your turn," Mom says.

He puts his pad and pen down and accepts the bag. After taking a polite fistful of the craisins, he walks to a row of hedges and drops the remains at the roots. I see his mouth move as he buries them. He's whispering to himself.

At first I think he might be doing something religious, maybe saying something he knows from church, but then I realize he's talking to her. I see his lips form the name Sheryl, and he's telling her something.

I'm done for. It's tears again for me.

His eyes are closed, and he's smiling as he speaks, and I'm desperate to know what he's saying, but I won't ask. I will let him have this moment.

Sometimes I forget that Chris met her when he was a little kid, and that they had their own history together.

There's a little bit left in the bag when Chris hands it to me. I give it straight to Bill. Honestly, why not? I think.

"I . . . wow. Thanks, Lori."

Bill—who is clearly humbled by my gesture, which is sweet, I have to admit—takes the rest of the bag and walks to a patch of dandelions growing nearby. He sprinkles what's left on the yellow flowers.

And it's done.

Chapter 16

Seth has found a cheap room at a hotel near Bill's house, which is, as mom said, right by a mall. It is not nearly as majestic as the Natick Mall. We drop him off, and Chris and I follow Mom back to Bill's condo, where we stare at the wall of corkscrews.

"I know I've seen pictures, but it's somehow worse in person," Chris whispers.

I point to one that forms the shape of Micky Mouse ears. "I can't," I say. "I think Mickey died for that one."

"That's dark, Lor."

"Finding everything you need?" Bill asks, coming out of nowhere.

"Yep, we're good," I tell him.

"The guest room is all made up upstairs. There's a bed and a cot. I'll let you fight it out."

"I'm happy on the cot," Chris says, and heads upstairs.

I go into the living room and am still on the couch when Mom comes down.

"You're staying up?" she asks.

"Just for a little," I say.

"Babe," she says, "can we talk about what happened with Seth?"

I answer with a loud exhale. "He told you what he did? Or what I did? About the manuscript?"

"He did." She tucks a piece of my hair behind my ear.

"You're not wearing your cat eyes," she says.

"I don't want to look like the girl in his book anymore."

Mom smiles. She gets it. "You feel like he betrayed you."

"He did betray me! He was acting like my new best friend, and all he really wanted was material."

"Hmm," Mom says. "It's not okay, and I understand why you're angry. But . . ."

There are no buts here, I think. When I say it all out loud, I'm even more upset by what Seth has done.

"It felt so embarrassing," I say. "It's a violation, but also, I felt so duped. I assumed he was asking me things because he cared about me. I was all excited about it. But I was being mined for ideas."

"Right," Mom says, hesitating. "This might sound strange, Lori, but when he told me what happened—what he had done —my instinct was to be jealous."

I lean back, surprised.

"Jealous of whom?"

"Of you."

"Why?"

"You've read Seth's books, right?" she asks.

I have. I mean, I did, long ago, maybe before I was really old enough to understand them. My mom always said they were for adults, but when I moved in with Grandma Sheryl when I was fifteen, she said I could read anything, so I took them from her shelf and tore through them, not because they were fast reads — they're pretty slow, actually — but because I was curious to know how my uncle told a story. The characters were all sort of miserable and longing for things beyond their small suburb. It all felt very tense in a way that didn't interest me.

Also, there was nothing supernatural about any of it. Still, I was happy I read them.

"The writing was good," I tell Mom, "but they weren't my thing."

"Right," Mom says.

We hear the sounds of television coming from the second floor.

"Bill's watching his news," she says. "Every night with Rachel Maddow. I'll have to get used to it."

"Rachel Maddow's cool, though, right?" I ask.

"I don't enjoy current events before bed. We'll have to find a compromise."

"Back to Seth's books," I remind her.

"Right. I was going to say that my brother has never written about me," she continues. "Everyone else — our mom, our dad, our cousin Dick, who died when we were teenagers — I can see how these people inspired Seth's characters. It's all rather transparent. But I'm not in there at all. And did you notice that not one of his main characters has a sibling? Not one."

"I don't remember that," I say.

"Yes, well," she says, "take a closer look. They're all only children. Which is fine. But I guess I thought that just once I'd open one of his drafts and read about a character who sounded like me. He'd written about everyone else, but never me. God, it sounds so childish and selfish to say it out loud."

"It's not selfish," I say after a swallow.

"And considering all the hours I spend talking to him about these drafts," she says.

This is new.

"He shows you drafts?"

"Always," she says. "That's how I wound up going into life coaching. He's the one who said I should try it. He said I helped his books so much. It wasn't that I was a great editor, he said, but I could listen and help him figure out what he needed to write. How to teach and write at the same time . . . I don't think he believes I'm a very compelling character. But you . . ."

She taps my chin.

"Clearly he thinks you deserve a whole book."

"That doesn't make it okay," I say.

"I know. And I shouldn't be trying to spin this so that you're not entitled to your anger, but please understand—I wouldn't mind being someone's muse."

I have to laugh at the way she says the word *muse,* like she just turned French for a second.

"I still have the story you and Chris wrote about me," she says. "Do you remember? What was it called?"

"'Mom-Bot'? It wasn't flattering, Mom. I feel bad we ever wrote that."

"No, it was not flattering at all," Mom agrees. "You made me a robot."

"It was one of our first stories," I say with a groan. "It barely made sense."

"I didn't care. Did you know how happy it made me? You wrote that story, and I thought, well, I'm in the narrative, at least. My daughter is living with my mother, and I cannot keep a relationship together, but I'm worthy of being Mom-Bot."

"Mom-Bot wanted to make better children, the kind who could take care of themselves."

"By removing their insides and filling their bodies with machines. I remember."

I am giggling now. "Mom-Bot" was not quality material.

"I wrote it to be mean," I admit.

"I didn't mind. It meant you were paying attention to me." She squeezes my foot.

"Are you telling me to forgive him?"

"No," she says. "I'm just pointing out that your uncle Seth is paying attention."

I nod, even though it's not an answer.

She clears her throat.

"He says he'll stay, Lor," she tells me, her voice barely loud enough to hear. "He says he'll move to Natick and help maintain the house for a year. He'll watch you until graduation. Then we'll sell it. And if it's what you want, I'm not going to pull you away, as much as I want you here."

It takes a second for this to sink in.

"Are you serious?"

"I told Seth I'd approve — with rules. And more visits, both ways."

I scramble closer to her. "What are you saying?"

"If you'd listen for a second, you'd know."

"Sorry, sorry," I say. "Keep talking."

"I was making decisions too quickly," she says. "You only have a year of high school left, and you're right about consistency and college applications and being able to tell these admissions people that you're the editor of your magazine. I do believe that." She squeezes the turquoise around her neck.

"I need to meet you where you are and see your human needs in the present, through *your* lens."

Mom is starting to use self-help speak, but instead of making fun of it, I try to understand.

"Seth has human needs too," she continues. "He needs a new purpose. He also needs to move out of that apartment. Ethan needs to start over."

"You know about them?" I ask her.

"Yes," she says. "He and I do talk. He's my twin brother, Lori. He probably didn't tell you, but he came to stay with me for a week after they broke up."

"He didn't tell me anything," I whisper. I can't imagine Mom advising Seth on his career. I can't even picture him at her house, bonding over whatever was happening with Ethan.

All these adults have secret lives.

"Listen," Mom says, moving on, "I've told Seth that it would be helpful for him to catalogue the house, prep it for sale, and help with you. He could use the time to write. And as long as you came to see me once a month and for holidays, and I could come up to you once a month . . ."

"I want this," I tell her. "But he'll be watching me. Writing about me. I'd have to forgive him."

I'm so confused. I am still hurt by Seth, but also so hopeful that I'm tapping my toes the way Chris does.

"At this point," Mom goes on, "Seth plans to move to Natick for the year no matter what, to figure out what's next for himself. He wasn't sure if you'd still want to be around him. You should think about what you want from him and what you're willing to live with. He is who he is. None of us are perfect parents."

"I wouldn't expect you to be," I tell her, and I finally get that.

Chapter 17

Jessica, Jason, Chris, and I have been taking turns jumping on Devin Coogan's trampoline for the past hour.

The invitation has always been open to do this, but I've never wanted to. After coming back home, for whatever reason, I wanted to try.

Jason flops to his back. "I gotta go," he says. "I'll come over tomorrow, though."

"Sounds good," I say.

Jason has volunteered to help Seth and me take Grandma's coats, the ones in the front hall closet, to the donation center. We're starting there, to make room for some of Seth's things.

"And I'll see you tomorrow night?" Jessica says, moving to follow him.

"Sure. At like six," I say. We're going to the mall together to get new stuff for school. We are going alone, as a duo, and I am excited.

I lie back on the trampoline next to Chris, who's in no rush to run off.

"So," Chris says.

"So."

"I've been thinking. How is Seth going to get around?" Chris asks. "You can't drive him everywhere."

"He has a license—technically," I explain. "He just hasn't driven in more than twenty years. He says he's going to learn all over again."

"Has he shown you any more pages?"

That's our agreement. I get to see what he's writing.

"I think I'd rather let him get some more chapters together," I say. "I know a lot of what he wrote won't stick."

It wasn't a long talk that got Seth and me to this place, where we are roommates. Where he is a guardian who's just trying to figure it out.

He apologized, and I listened. He told me how much he wanted me to stay.

I realized that Grandma would always seem like the better parent because she'd already answered the big questions about her life. I got to be her do-over. Mom and Seth are on their first drafts with parenting—they're working out the details in real time.

I feel like I'm getting to know the real Seth now. The genuine one, as opposed to the one who had to be my idol, showing up with gifts on holidays.

Chris says, "hmm," and then we're quiet, looking at the stars. The evening is clear and cool, and it smells like fall is coming.

I am getting everything I want. I don't have to leave.

And yet.

I feel sad. It's about Grandma Sheryl, I'm sure. It's finally becoming real that I'm here and she's not. The house—and my life—will become something else without her.

"I've decided I don't want to be your best friend anymore," Chris says, startling me.

"Excuse me?"

He pauses long enough for me to let out a nervous laugh.

"You're demoted," he continues. "Jason is my best friend now."

"Wow," I say, giving his right leg a little kick with my left. "I didn't realize I could get demoted. Or that you had a ranking of seconds. I guess Jess will have to be mine."

We both start laughing, but I'm a little uncomfortable because I don't get the joke. I wiggle an inch away from him, which is difficult to do on the springy trampoline bottom.

He turns to me then, which makes me roll back in his direction, facing him.

"I won't let you screw this up," he says, now serious. "This year is a gift. We should be together."

I hold my breath.

"Together?"

"Yes," he says.

"Nothing has changed, Chris," I tell him after an exhalation.

"I just changed it," he tells me. "You don't want to lose whatever we have, but I'm telling you it's gone. The minute you told me how you felt, it was over. It's different now—and now, lying here like this, pretending . . . it doesn't work."

"Chris . . ."

"Lori, I'm not supposed to be the stable thing in your life, the person who's there like family, always, no matter what. I didn't ask to be that. And I quit."

He takes my hand, which has been resting on my hip, and places it on his neck. I'm confused at first, but then I realize where he's put it.

My eyes widen.

"Christian Burke," I say.

He laughs, and I feel the movement in his chest.

"I don't get it," he says, his voice hoarse.

"I can't explain it," I say, tracing his clavicle for the first time.

He places his hand on top of mine, stilling it.

"What if we break up?" I ask, swallowing my nerves, feeling the arrival of new tears.

"Well . . . that would make a really good story," he says. "I'm sure I could come up with an illo for it."

We hear a rustling, and we sit up, startled. Devin Coogan is staring at us.

"You guys," he says. "I gotta practice now."

"Sorry, my man," Chris says. "Get to it."

We both slide off the trampoline, and Devin pounces on top and begins jumping. He has his soccer ball with him, and he bounces it off the mesh that surrounds him on all sides.

"Why don't we go write for a bit," I say, my heart beating

wildly, and Chris nods and follows me across the street and up to my house. We pass Seth, who's on the couch in front of his laptop. He grunts a quick hello.

We go straight upstairs, where my floor is already covered with Chris's first-draft drawings of what could be the *N-Files*'s first cover of the year. There is a ghost floating over a building. Her name is Marge.

I close the door, and Chris stands by the bed. I know he's wondering if I'm going to change the subject or whether I'll let him keep talking about what we started on the trampoline.

I'm not sure I have anything else to say. Also, I am tired. He has quit, and I have too.

I look at him. He has a few more freckles because it's the end of summer. They'll be gone in a month or two. His fingernails are messy from pens. He is tapping his foot. Slowly.

I turn off the overhead light, which seems like the thing to do. I get into bed and turn on the small lamp on the end table. Chris joins me under the covers.

Our kisses are awkward at first, because it's new, and I find it so interesting. Even though I have learned to predict every word he says, every drawing he'll make, I have no idea what he will do next with his hands, and his body. I sweep my hand across his chin to see if he's shaved.

He surprises me by getting on top of me.

I start laughing because I've imagined it too many times.

Everything he does makes me dizzy, and when I look beyond him, behind him, I see the drawing on the ceiling, the one of the mall and the portal, the most important place in my universe, and I can't help but grin.

Chapter 18

Chris is leaning against my bed, his sketchpad on his knees, and when I lean over to see what he's drawing, I find that it's an illustration of a bunch of people who have animal faces. Like dog ears on their heads or cat whiskers on their noses.

"What is it?" I ask.

"Just playing with something," he mumbles. "Like, what if everyone's face filters—the ones they posted—just stuck and became their actual faces. What if people woke up one day and they were puking rainbows forever, or they looked like a tiny dog with baby ears."

"How about those people who use filters that show you what you'll look like when you're old," I offer. "Those people would wake up and their faces would be all wrinkly, but their bodies would still be young."

"Oh, that's good," he says.

"We can fine-tune it some more," I add because there is no rush right now.

He starts to put his pencils away, and I sigh. Our second week of school starts tomorrow, and now that I am not going anywhere, we are back to rules. Chris has to be home by dinner on weeknights, unless he has permission to stay, and Mrs. Burke has told Seth that we are not allowed in my room alone with the door closed.

Seth does not enforce that second rule, but he does request that we try to be discreet.

"Imagine the rules my mother would have set, and follow them," he tells me. "For god's sake, don't get it on with the door *open*," he adds. "It feels like *that* should be the rule, right?"

"It's time," Chris says, and I know we're done for the night.

I nod and stand up so I'm facing him. He leans in and gives me a long kiss.

Then I follow him down the stairs. I'm hungry, and I have a writing date with my other story partner.

Seth does a lot of his work while I'm at school. He wakes up, writes for four hours on Grandma's bed, teaches a class or two online, and then gets to work on the house. He's starting with the basement, which will take him a while. Yesterday he found cans of beer that he hid behind a dresser in the '80s.

That's like forty-something years of life in this home to dispose of and organize. Some days are really hard for him because of all the memories. Sometimes we find fun things, like my mom's diary from when she was a teenager and loved Keanu Reeves.

"Good taste on her part," I'd said. "Stood the test of time."

"Whatever, I loved him first."

I have more homework than I used to. College essays and applications. Math is really hard for me. On Wednesdays I stay late to get tutored. On Tuesdays I stay late to work on the magazine.

On Thursdays, though, Seth and I have a standing appointment. We order take-out from the mall and sit across from each other at the dining room table, sometimes looking out the window at the Garden Girls, who meet here weekly, provided it's not raining, to trim trees, water plants, and take big clippers to whatever needs pruning.

While they work, sometimes coming inside to check on the houseplants, Seth and I bring out our laptops and work on the same story. Well, two stories—very different stories—about the same thing.

Both tales are about a beautiful matriarch who dies and leaves her family a list of gardens where she'd like them to place her ashes.

I'm pretty sure both stories are about the way a family changes when someone has to leave—how a death reshuffles everyone's duties, and how people who love one another have to learn to lean on one another in new ways.

Seth will write the story his way. It will be real and poignant, and based on recent drafts, I love the heroine. She is loud and sarcastic and has very good style. She can apply eyeliner without a mirror.

My version of the story is a bit different. There are haunted flowers that seek revenge, and three ghosts named Dorothy, Edith, and Sheryl. There's also a team of magical people made of petals who know how to cast magic spells. One is named Jill. Another, Kevin.

Seth says it's okay that we're both telling similar stories in different ways. So many great writers do.

He tells me not to rush my work, that he will read the drafts when I'm ready.

It is not a competition, he says. A good writer takes her time.

Still, I'm pretty sure mine will be more interesting, especially because of the illustrations.

And I know this much: I will be done first.

Acknowledgments

Leslie Goldstein—my talented mom—was an incredible piano teacher, mother, and friend. She left a note in her will saying that she wanted to be cremated and placed near "things that grow." I, a very confused Jewish woman, wound up at a very Irish-Catholic Boston funeral home with my sister Brette, my aunt Nancy, and our friend Brian Taylor (an honorary Goldstein). It was a surreal day—and a painful one—but it sent me on a joyful adventure that continues. Thanks, Mom, for giving us a reason to explore the world in bloom. Readers, if you would like to visit *some* of my mom (there are multiple boxes of her, of course), I'll give you two hints: Paris and Chopin. We didn't have a permit, but I promise we were respectful. The view there is gorgeous. Bring her some espresso.

Please know: I did not bring any real cremains to the Arnold Arboretum. It is a beautiful, perfect place. Please visit when you're in Boston—and go see The Mount and Green Animals! —but keep your craisins to yourself.

This book exists because my agent, Katherine Flynn, said I could write it. Katherine, thank you for believing in my ideas and for your unwavering support. Nicole Sclama at HMH Teen, you are a treasure of an editor. You made this book better—and during a pandemic. Emilia Rhodes, I am grateful for your editing and humor. What a team.

Just *some* of the people/experiences that made this book possible (I will forget many; please forgive me): my colleagues at the *Boston Globe*, including the kick-ass Linda Henry; the magnificent Ellen Goldsmith-Vein; every long phone call with D. J. Goldberg; high school friends Elizabeth McQueen, Laura Heffernan, Kyle Hubbard, and Desaray Smith; Janice Page and burgeoning editor Zoe Tseng; Emily Procknal; Marge Cox—yes, there is a real Marge!—at The Mount; forest therapy guide Tam Willey of Toadstool Walks; and India Artis, who's been with the NAACP for more than thirty-two years and was an incredible person to talk to about Dorothy Parker's longtime home in Baltimore. India, thank you for documenting so much and for sharing. To Gina Favata, who helped make this book work when I feared it wouldn't; Jenn Abelson and Paul Faircloth, who have been giving me shots of bravery and love for years; Jon Gorey and Kirk Woundy (heart emojis); World's Best Duo Lauren Iacono and Allie Chisholm; support human Pete Thamel; treat Bryan Barbieri; Heather Ciras, Lauren Shea, and *the* Matt Ellis; Stacie Vollentine, a forever friend who talked me through cremation so it was less scary; my dad, Dave Goldstein, and his saxophone; Rachel Zarrell and endless texts that make me smile; Paul Bernon, who sings me voice memos and makes me laugh so hard just when I need it (and this thank you also goes to Rory Uphold, of course); Fran Forman and Bob Flack and Nicole Cammorata and Sophie and Josh Charles, who give me love and countless good days; brave and whip-smart Trenni Kusnierek; Devin Smith and Jenna Cirbo; Susanna Fogel, Mark Feeney and Wesley Morris; Joani Geltman and dinners; Linda Resiman and Jack and movie theaters; Mark Shanahan and my aunt Nancy, who traveled with my sister and me to take my mom where she needed to go . . . she loved you both, and I do too; my extended family, including Michelle McGonagle and Julia and Beckett Shanahan; my late grandma Lorraine, who had Grandma Sheryl's bookshelf; Jaime Roberts and her family; Ale Checka and her students; snacking before family dinners with Tim, Elana, Ariela, and Sarah Knight; Brad, Julie, Nate, Shula, Yael, Jake, and Sam Goldstein; Sarah Grafman; Julian Benbow; James DiSabatino (in a track suit); Love Letters podcast team (please listen!) Amy Pedulla and Scott Helman; the most formidable of friends, Jenny Johnson; creative soul mate and life travel spouse Sara Faith Alterman; Jenni Moran Krepp; baby shark Lilly Brown; the editing and thoughtfulness of André Wheeler; my brilliant and loving brother-in-law, Ben Barocas; uber-cousins Tina Valinsky and Shirley Craig; and Sara Farizan, a friend with whom I have watched more than one thousand hours of television. You are a Maven, Sara, and I don't regret one minute of it. Rachel Raczka, you cared for me during this book process, even when I became a monster, not unlike one that Lori might invent. I am forever grateful for you. Sarah Rodman, you are the best product of Natick; you are all the things that are home. Let me be clear: I would not have finished this book without support from Benielle Sims. Writers: get yourself a friend who loves romance novels and knows when people should kiss. Benielle, you are the Bonnie, the Caroline, and, on some of my favorite days, the Katherine. You are simply the best. Thank you to Danielle Kost, who renovates *everything* until it's better. I'm forever in awe of you. Jess, this book is dedicated to you because you are my heart. Is there any other way to say it? Thank you to Santo, Alex, and Gabe Perez for sharing her, and for years of joy, and more to come. To my sister, Brette Goldstein: you inspire every good character I write, their dirtiest jokes and most human and hopeful moments. You make my best memories. I love you.